Glynis Peters lives
was shortlisted for

When Glynis is no ... ...joys making greetings cards,
Cross Stitch, fishing and looking after her gorgeous grandchildren.

Her debut novel, *The Secret Orphan*, was an international
bestseller.

www.glynispetersauthor.co.uk

X x.com/_GlynisPeters_
f facebook.com/glynispetersauthor
⊙ instagram.com/glynispetersauthor
BB bookbub.com/authors/glynis-peters

Also by Glynis Peters

THE ORPHAN'S SECRET LIBRARY

GLYNIS PETERS

One More Chapter
a division of HarperCollins*Publishers* Ltd
1 London Bridge Street
London SE1 9GF
www.harpercollins.co.uk
HarperCollins*Publishers*
Macken House, 39/40 Mayor Street Upper,
Dublin 1, D01 C9W8, Ireland

This paperback edition 2024

3

First published in Great Britain in ebook format
by HarperCollins*Publishers* 2024
Copyright © Glynis Peters 2024
Glynis Peters asserts the moral right to
be identified as the author of this work

A catalogue record of this book is available from the British Library

PB ISBN: 978-0-00-870760-6
TPB ISBN: 978-0-00-871532-8

Printed and bound in the United States

To the volunteers of the 100th Bomb Group Memorial Museum
With my thanks.

So, when you see mighty aircraft, as they mark their way through the air.
Remember the grease-stained man with the wrench in his hand
is the one who put them there.

Anonymous

Prologue

Falling in Love With Books

The moment five-year-old Alice Carmichael lifted down her first book from the highest shelf of her father's bookcase, she was in love.

She traced her finger in admiration across the gold-embossed lettering and lifted open the green cover to stroke the creamy paper on the inside. In wonder, she turned the pages knowing they offered words waiting to transport her into another world. Alice sniffed them and closed her eyes, imagining the author deep in thought at a large leather desk much like her father owned.

It was when Alice was invited to live with her grandmother in 1941, at the age of fifteen, that she discovered the library. One afternoon, feeling overwhelmed, she had walked into a room full of ancient books that had not been given up to the war effort. Alice stood staring, as if she had walked into a treasure trove of words encased in wondrous covers of colour. She started to count the books, but when she reached 100, she stopped, seeing that there were at least another hundred awaiting her attention. She vowed to read each book to give it the respect it deserved and to honour the author. Her grandparents' collection would keep her going for several years.

Time in the room was spent drifting into another world, curled up and transported away from the war. Here, Alice could fight a whale, kiss a prince, run through dark woods with a handsome man, and climb a snowy mountain in a country she would never visit in real life. This library was a magical home for her heart and mind, a place to breathe, not hide away frightened by the noises around her. It was not a sparce room with grubby, torn books like she had seen at the orphanage. It was a place to heal. To start a new life.

Dear Diary

Life is certainly different in Great Yarmouth to that in the orphanage. My grandmother, Mary Fenn, is a kind and generous woman. Nothing like I remember about my mother. She has a library, oh my word, a beautiful room with leather chairs, large wooden bookcases, and colourful drapes at the windows, which remind me of autumn. It is a beautiful room, filled with beautiful books. I am going to be sixteen after Christmas and I just know I am going to be happy here for the rest of my life!

Chapter One

May 1943

In a state of exhaustion, Alice pressed on through the narrow lanes of Norfolk, her sore feet, weary, bruised limbs, and overwhelmed mind making each step a challenge.

'What if I don't find Jane?'

'Where do I go from here? What happens now?'

Questions shouted out into the wilderness of empty tree-lined lanes remained unanswered. Shadows stretched across the small lane and when the sunlight tucked itself away, Alice was tempted to put the fur coat hanging from her suitcase, across her shoulders. A few minutes later, a sweat formed across her top lip and brow, and she was glad she had not.

Alice stumbled, her slightly large, heeled brogue shoes inadequate for the long walk. She tried hard to ignore the blister blooming on the side of one foot, now protected with two leaves from a dandelion plant. Her knee, already grazed from a fall, ached with emerging bruises.

'What am I supposed to do!?' She cried out as she regained her balance and continued walking.

'Why is this happening to me? Haven't I suffered enough?'

Two days previously, German bombers had destroyed her home in Great Yarmouth, trapping her beneath the rubble and killing her grandmother. At seventeen years old, Alice had become a desperate, homeless orphan.

After spending ten years hoping her parents would come back to take her from the orphanage where they had left her at the age of five, the then fifteen-year-old Alice found herself living in the cosy home of a previously unknown grandmother. Neither of them had known the other existed until a friend of her grandmother's visited the orphanage and suspected they were related.

Alice discovered her parents had passed away two years before, when their bodies were found. Debt collectors were not tolerant people according to her grandmother. The news angered Alice. She had lived in an orphanage unclaimed while they were still alive. With no paperwork and being so young, when Alice first arrived in the home, she did not know the date of her birth, only that she had just turned five. She knew it was after Christmas and recalled her mother used to say she was a New Year baby, so the orphanage dated her as born on the 2nd January 1926. Her grandmother tried to trace Alice's original birth paperwork, but the enemy bombing put an end to her search when official buildings were blitzed and burned out.

Alice had been informed of a relative linked with her deceased grandmother and found a chink of hope, hoping the loneliness she endured was coming to an end. However, as she walked now, she failed to see the day ending and a new relationship building with a great- aunt by the name of Jane Lovett.

'Please let the next lane be a short one!' She yelled out,

uncaring if anyone heard her, though the chances of that appeared very slim. Alice had not met one person in over three hours.

The spring showers which now dripped from trees seemed to mingle with her tears. She caved into the crying. It was a rare event for Alice to feel sorry for herself, but as she entered another lane as long as the last, her resolve crumbled. Her bags, heavy, rubbed against her calves and each movement stung her flesh.

Alice carried all she had left in the world, including the old fur coat – which added to her load and which she now contemplated discarding in a ditch – and her diary, which she had tucked beneath her nightdress at the time of the attack and which had protected her against a jagged pipe.

She had also managed to rescue nine tattered paperback books and ten hardback copies of non-fiction, originally belonging to her grandfather. And jingling in her purse was the remaining travel money, given to her by the Women's Institute to get a bus to the village of West Tofts.

'I will carry you to safety, I will. And one day I will read you all, but why do you have to be so heavy?' she muttered to the books inside the suitcase as she placed it on the ground to rest her arms.

Although Alice could happily sit and read or sleep under a tree, her mission now was to track down her only remaining relative in the world. She picked up the case again and took another step adjusting the weight for comfort.

'I wonder what Jane is like.'

'I need money. I hope there are jobs are available for me.'

'Where is this place?'

All the while she walked, she threw these questions at the birds, anything to keep her focused on seeking help.

'I think it would be easier if I was Agatha Christie's detective, Miss Marple. Investigating a dead body seems easier than tracking down a live one!'

Alice sighed as yet another long stretch of road lay ahead, the leafy lanes were no longer pretty with their hawthorn blossom shining white, they were an endless road to nowhere.

'How many more miles? This is like the title of one of the books in this case, *The Road to Nowhere*! I bet Maurice Walsh knew where his characters were heading, though!'

When she reached the end of the lane and ventured out into more open land, the noise of plane engines overhead filled her ears and her stomach churned with fear.

Alice watched as two planes flew low, and she felt the engines' vibrations throughout her body from the ground up. As one plane turned, she saw the insignia of the enemy and when the planes dipped above her, she felt seen and a target. They swerved the treetops and loomed her way. Alice hit the floor behind a clump of trees.

While she laid low on the floor, peering from behind a grassy mound at the planes firing at every angle, Alice saw a squirrel run out from behind the trees. It sat bolt upright, ears pricked and alert, then it abandoned the tasty morsel it had found as it raced to safety. The sound of pigeons cooing became a frenzied wing-flapping affair as they fled the fields. A horse whinnied nearby, and a dog barked. Each one of them an innocent caught up in the war of politicians.

'Haven't you done enough damage? Now you are frightening innocent animals!' she yelled at the planes still strafing bullets across the field ahead.

A hare scampered across the field, darting one way then another.

'Run!' Alice cried out, closing her eyes for fear of seeing it caught in the crossfire when gunfire echoed from the ground. Much to her relief, the planes suddenly turned tail and swiftly returned to the safety of the clouds.

Taking a moment to compose herself, Alice breathed deeply

then lifted her luggage ready to take another painful step forward. She headed to where she could hear loud male voices calling out to one another, while the sound of machines chugged in the background.

Five minutes later, she stood in front of a sentry post, facing a soldier with his arm outstretched.

'Papers!' he demanded, his face stiff in an attempt to look fierce and in control.

Alice gave him a smile.

'I have temporary papers,' she said, holding them out, along with a letter from the officials in Norfolk explaining her position as a displaced person.

Alice's eyes met the soldier's as he handed back her papers.

'Sorry, but I cannot allow you through. All residents have been evacuated,' he said.

Horrified, Alice gaped at him.

'Where did they go? Jane Lovett. Do you know her?' she asked, desperate for the journey to end.

'We have no names, and it is not safe for you to walk around here,' a second soldier said, stepping out from the guard room, and just as he did so gunshots rang out.

Alice jumped but the men stayed focused on her, waiting for her to walk away, but she remained on the spot.

'Maybe I can find someone who might help, the vicar. Look, the church is over there. Let me through and I can ask him,' she said, pointing across a field to the large church nestled in a field.

'A no-go zone I'm afraid. Evacuated. There are no residents inside the boundary. You need to leave,' the second soldier said firmly.

'What, even the church?' Alice asked in amazement.

'Four churches in the area are closed and the villages are shut off to the public, this is a strictly controlled military base,' came the stiff reply.

'No more lingering, move along now,' the first soldier said, his voice now even firmer with authority.

'Go around the back lane that way, it is safer. Away from the firing range.'

Not wanting to stand still for too much longer, and feeling slightly dizzy with thirst and hunger, Alice simply gave them a nod and walked back the way she came, then turned left following the tree-lined lane. She had no idea where she was heading, and of how to find Jane Lovett.

At the end of a narrow lane, she saw a small row of cottages. The first in the row looked welcoming so she decided to ask for a drink of water and find answers as to where her great-aunt might live since the evacuation.

Looking into the front garden, Alice stood surrounded by small bushes tipped with yellow and coral-pink flowers, all complemented by variegated green foliage surrounding the neatest vegetable garden and hen house she had seen during her travels from Great Yarmouth to Mundford, and her walk from Billingford to the edge of Thorpe Abbotts.

A large golden-haired dog plodded from behind the cottage and gave a half-hearted woof.

'Hello, how friendly are you?' Alice said warily, as she put her hand on the wooden gate.

With a huff of a sigh the dog sank onto the grass and laid his head between his front paws. With caution Alice opened the gate and stepped into the garden. The dog never moved. But as she walked towards the door sited on the side of the building, he plodded behind her, his nails clip-clipping along the flagstones. Alice raised the door knocker and tapped it lightly. From inside she heard a female voice.

'Teddy!'

The dog took himself off around the back of the building again, and Alice heard a door banging shut.

With a pounding heart, she wondered if her great-aunt would be the one to answer the door, but she also knew fairytale situations did not happen in her life and waited for the female inside to answer.

Eventually, the door creaked open and a tall middle-aged woman with greying hair pulled tight into a bun, wearing a pair of men's dungarees, peered out into the sunshine.

'Can I help you?' she asked in a clipped voice.

Alice, fully aware she looked like a battered waif and stray, tried to speak, but her words faltered at her lips.

'Speak up, girl.'

'I ... um, sorry. I have a note from the Great Yarmouth WI which explains why I am here in this part of Norfolk, I need help,' Alice said, and her hand shook as she handed over the letter.

Chapter Two

Alice stood still, barely breathing with the hope this was nearly the end of her journey. Her arms, neck, and shoulders ached. Her legs felt like jelly and her feet were so sore she doubted she could walk another yard.

But Alice told herself she had hope on her side. If the woman knew someone who knew of her great-aunt's whereabouts, then she could be resting in under an hour.

The woman finished looking her up and down and took the envelope. Alice watched her every move as she opened the letter and read the message, then looked up at Alice.

'You'd best come inside, you look done in, Alice Carmichael,' she said, and Alice followed her down the narrow hallway into a dark, but comfortable room.

'Take a seat. Would you like a glass of milk?' the woman asked.

Alice nodded her head. 'Yes, please,' she said shyly.

The woman busied herself with cutting up an apple and pouring a glass of milk from a jug on the table, then sat down.

'My name is Hilda Jones, and by incredible coincidence I was once a neighbour of the woman mentioned in the letter. She stayed here for two weeks when West Tofts was taken over by the military. I don't like to speak ill of the dead, but…'

Alice gasped, and a slice of apple nearly choked her.

Hilda looked over at Alice, who was dabbing tears from her eyes after the choking session.

'Oh, my dear, sorry, but yes, Jane Lovett is dead. Heart attack. However, she would never have taken you in. Mealy-mouthed and selfish. I'm sad to say this, but Jane Lovett was an ungrateful woman who thought only of herself. I was the only person at her funeral.'

Alice sat in shock.

'I'm sorry, dear, but it's the truth,' Hilda said. 'And I am not one to sugar-coat the truth. You deserve to hear it.'

To Alice, Jane sounded like a woman who was the exact opposite of her grandmother. She had never heard her gran speak ill of anyone, and if she felt any animosity towards her sister, she had never made Alice aware of it. She never spoke about her.

'That's sad. I wonder if Gran and she fell out, I never knew she existed until a neighbour mentioned it to the lady helping me. I assumed my gran was an only child like me.'

Alice tried to control her breathing. A panic set in. 'I don't know what to do now. I've no one else left in my family and nowhere to go,' she said, tripping over her words as she became overwhelmed with sadness.

She struggled holding back tears, but did not want to make the situation awkward between her and the stranger in front of her.

Hilda stood up from the table. 'First, we will tend to your bloodied knee,' she said, and fetched a cloth and a bowl of warm water for Alice, who dabbed at the stinging wound.

'My beds are full, thanks to the RAF billeting their men wherever they fancy,' she went on, 'but fortunately, young lady, all is not lost. I have a sister who lives on the other side of the military base but inside its boundary. On the edge of Billingford. I know she has one small room free.'

Alice's heart sank.

'I have just walked from near the pub in Billingford, and from Swaffham to West Tofts. Hours of walking – over four I think, going by the last church clock I saw. An army truck gave me a lift to Thetford, then I took a bus to Mundford, and it's taken me over another two hours to walk here. Wherever here might be. Six hours and I am going around in circles.' she said, and winced as she tended to the large blister on her foot.

Hilda handed her a small bandage.

'Wrap it around your feet. Those shoes are too loose, you will get more blisters if you are not careful,' she said, and Alice gave her a grateful glance.

'Small pickings at the table after the bombings, but I was grateful for anything. I stood in a tattered nightdress for hours,' she said.

'We all have to be grateful for what we can get hold of nowadays,' Hilda said.

Alice nodded her agreement as Hilda continued speaking.

'A lot of families were split up and evacuated all over the place. As I said, Jane would not have entertained you anyway. The village you are in now is Thorpe Abbotts, and sadly I do not have the transport to take you to Billingford. Still, you are young with strong legs, and it is only a forty-minute walk.'

Alice's heart sank. The seat beneath her was comfortable and the pain in her legs throbbed. Her back ached and her mind was foggy with worry. She sat quietly, it was not the woman's fault, and she was trying to be helpful.

'I will write a letter to my sister and explain you need a bed for the night and see if she can help in other ways. The quickest route is through the airbase, though sometimes you need a pass to get in and out, but I will also write a letter explaining the situation. I'm the post woman for the area, so they know me well enough. Just say you are visiting a relative – makes life easier.'

'Thank you,' Alice said. She felt totally bewildered by the unfolding events.

Something inside nagged at her again. She should have stayed at the orphanage and just visited her grandmother. She would still have a roof over her head and probably a job. Everything was becoming a nightmare, and Alice was not sure how much longer she could keep moving from one place to another and stay strong emotionally.

She knew she was not in a position to turn down a bed for the night, so she thanked Hilda, and followed the road as instructed.

Her suitcase banged against one leg, and a string bag of vegetables and eggs for the woman she was about to descend upon, tangled itself against the other. But Alice was thankful the weather and mid-afternoon light were still on her side, and that six o'clock in the morning was a distant memory. She tramped her way through the narrow roads, only stopping to relieve the ache in her arms.

'Halt!'

A male voice barked out the instruction, and although she could not quite see him, Alice guessed it was a someone from the airbase. She stopped, placed her goods on the floor and reached down for her identity papers.

'I've got papers. I'm going to, um, my relative in er, Billingford,' she called out.

The crunch of boots on stones made her heart beat fast with anxiety and she waved her paperwork in the air.

'Found them!' she called out.

A smiling young male in a blue RAF uniform walked towards her. He held out his hands for her papers and read the letter from Hilda explaining her journey.

'Alice Carmichael. That's you? And your relative is Hettie Saltfield of Billingford, I take it?' he asked.

'It is, yes. I ... yes,' she said, giving the white lie Hilda encouraged her to use. 'I've walked all day and have no idea how much further I have to go.'

Alice sighed. Now that she had stopped walking the aches and pains in her arms and legs had kicked in and she rubbed her forearms.

'It is a bit longer following the road, but as your papers are in order I can allow you across the base. We all know Hilda, the postie,' he said, waving the letter Hilda had written.

'Thank you.'

'I will speak to my mate at the gate, and escort you over. It will save your legs a bit, and I'll even carry your case for you. Ready?' The airman said with a wink.

'I ... er, yes, thank you ... sir,' Alice replied.

'Not sir. Private Turner will do. Quick march, Alice Carmichael,' Private Turner said with another wink, which helped Alice relax into the situation.

'Blimey, this case is heavy, what you got in there, rocks?' He asked.

'Books,' Alice replied. 'My gran's.'

'Yer gran's whole library, I guess, going by the weight of this.' Private Turner moved the case into his other hand for comfort. 'You're stronger than you look,' he said, laughing.

'What's left of the library. Nineteen books,' Alice explained. 'Gran's dead. Great Yarmouth bombings a fortnight ago,' she added bluntly, and the airman swung her a look.

'Oh, sorry ... I, um, right this way, Miss Carmichael,' Private Turner said, and strode away.

Fifteen minutes later Alice's cheeks were red from walking fast to keep up with her escort and they burned with blushes from the endless wolf whistles sent her way.

'Don't mind them, they ain't seen a pretty face since the pub last night,' Private Turner said.

Along the pathway leading to her destination, Private Turner placed her case on the floor.

'I'll leave you here or I will be accused of leaving my post without permission. I can see a Home Guard over there, show your papers and I bet he will know exactly where your relative lives. Good luck, Alice. If you need anything ask for Pete Turner. Not sure how much longer I'll be here as the Americans are heading our way, but I'm always happy to help a pretty damsel in distress while I can. See you about.'

Before Alice could thank him Private Turner saluted, turned heel, and marched back across the base.

Alice took in her surroundings and saw vast machinery digging and cementing what looked like long roads that she assumed were new runways. Everywhere she looked was a hive of activity, right down to a farmer working his field on the outskirts of the airbase.

Taking a moment to gather her thoughts and find more courage to get her through the next possible rejection, Alice wanted the world to stop, to slow down and let her head clear itself of the dark thoughts of war.

Around her were large trees, shrubbery, green fields, large huts, small huts, the odd bird or two, and noise; a lot of mechanical noise. Above her, Alice heard an engine whine in the distance and saw everyone turn their heads skyward, then turn back to what they were doing.

The plane was going home and not about to attack. It dipped and bobbed, balancing its wings like a bird of prey on the swoop. Alice watched in awe as the pilot guided his plane clear beyond the buildings and across the fields out of sight, heading for his own airbase.

What skill it took, and Alice stood a while taking it in. She had possibly watched Royal Air Force heroes return from defending their country. Her country: a place where she was desperately trying to find a spot called home.

She turned her attention back to the man and woman standing chatting beside a hedge, and taking a deep breath she summoned courage to speak with them and find the address of the woman who might take her in and help her back on her feet.

Chapter Three

'Excuse me!' Alice called over to the couple who immediately turned her way. The man, older and dressed in Home Guard uniform gave a smile and stepped towards her.

'What can I do for you, miss?' he asked, offering Alice a smile.

'I'm looking for Hettie Saltfield. Her sister said she lives this way,' Alice said, offering him a smile.

'Are you, now? Well, Hettie lives just over there,' he said, pointing to a large clump of trees. 'Through the woods onto Wood Lane, and it is the first house you come to, sits on its own.'

'Thank you for your help,' said Alice and lifted her bag and suitcase from the ground.

'Happy to be of service, young lady,' the guard said, and turned his attention back to his companion.

Alice walked through the woods, grateful for the cool shade. Although she was tempted to sit on a moss-covered felled log, she took one slow step after another. As the edge of the woods came into sight, she braced herself and stepped out onto the edge of a ploughed field.

Fields and trees featured for miles as she looked around for

Hettie's house. At the end of the rough pathway, she stepped out onto Wood Lane and continued her walk on sore feet and aching legs. Rounding the next bend, nestling on the edge of the vast expanse of fields and trees stretching out for miles, a large red brick building with a porch and four large windows came into view. Finally, heaving a sigh of relief, she had reached Saltfield Cottage. Although she knew this might not be the last part of her journey, it was a moment she could stop and catch her breath. The garden surrounding it was as cared for as Hilda's. Both women obviously took the Dig for Victory instruction seriously, as vegetables and climbing canes filled soil beds.

Tugging on the bellpull inside the porch, Alice waited. Again, her heart pounded. Was this to be another dead end?

A short, stout woman opened the door, her face and her pinafore powdered with flour.

'Mrs Saltfield? Hettie?' Alice asked.

The woman frowned at her. 'That's me, what can I do for you, dear?' she asked.

Holding out the vegetables and egg bag Hilda had given her, Alice smiled.

'Your sister sent you these, and wondered if you could help me. I have a letter from her,' she said.

Hettie gave a laugh, a loud boom of a laugh which startled Alice.

'My sister and her vegetables. She thinks hers are better than mine and her eggs are golden, bless her. What does the letter say, give it here.' She held out her hand out, still keeping Alice standing on the porch.

After a few minutes of silence, the woman folded the letter and placed it into her pinafore pocket.

'A relative of Jane Lovett. I see. Well, you are lucky I am not her or you would be torn to shreds by her sharp tongue. Never heard her say a kind word about anyone – especially her sister.

Jealousy does that to people. Now, let's not stand here chatting. I've got a bed to make up – you can go and pump water ready to heat for a bath. You look done in, child. Come in, come in. My sister was right to send you my way.'

And before Alice could finish taking in the words thrown at her at great speed, she was ushered inside the house. The entire place was neat and organised, except for the kitchen, where the worktops were covered in a thick layer of flour and trays of baked goods.

'Don't mind the mess,' Hettie said. 'I'm the allocated baker for the Women's Institute delivery tomorrow.'

'It all looks and smells delicious,' Alice said, her mouth watering.

Hettie tapped a plate.

'I'll just finish the last of the scones, you get yourself a potato pasty from the last tray over there. Warm and tasty. Eat while we get to know one another.'

Grateful for Hettie's hospitality and some food, Alice listened to more about her grandmother and Jane. She discovered Jane had been envious of her grandmother all her life, and had attempted to steal Mary's fiancé. Consumed by jealousy, Jane made it her mission to ruin the wedding day as well.

She led a spiteful campaign to destroy the relationship with false allegations against Mary's husband. Eventually, Jane's parents had banished her from their home. The villagers she had lived here with suffered from her gossip and spiteful ways. Jane was sly and found ways of finding out secrets and making threats which gave her control over many residents.

'I'm sorry to say she was an enemy to so many, Alice. You will never hear a kind word about her around these parts. And if I was you, I would not mention you are related.' Hettie gave her a sympathetic look. 'Some people have long memories and have suffered so much because of her. Mind you, it could be worse, because if that woman was still alive, she would use you for her own gain. Put her out of your mind.'

'I think I'm so lucky she wasn't my gran. My grandmother was kind and gentle,' Alice said.

'You are lucky, believe me. Now, tell me about how you came to be here and not with your parents,' Hettie said, as she bustled about cleaning her kitchen, refusing Alice's offer to help and insisting she sit and tell her own story.

Alice had minimal memories of her parents, but even after so many years since she saw them last, she could still recall the year she turned five.

That was the year they left her alone in a wild rainstorm and never returned.

It was the year she felt unloved.

A period in her life when she understood the word 'unwanted'.

'My parents were Sylvia and Frank Carmichael, they abandoned me outside an orphanage in Sheringham. According to my grandmother they were dreamers, with money worries. My father was an author, and they were killed over their debt, from what Gran learned. I grew up thinking I was Alice Smith. Apparently, I am dark-haired like them both, and my eyes are brown, and my skin tanned like my father's. He was a horrible man. I remember not loving him, even at the age of five. He had a violent temper. I learned to read very early on just to avoid him.' While she was talking, Hettie gave soft tuts of disapproval and sympathetic glances at Alice.

Alice's voice petered off as she thought about how much she had shared with a stranger. But it was the truth. When reading had become her escape from reality, she had created an imaginary friend, Lilly, and spent her time reading to her. This and the books she read gave Alice her magical moments and helped her switch off when her parents raged at one another, their tempers so heightened they no longer held back on the loud insults. Alice would hide in a small nook in the house and read her way out of the atmosphere.

'That's a sad state of affairs, not loving your child to the point that at such a young age they know,' Hettie said softly.

Alice gave a sad nod.

'According to my grandmother, the police found them in Scotland in nineteen thirty-nine. Dead. It was definitely them. My mother was carrying a letter Gran had sent her when she first married. That's how the police found her. There were also papers which showed an enormous debt. The lenders demanded their money with interest. The police reassured my grandmother they are all under lock and key for murder, and the debt died with my parents.'

'Well, it is a sad past, and a recent sadness added to it, Alice. You need to rest. Enjoy a bath, then a glass of hot milk before bed. We will see if we can make the world a little brighter for you tomorrow,' Hettie said softly, her kind words unburdening Alice of her major worries for a short while.

Chapter Four

Once bathed and semi-refreshed, Alice sipped her milk, then gave a slight yawn and tried to cover it up, not wishing to appear rude.

'You are making me feel tired. Up to bed with you. I'll leave you to make up the bed. It's a small room, but it has an unobstructed view across the fields,' Hettie said, and ushered her upstairs into a small bedroom.

She pulled fresh bedding from the wardrobe in the corner of the room and placed it on the mattress – the mattress calling Alice's name. Hettie beckoned Alice to the window of the bedroom.

'Isn't it beautiful out there? Well, aside from the airfield. We will be able to see the planes take off and land from here when the runways are finished – and hear them, of course, but we have to be grateful for their protection,' Hettie said, turning back to face Alice.

'I will make breakfast for my guests tomorrow, so Hilda's eggs will come in handy, they won't mind them being smaller than my usual ones. And you can tell her how wonderful they were,' she said with a gusty laugh, and Alice giggled. She got the impression the sisters loved one another and had a good-humoured relationship.

Hettie left Alice to organise her bed. Although the room was much smaller than the one at her gran's, it was pretty, clean, and well decorated. Alice could not wait to climb into the bed along one wall, the sheets smelled of fresh air and were very inviting.

Hettie had explained she had RAF engineers billeted with her, but they would not be home that evening as they were busy overseeing something on the base, so Alice might run into them around the house in the morning. Alice was slightly nervous about meeting them, but had to accept she was in a different environment to the one she was used to in the past.

Watching men in the field beyond clamber over the large machines, Alice opened the window slightly and heard their voices and laughter echoing across the field. Friendship and unity whilst dealing with such difficult tasks was something she envied. In the orphanage she'd had people around her, noise, routine, and discipline. Again, she squashed the nugget of regret leaving the home she had lived in for the longest time in her life to live with a woman she barely knew.

Even meeting Hettie and preparing to sleep under her roof, Alice felt very alone in a strange world and closed the window against the laughter in an attempt to dilute the envy.

Dear Diary

Today was the most tiring day since the bombing. I've taken more bus journeys than I care to think about and met generous, kind people along the way. From a ditch, I watched and listened to two enemy planes and wished I had my own gun to bring them down!

My body is sore, my bones ache, and my heart is struggling to find a positive beat. It has fluttered, dipped, and dived all day today. It is exhausted, too.

Gran's sister, my great-aunt Jane Lovett is dead. From what I have learned, she was an unpleasant woman and does not sound anything like my gran. This means all relatives on my mother's side are dead. I am all that is left of her family. I do not know about my father, Pablo Marin, who apparently changed his name when he arrived in England from Spain. I am sad and feel lonely, but the two sisters I met today (Hettie Saltfield and her sister Hilda) are kind, and have ensured that tonight will be comfortable, so I should not complain.

Hilda seemed blunt and to the point, whereas Hettie is busy, and sweet. Hilda strides and Hettie flits. Two lovely, lovely ladies. My gran would have enjoyed their company. She certainly would be grateful to them for taking me in. I know I am!

What a strange life I have led so far, and I wonder what will happen tomorrow. My aim is to return to the orphanage where I might be able to find work again. I have enough for the ticket back to Sheringham, and my fingers crossed for my future.

I cannot keep my eyes open. Time for bed!

Beneath the comfortable eiderdown, Alice allowed her body to drift into a natural sleep, but found her dreams flashed into reality and back to the night of the bombing. She tossed and turned trying to ignore the event, but the nightmare took over and she relived the end of April.

Her memory dived right into the moment she had been enjoying time in her grandmother's library. Seated in a green, winged-back chair, she lost herself in listening to her grandmother's life story after they had enjoyed an afternoon of reading together. Her grandmother impressed her with her knowledge of authors and their characters. Her words, 'I believe books hold the beating heart and soul of an author,' had impressed Alice, and that is when she had made up her mind she would read as many books as she could throughout her lifetime.

She remembered a nagging character in *Pride and Prejudice* had called out to her and she had to find out more about Fitzwilliam Darcy and Elizabeth Bennet. Why was he so rude? So arrogant? Why did he refuse to dance with Elizabeth?

The more Alice read, the more the plot drew her in, and the complex characters puzzled her. She knew her life inside the orphanage had held her back from life experiences, and Alice challenged each book and character she read to show her real life. Even though it was fiction, she was certain a lot was drawn from true-life experiences, and Jane Austen was certainly giving Alice food for thought with each exciting sentence she read.

After an hour of reading one evening, she'd shifted in her seat with the need to stretch her numb legs. She knew if she did not stop reading about the awkward and shy man she would continue reading until the early hours.

As she stood upright, a sudden blast from a siren pierced through the room from outside, and she listened out for movement from her grandmother in the room above. Nothing. Then the definite sounds of bombs dropping filled the air. It was time to go to the shelter.

'Gran! Gran! Grab your bag. It's a raid!' she called out and briefly listened as her grandmother moved around her bedroom above.

Alice ran around the library and quickly stroked the spines of the books, selecting two more to take with her to the shelter. She imagined the other books awaiting her return, ready to teach her, transport her, and fill her mind with their messages of hope. Her dream flashed back to before that night, to the first time she'd ever stepped into the room.

'Stay safe, books,' she whispered as she rushed towards the door to help her grandmother who was descending the stairs armed with her knitting and the night flask Alice had prepared for her earlier. Her grandmother enjoyed a cup of tea before daylight.

'I've got everything, Gran. Careful on the—'

Neither of them stood a chance to escape the house when a torrent of bombs exploded above and around them. The ground shook, and everything shattered around Alice and her grandmother.

'No!'

Startled by such vivid memories, Alice woke herself from the nightmare. A chill ran through her body, and she managed to stop herself from screaming out again. She lay listening to the noises outside, trying to calm herself. A sweat had formed across her brow, and she breathed in and out until a more comfortable, if fleeting, form of sleep overcame her.

Chapter Five

By the time a cockerel suggested it was early morning, Alice was wide awake. She stretched out her limbs, which were still aching from the previous day. In general, though, Alice felt more alert and energetic despite the vivid dreams.

She quashed the merging images from her nightmares and went to the window and opened it, allowing the springtime floral fragrance in, and letting the noise of another day fill her ears.

After washing and dressing, she made her way back downstairs, but when she heard voices she stopped.

'Morning! Sleep well?' Hettie said over the sound of bacon sizzling in a pan.

'Yes, thank you.' Alice gave her a short nod and then smiled shyly at the two airmen seated at the table.

'My niece, Alice,' Hettie said quickly and gave Alice a warning frown.

'Morning,' Alice said.

'Morning, miss,' they said in unison then returned their attention to the plates of food in front of them. They both looked as tired as Alice had felt the previous day.

'Alice, do me a favour: can you let the chickens out of the pen and feed them while I cook your breakfast, dear,' Hettie said, and looked to the back door. Alice nodded and walked into the garden bewildered. Why on earth had Hettie introduced her as her niece? Then she remembered the letter her sister had written.

If Alice had the good fortune of having an aunt in her life, she would undoubtedly choose Hettie. She came across as a kind woman. Definitely not as staid as her sister, Hilda.

After successfully chasing out the chickens from the coop, Alice happily collected the eggs, smiling at Hettie's comment about Hilda's golden one, as she playfully scattered grain and scraps around the chicken pen. As she finished, Alice caught sight of Hettie carrying out a large linen basket filled with what appeared to be a mound of white bedsheets. Alice, with her hands still wet from rinsing them under the water pump, called out to her.

'I'll peg those out for you, Hettie,' she said. Rubbing her hands down her dress, she walked over to the clothes line, where Hettie was taking pegs out of a cotton bag.

'Here, give me a sheet,' she said.

Hettie smiled. 'I'll manage, dear. You get yourself inside for your breakfast. I made you porridge. Hearty and healthy for a young girl with a long day ahead of her.'

Alice's heart sank, remembering she'd decided to take the long bus journey back to the orphanage today.

'The men have gone to get some rest. They are done in, poor things. Even those who have to plan and organise are working around the clock to save us. Just be aware they'll be in and around the house today. Use the outside privy, if needs be.' Hettie picked up the empty laundry basket and then looked beyond Alice. 'Looks like we've got a visitor,' she said and nodded to Pete Turner who was walking through the gate.

Looking over at Pete, Alice gave him a quizzical look.

'Private Turner? Is there something wrong?' she asked, her nerves twitching.

'No, nothing. I came to check with Mrs Saltfield that you had found her. A security check I'm afraid,' he said, with an apologetic quirk to his lips.

Alice looked over at Hettie and gave a gentle smile, then back at Pete Turner.

'I found her, and I have enjoyed a good night's sleep, for which I am truly grateful,' she said swinging another smile at Hettie.

Pete gave a nod of approval.

'Grand. I'll be off then. Take care, Mrs Saltfield, and good luck, Alice,' he said, and turned to leave.

'Security check my foot,' Hettie said once his footsteps faded away, and she laughed. 'He's taken a shine to you.'

Alice felt her face flush and chose to say nothing. Private Turner was pleasant enough, but she had no intention of getting involved with anyone when she was struggling to find a permanent home.

'Are there many buses to Norwich from here?' she asked Hettie, changing the subject.

'Buses?'

'Yes. I think I'll try and find my way back to Sheringham, to the orphanage. I lived there for so long, and if I explain my situation…'

'You are too old. They will not take you in again, dear,' Hettie said swiftly.

'I had a little job there in the laundry after I turned fourteen. I'm sure Matron would take me on again. I'm a hard worker,' Alice said earnestly. Negativity and obstacles were not going to block her way forward into a new life. With no one in her life to make decisions for her, she was aware she had to make her own way in the world. She was in survival mode.

'Well, have something to eat and drink first,' Hettie said and ushered Alice into the kitchen.

As they sat eating in silence, Alice listened to the sounds of a blackbird, the hammering and banging from the airfield, and the farmer's tractor. At her gran's house, the odd bus or car, people chatting and the clipping of shoe heels on the pavements, maybe a bird or two, and the paperboy calling out the headlines were the sounds she had grown used to. Noises in the orphanage were different: loud squabbles, firm and instructive voices, laughter, crying, seagulls, the trains, and people's distant voices at the perimeters of the grounds. Here, nature battled against the vehicles of war. Birdsong against engine whine and drills. Life for so many will never be the same again, she thought, and let out a sigh as the harsh noises stopped for a brief time and the birds and the kitchen clock ticking were all she could hear.

'Was it always this peaceful, before the war started, I mean?' she asked Hettie.

Hettie took a moment to appreciate the virtual silence, too.

'It was. Apart from when the farm vehicles trundled by – but most of the time it was an area filled with bird and animal noises. Bliss. I cannot wait for the day the quiet returns,' she said, with a wistful sigh.

Once they had finished eating, Hettie cleared the table.

'I'm going to the farm to find out about transport for you back to Sheringham, and I will visit my sister – take her some large eggs!' Hettie laughed, and Alice grinned back at her. 'Do not go anywhere until I get back because you don't know the military boundary yet. Can't have you shot, can we?' She smiled to soften her words. 'Enjoy the rest, sit and read. Make yourself comfortable.'

As Hettie walked away, Alice giggled, but was grateful for the warning.

She tiptoed into the hallway where she had stored her case

earlier and pulled out a copy of *Kidnapped* by Robert Louis Stevenson and turned to the page she had last read. She struggled with the adventure story but was also fascinated by the quest of David and Alan Breck Stewart. The lives and adventures of the characters gave her an insight into places she had never heard of, and some she had, and wished she could visit.

An hour later Hettie returned, and Alice reluctantly closed the book.

'I'm back!' Hettie called out.

Alice went into the kitchen and waited for a smiling Hettie to speak first.

'Sit yourself down, Alice. Don't hover,' Hettie said and pulled out a chair for herself. 'Now, I've just spoken to my sister about you, and she agrees with what I am about to suggest. As far as everyone will be concerned, you are my niece, on my dead husband's side, and neither of us knew the other existed until your grandmother's death ... then the rest is the truth. I need more help with my sewing service than Hilda can offer, and wondered if you would be interested in working for your bed and board? I will of course give you a small wage. What do you think? Is it something you might consider rather than returning to the orphanage?'

Alice took a moment to absorb what Hettie had just said. A home and job offer were hers for the taking, but it felt too good to be true.

'I don't know what to say, except ... I can't sew,' she said with a shy smile.

'I can teach you, and you can deliver for me. You can also clean the house to give me more sewing time?' Hettie looked intently at Alice as if she was willing her to say yes.

Alice grinned. 'Of course, I'd love to live and work here with you, but ... you hardly know me,' she said.

'Nor you me, but I've a feeling we'll get along grand. You would be good company,' Hettie said. 'You already have been.'

Alice gave a slight shake of her head. She struggled to understand her luck after receiving so many blows in the past. Her heart pounded with excitement as she considered the offer. She knew she was capable of repaying Hettie's kindness, and her home was comfortable and clean, and the surroundings – despite the airbase – were beautiful. 'I don't know what to say. I am grateful to you for helping me, truly.'

Hettie got to her feet and leaned her hands on the table.

'Say yes, Alice. The small room is all I can offer at the moment, but when one of the larger ones is free, I'll move you in there. I would not rest knowing you were out there alone again.'

Alice considered the offer. The bedroom would be a small sanctuary and better than an orphanage dormitory.

'The room is lovely,' she said. 'I can see the woods and fields – I even saw a little deer rush across the runway this morning, the men were chasing it off, so I guess it was near their fresh laid concrete. Another brave creature.' She laughed. 'Thank you, Hettie, I accept your offer.'

'That's settled, then,' Hettie said. 'Now. Let me show you my sewing room.'

Along the hallway were two doors, Hettie pushed open one.

'This is the sitting room. The men gather here with their newspapers whenever they get a moment to themselves. Feel free to sit here yourself, anytime. And this'—Hettie turned and pushed open the other door—'is my workshop.'

The room was filled with clothes in piles, a large sewing machine and a table filled with buttons, lace, and large pieces of fabric.

'I restyle and repair. "Sew for Victory" is my motto,' Hettie said laughing as she walked over to the clothes pile.

'These are donated clothes, some with marks or that are torn in places. I mend and refashion them and sell them on once a week in the church hall. With clothing rationed, I do a roaring trade, but I keep my prices low.'

Alice walked over to a dress draped over a mannequin. The top half was a pale blue cotton, and the skirt was a similar blue but with lemon-coloured flowers. In Alice's eyes, it was the perfect summer frock. She stood admiring the pearl buttons on the three-quarter length sleeves.

'You are clever, Hettie. This is beautiful,' she said.

'An old shirt and a dress came in handy for that one,' said Hettie. 'The buttons were from a drab black dress, which became a small jacket. Our mother taught both Hilda and I to sew. I love it, but Hilda is not so keen. Instead, she scouts out the fabrics for me on her rounds.'

Hettie started lifting garments from the pile and checking them over. She held up cardigans and blouses, then moved over to a pile of clothing neatly ironed and folded.

'I don't wish to be rude, Alice, but did you manage to save your clothes in Norwich?' she asked.

Alice shook her head. 'I'm afraid not. I have this dress and another brown one. They were given to me by a lady from the WI. I've also one cardigan, a nightdress, and the coat is from Gran's landlord.'

Hettie handed her a blouse and skirt, then picked up a large wool needle.

'The blouse is roughly your size; the skirt definitely is, and this cardigan just needs the edge of a sleeve repaired. Take them for now and we'll sort you out a better wardrobe later,' she said.

Alice took hold of the items. 'I have a little money, so I can pay for them. Thank you.'

'Don't worry.' Hettie waved her offer away. 'Go and hang them up and we'll chat about what I want you to do each day. You will not be idle, that's for sure,' she said with a grin.

Two days later, Alice put three new dresses in her wardrobe. One, a pretty green, was for Sunday best. Hettie had also found her new shoes, a small handbag, and a brown jacket. On her dresser along with a new hairbrush and four ribbons, sat a pot of moisturising cream. Hettie had insisted she protected her face from the sun and wind.

On her bed was a new nightdress and in a drawer were three more. Hanging on the back of the door was a yellow flannel dressing gown. Hettie's generosity overwhelmed Alice and she stood looking around her compact private space. On top of the wardrobe was her suitcase and her treasured books, plus the fur coat. Inside her handbag was a small purse which held the last of her money from the WI.

'Well, Hitler, I am safe, warm, and fed. Stay away!' she said and thrust her fist into the air in defiance.

On her bedside table was a new ink pen, pencil, and notebook. Aside from writing her diary, Alice had decided to write down anything Hettie taught her, to remind herself of the process, or of ingredients. Hettie deserved the best of Alice, and she was determined to repay her new friend and employer with the respect she deserved – by becoming a loyal employee and companion.

Dear Diary
    I cannot express how I feel inside. Hettie Saltfield is someone who has shown me the greatest kindness by offering me a roof over my head and the comforts of a home. I promise to do my best to

repay that kindness with hard work. I am writing this sitting by a window in a small bedroom of a large house in Billingford, near Thorpe Abbotts and Dickleburgh. It is close to a town called Diss, which I remember Gran talking about. I think it is where my grandfather's family once lived.

Hettie is keeping me safe by pretending I am her niece, which means her sister will have to do the same. Hettie reassures me that Hilda will. So, it already feels as if I have the new beginnings of a family to support me through this dreadful war. I have a wardrobe filled with lovely clothes, Hettie is so generous and thoughtful.

There is a British airman who helped me, and he has checked whether I found the help I needed. He is what Matron would have described as a cheeky chap. I think he has a lovely smile.

I must be positive and remain grateful for the people who help without question.

I do have one thought about my past, though. I assumed Gran was an only child, and I now know differently. Which made me wonder if I have a sibling out there that I do not know about. After all, neither Gran nor I know what my parent's life was like after they left me. They might have done the same to another child. I truly hope not!

My new life in Billingford has begun and

although I am a little excited, I am also extremely nervous. If this does not work out for Hettie and she finds I am a responsibility she would rather not have - what will happen to me? Where would I go? Perhaps the orphanage? But will there be a life for me there? I know there is always one of the services I can join, but in the meantime, I will have to have faith this new situation will work for us all. My mind is in turmoil, but I must remind myself I am a survivor and have received a second chance at finding my way again. Whether I am fortunate or not, only time will tell.

I am reminded of the novel my grandmother was reading when I first arrived in her home, Lady Windermere's Fan, and the quote she read out from the book, "We are all in the gutter, but some of us are looking at the stars." I knew immediately what it meant, and they are words I shall reflect upon today. I was down on my luck, but now I am looking at a brighter future.

Chapter Six

D ay after day, Alice's confidence grew. She got on with Hettie's village friends and enjoyed walks to Hilda's, and slowly her mind and body relaxed into everyday living.

Although Alice found some days hard and missed her grandmother, she tried to focus on a future within the small village. Gran would want only the best for her, and Alice had to ensure she did not ruin her new opportunity of a better life.

During her reading time in the sitting room one evening, Alice was joined by one of the airmen.

'You have certainly cheered up Mrs Saltfield, Alice,' he said, after introducing himself as Flight Lieutenant Edward Munns.

Alice laid her book in her lap.

'She has cheered me up, too. Where I would be without her, I do not know,' she said.

Knocking his pipe against the inside of the fireplace and repacking it with tobacco, Edward lit it, took a few puffs, then nodded.

'Your aunt said you are orphaned, and you lost your grandmother during the raids in Great Yarmouth. I truly am sorry for your loss. What luck you have Hettie and Hilda in your life. Got hearts of gold, the pair of them.'

Alice nodded her agreement, politely waiting for him to pick up and open his newspaper, but he seemed keen on conversation, so she relaxed back in her chair.

'Do you have family?' she asked.

Edward crossed his legs and puffed on his pipe again. Dark rings underlined his eyes.

'A mother. Lost my father in the Great War. The war to end all wars – in some ways I am glad Dad's not around to see this one. I have a sister, two brothers, and a fiancée, Helen,' he replied.

'Are your brothers in the air force?' Alice asked.

'One is. The other is in the army – and my sister is a nurse in the navy. We *are* the British forces,' he said, laughing loudly. A laugh her grandmother would have described as a hearty bellow.

'Well, we are in safe hands, then,' Alice said. 'Your fiancée, what does she do?'

'Worries. Writes me letters worrying, day in and day out. Seriously, though, she is a clippie. That is how we met. She punched my ticket on my bus journey home, and I fell in love. I travelled the same bus every day of my leave. When she wasn't on there one day, I tracked her down at the depot and asked her to walk with me in the park the next day...' Edward's voice trailed off and a sadness fell around him.

'That's a beautiful love story. The bus conductor and the airman. It sounds like a title for a book,' Alice said and gave a light giggle to lighten the mood.

'Read much?' Edward asked, nodding at the book on her lap.

'Whenever I can – I'd read all day and every day, if I could. Gran had the best library; this is one the gas explosion didn't get to destroy. I've more in my case. Some were my grandfather's, and I think they may be a bit of a tough read, but they are all I have left of my family, so they are more than just books to me,' Alice said passionately.

'Then my advice is to keep them for yourself. Do not lend them out or you might never get them back.' Edward glanced at his watch. It was nine o'clock. 'Right, that's me done in for the night – early start in the morning. Night, Alice,' he said and got up for the door, calling out for Hettie.

Lifting the book from her lap, Alice thought about what he said, and she thumbed through the book in her hand. As she did so, a piece of paper fell from near the back and fluttered to the floor. When she picked it up, Alice noticed it was headed with an address in Canada. She had heard the country mentioned, but knew very little about it, and wondered who her grandfather might know in a country so far away.

Miss Gabrielle Claudette
    Home Farm
    Ontario
    Canada
    Dear Mrs Fen (Mary),

My brother asked that we write to you, and he promised us he has also written his thanks. When my brother read your note and unwrapped the warm knitted socks, he was overcome with gratitude that a stranger could send such a welcome gift.

We learn of deaths by the hundreds when your country is bombed, and I admit it brings my family to tears and breaks our hearts, so for you to take the time for a young Canadian soldier is a true act of kindness. We hear news from Great Britain about our boys fighting to help against the German enemy, and it spurs us on to keep writing to the servicemen and women involved in the battle for freedom.

I would enjoy reading more about your part of England and of your life before the war, so please would you consider writing to me, too?

Stay safe.

Yours truly,
Gabrielle Claudette

Alice folded the letter and placed it back inside the book for safekeeping. The date was marked as 1941, and she wondered if her grandmother had replied to Gabrielle. She mused over the beautiful name and handwriting and imagined someone with film star qualities.

Glancing at the clock, she decided to finish the last of the chores for the day, and write a letter to Gabrielle informing her of her grandmother's death. The woman might not be interested in knowing, but Alice felt it the correct thing to do.

Dear Miss Claudette (Gabrielle),

I came across a letter tucked inside a book belonging to my grandfather. My grandmother must have used it as a bookmark.

You wrote to my grandmother, Mary Fen, thanking her on behalf of your brother. It is with great sadness that I inform you that Gran was killed in April this year, when our home was destroyed by enemy bombs. We had less than two years together. She found me in an orphanage (a place where I have fond memories of delicious Canadian jam given to us by Canadian soldiers serving in Britain), as my parents abandoned me, and a neighbour thought I was Gran's long-lost daughter. It is a long and troublesome story, but I am now safe with a lady who has offered me a home.

I am not sure whether you and my grandmother wrote to one another again. Sadly, all papers were destroyed. But I wanted to let you know about her death and thank you personally for reaching out to her. Knowing my grandmother for only a short while, I do know she would have been delighted as she enjoyed writing letters to friends.

My kind regards,
Alice Carmichael.

Later, after showing Hettie the letters and wishing her goodnight, Alice went to bed. Wondering about Canada and what life was like out there during the war, she opened her diary.

Dear Diary

I am tired but wanted to write down my thoughts and feelings.

How can I be so very lucky to have found someone like Hettie as a friend. She has a way of healing some of my pain with her kindness. I am afraid of my future and where my place in this world might be, but I must cling onto hope. Hope is all I have left. I have also written a letter to a lady in Canada! The war brought her into Gran's life, and I look forward to seeing if she responds. Tomorrow, I will try and find out where Canada is in the world.

So far, I have spoken to more people here in Billingford than I have in my whole life! Sometimes I feel like a young child, I am so naïve, and another moment I am dealing with things someone older than me would normally handle. Life is so confusing. Without my parents here, I often wonder who I take after, not in looks but in personality. I do not feel bad-tempered every day, so I would suggest to myself I am not like my father – but am I like my mother? I only remember a worried woman, flitting from room to room trying to please a loud and commanding man. I cannot imagine I am like her either. Their daughter is determined to be strong, kind, and forgiving. I like to think I take after my grandmother, Mum's mother. Our short relationship bloomed quickly because of our love of books - and, of course, one another. She taught me English to a higher level than the orphanage. I thrived with her support. I have to be brave for her sake and do well, but will life during wartime allow me to honour her in such a way? One day I am afraid, and another, I am overwhelmed, happy, and then nervous again. I must find a balance to bring about a stable life; a safe one. Some days I would like to sleep and wake up to the days of sitting in the library room in Gran's house and life moving forward without war. I know I am fortunate to have stumbled across caring people, but I want a caring family. My heart needs to love people and call them my own.

Chapter Seven

Waking the next morning, Alice reminded herself again of how lucky she was, and that she would do whatever was asked of her, no matter how tedious it might be.

She intended to show Hettie she was comfortable enough to get on with her chores and not hover around waiting for instructions.

'Good morning, Hettie. I'm off to feed the chickens,' she said brightly, and snatched up a fresh pinafore.

Hettie looked over from the stove and grinned at Alice as she headed out to tend to the chickens.

'Good morning to you, Cheerful Charlie. A good night's rest worked for you, I see. Breakfast will be on the table in five minutes, so don't dilly-dally out there,' she called after her.

Once finished, Alice took a look at the airfield from the side fence. Peering through a gap in the hedge, she watched the workmen going about their duties.

'You will be charged with spying, if you keep that up'— Edward's voice came from behind her with a jovial tone—'but I won't say a word.'

Alice stepped away from the fence.

'That's enough to put me off. I would make a dreadful spy, I'm caught already,' she said. 'The runways look so small, how pilots land their planes on them amazes me.'

'Clever and brave, every one of them,' Edward said, and smiled.

'They are, take care, Edward,' Alice said. As she went inside for breakfast, she wondered if his mention of spying was him warning her off in a pleasant way.

After breakfast, Alice and Hettie set off to walk to the Brome and Oakley school, to sell Hettie's clothes from one of the classrooms. It was a thirty-minute walk pushing prams filled to the brim with clothing.

As Alice opened the doors to let people inside, she felt the excitement inside the village hall reverberate around the walls. Women of all ages made appreciative noises over the range of dresses, blouses, and skirts refashioned by Hettie, and the neat repair work she'd done to their own clothing.

Alice felt a touch of pride for the woman she had only known a short while, who spent hours ensuring life in Billingford and the surrounding villages was brightened with her handiwork. She also noticed Hettie refuse payment from women with several children in tow and was touched by her friend's generosity.

Hilda arrived to help after her postal round, and Alice went to greet her.

'Hilda! How are you?' she called out over the noise, 'Isn't this wonderful?'

'Alice, I'm footsore and thirsty after my round but always happy to come and help Hettie in here, she does a wonderful thing for so many.'

With a nod, Alice agreed. 'Both of you have done a wonderful thing for me, too, that I know. I will always be grateful. The urn is on in the kitchen, come through and get a cup of tea before you help her.'

They stepped into the quiet of the small kitchen and Alice made Hilda a drink.

'I'm glad you are happy, Alice. You've filled a gap for Hettie, too, and I'm grateful to you. When my niece died I tried my best to help Hettie through it all. Her sewing helped, but there was always a sadness about her. Sarah left a wound I never thought I would see healed, but here she is, happier than I've seen her in years, thanks to you. I knew you would be the medicine she needed, someone to fuss over again – she will stop fussing over me now, thank goodness.'

She and Alice watched Hettie through the serving hatch, giggling and chatting as she pulled a pretty dress over a little girl's head.

Reflection suddenly settled around Alice. The pain of losing her grandmother still crept into her daily life, but since living with Hettie for the past few days it didn't consume her as it once had. For Hettie to lose a child must have torn her apart.

'She didn't say she had a daughter. I didn't know. How sad,' she said softly.

'It doesn't surprise me. Hettie probably wanted you to stay out of your own choosing not out of pity for her. Sarah was fifteen when she drowned in 1935 – the worst year of our lives. Please never ask Hettie to go to the seaside, or mention her girl unless she encourages you to. Hettie's husband never returned from the Battle of the Atlantic at the end of 1941, life has been unfair to her, he was a good man. Do right by my sister, it is all I ask of you, dear. Keep her smiling.' Hilda patted Alice's shoulder.

'I promise. I will try my best, Hilda,' Alice said, and went over to Hettie's side, helping her until the stock was practically depleted. Surprised by Hilda's affectionate tone she also realised Hilda had also suffered deeply from the loss of her niece, but had to be strong and support her sister.

The atmosphere eased into a gentle quiet as the selling event came to a close. Alice was even more determined to support Hettie.

'These will be lighter when we push them home,' she said to Hettie and Hilda after folding and packing away what was left and placing it into one of the two prams.

Hettie laughed and pointed to a pile of clothing on a nearby table.

'I am afraid repairs and alterations always balance it out, Alice.'

On their way home, Hettie pointed at houses and told Alice the names of the residents, and a little bit about some of their lives and quirks. Women whose husbands were fighting, who were missing or dead. Men who were widowed, injured, in the Home Guard or fire-fighting volunteers, women with children, those who worked in surrounding villages and those locals who kept The Horseshoe pub busy during the evening. Alice took it all in, and was thrilled she lived in a close-knit village with character and characters. A sense of belonging had snuck inside her, and she thanked fate for finding her a home with a heart.

The following day, Alice ventured into Billingford alone. She had errands to run for Hettie and a trip to the post office for herself.

After delivering a repaired jacket to a lady who insisted she took home a cauliflower as large as a human head for Hettie, Alice was grateful for the bicycle Hettie had pulled out from the garden shed that morning, carrying the oversized vegetable would have taken every ounce of strength from her arms.

Once three deliveries were done, Alice pushed her bike to the post office.

Inside the red brick building she was greeted by a woman she assumed was the postmistress.

'Morning. I've a letter to send to Canada, please,' Alice said with a bright smile.

'You must be Hettie's niece. Nice to meet you dear,' the woman said and took the letter from Alice.

'Family?' she asked as she looked at the front of the envelope.

Alice shook her head. 'No, it's to my grandmother's penfriend. It's just to inform her Gran is dead.'

'Very sorry about that, dear, but it is good of you to make an effort. Let me look up the stamp for you,' the woman replied.

After leaving the post office, Alice explored the unfamiliar streets, feeling the warmth of the sun on her skin and exchanging smiles with the locals as she pedalled by their neat houses. As she reached the end of the lane, her new home came into view, nestled amidst its picturesque surroundings.

Alice took a moment to appreciate the beauty and wondered what it was like before the air force arrived. She decided the next time she had a moment, she would take a walk through the woods.

Back home she set about cleaning as Hettie had asked her. She started on the upstairs and gathered fresh bedding for Hettie's room. Inside was painted soft green with a green paisley eiderdown on the bed. On the dressing table, stood two photographs, one of a man and one of a young girl, and on a bedside table was a photograph of Hettie with them both. Alice gently dusted them and carefully placed them back into their places. The people Hettie loved might be images behind glass, but they deserved respect.

Inside the rooms allocated to the airmen, more photographs sat on the dressers and bedside tables, and Alice gave a soft sigh. All around the world there were photographic memories keeping hope alive or offering love from beyond the grave.

A sudden blackness came over Alice and her bright mood slunk away as she realised she had no photographs for her room.

Shaking off the melancholy, she moved through the house room by room, happy to be useful and reassuring herself it was home for as long as she and Hettie wanted it to be, and she was not just a guest passing through. Hilda had invited her to tea the following day and Alice had a question or two about Great-Aunt Jane.

Dear Diary

I do not think there is one day where I have not been happy here. Even the shock of Gran's death is easing into a sadness, which does not sit as heavy as it did at first. I know I will mourn her fore ver, she was my saving grace, my family, but in Hettie's home I also feel safe and secure.

Today, although I was happy, I had a reminder that when the images of my gran fade in my mind, I will not have a photograph to look on and remember her sweet smile.

I will not write more as it might bring some of the horrors of what happened haunt my sleep again.

Chapter Eight

W hile making her way to Hilda's, a sudden cloudburst broke overhead and rain pelted onto the ground forming puddles the moment they landed, catching Alice off guard.

She was drenched within seconds, and realised it would be some time before the downpour stopped, when she spotted darker, threatening clouds scudding over the treetops.

Nearby, there was what looked like a small pocket of trees and bushes, and the tip of a small building roof. Pushing her bike as fast as she could, Alice decided to investigate rather than shelter under the trees, when a streak of lightning flashed in the distance. A small brick hut with a door slightly ajar sat within the dark shadow of a clump of trees.

Alice quickly leaned her bike against the wall and went to the door of the hut. She pushed it and the door swung open. The place was empty and dirty, it smelled of urine and animal matter, but the roof overhead kept her dry. It was pitch-black, and Alice dared not move for fear of standing in something horrid, the acrid smell suggested something rotten lay on the floor somewhere nearby. But Alice told herself that she had smelled worse when she'd visited the local farm. She struggled when the smell got worse and the air in the hut became damper, but outside the lightning flashed and she knew she was safer inside than out.

After fifteen minutes or so, the heavy rain eased and left behind an easing drizzle. Pushing her bike out into the open field nearby Alice took deep breaths hoping the fresh air would clear her nostrils. The hut was a useful stop-off point if it rained in the future and she made a mental note to ask the farmers who it belonged to and if she could clean it out to create a shelter for her and the post.

Making her way around the edges of the airfield to the entrance Alice had first used, someone called out her name, and for a second she froze.

Had she done something wrong, walked the wrong way? When she turned to her left she spotted Pete Turner striding towards her.

'Alice, wait!' he called out.

She let out a breath. 'You had me worried there, Pete. I thought I had crossed a boundary or something. I am still getting my bearings around the area,' Alice replied.

A group of his colleagues walked by and cat-called teasing remarks about Pete to Alice. Alice laughed as Pete cursed them away then blushed with a swift apology.

'Sorry, but they torment anyone who stops to talk to a girl. Idiots,' he said, then looked at her. 'I spotted you walking by. I remembered you liked books – or rather, carrying them in a suitcase...' Pete laughed shyly, and Alice smiled. 'Anyway, I was going to drop in with a book for you later, but you've saved me a journey.' He rummaged inside his jacket pocket and held out a book with a well-worn paper sleeve. 'It's a murder mystery adventure, not sure it's your sort of thing, but I enjoyed it.'

Alice took the book from him and looked at the title, *The Maltese Falcon* by Dashiell Hammett.

'That's very thoughtful of you, Pete. I haven't read this one. I have an Agatha Christie, which is a good read. I can lend it to you as it wasn't one of Gran's, one of the airmen at the house gave it to me. I can also recommend J.R.R. Tolkien's novel, *The Hobbit*. Sadly, I don't have a copy of that one to lend you. Mine was lost the night of the bombing.' She smiled sadly at him, but she was also enjoying the opportunity to talk about books with someone who held the same passion for them.

Pete grinned and pushed his hands into his trouser pockets.

'I'll look out for it, thanks. Books fill the time and I tend not to think about what is going on around me when I am reading.'

'Me, too,' she said, brushing her hands over her skirt.

'You off anywhere nice?' he asked.

'Aunt Hilda's for afternoon tea,' she said.

Pete smiled. 'You have two of the nicest aunts anyone could have,' he said.

Slowly nodding, Alice gave a gentle sigh. 'I have, and they have given me a fresh start in life. The world is a scary place for an orphan – even one as old as me.'

'Well, you don't need to be scared any more. You are in safe hands. You're strong. You'd walked miles carrying all those books the day we met. I still smile over you with that suitcase, and me struggling to lift it for two minutes across the field,' he said laughing.

'Well, if ever you need my muscles, you know where to find me,' Alice said with a grin. 'Seriously, though, my aunts are guiding me in the right direction. Hettie says she's going to find me a job to keep me close to her, in case the government starts recruiting anyone useful over the age of seventeen.'

Pete glanced across her shoulder and pushed his cap onto his head.

'Cripes, here comes my chief. I hope it all works out for you, Alice. See you later,' Pete said and took off, back the way he came.

'Stick to the boundary, that side, Miss Carmichael, it is safer there,' he called over his shoulder, and Alice grinned to herself. His final words were more for his chief than for her.

'Thank you, Private Turner,' she whispered, before setting off for Hilda's.

Teddy plodded along the pathway and greeted her with a woof. Alice stopped to tickle him behind the ears, before he raced to the back of the property, barking as he ran.

'Be like that, then,' Alice said laughing, and walked around the back of the building. As she tapped on the back door and pushed it open she called out for Hilda.

'In here! Help, Alice,' Hilda's strained voice came from inside the cottage.

Laying her bag onto the kitchen table, Alice rushed to where Hilda was calling from – the bottom of the stairs.

Hilda lay on her back, with her leg out at an odd angle and a streak of blood oozing down from her forehead. She looked pale and uncomfortable.

'What on earth's happened, Hilda?' Alice said as she rushed to assist.

'I tripped and tumbled from top to bottom. I think I've broken my leg. I feel sick and the pain is awful when I try and move. Typical me to do it when none of the men are around,' Hilda said, breathlessly.

'I will get help. Stay still and I'll be back soon.'

After she had covered the shaking Hilda with a blanket, Alice ran back to the airbase. At the guard hut she explained the situation and asked if they could help Hilda. Within the hour, a medic and an orderly had taken Hilda to the airbase hospital, a surgeon had set her broken leg and she was declared fit and not concussed from the fall. Originally, they were going to check her over and transport her to a civilian hospital, but the surgeon deemed it a courteous thing to do for the village postie, not to mention that by the time she had travelled the leg would be in a distressed state.

The crew took Hilda home and Alice had a message sent to Hettie. Back at Hilda's she settled her onto the large sofa.

'Thank goodness you have a bathroom downstairs, Hilda. The combination of you and crutches on the stairs is not a great one,' Alice said placing a cushion beneath Hilda's plastered leg.

'I have another problem: the servicemen and my deliveries. I have a bag of post for delivery sitting on the porch. I always collect it then walk Teddy before heading out. It will have to go back to the post office. Damn and blast!'

Hilda's outburst and agitation startled Alice, and made Teddy bark.

'I will take it for you. I have the bike with me. Once Hettie arrives, I will go and explain. She will have an idea about the servicemen billeted here too, I am sure. You settle here and rest, and I will wear Teddy out in the garden for a while,' Alice said, trying her best to keep Hilda calm as the doctor had suggested.

'There's a good girl, thank you Alice,' Hilda said leaning her head back onto a cushion.

Once Hettie arrived Alice explained the situation and Alice loaded the sack onto the bike. Inside the postal sack she saw that most of the post was local to Thorpe Abbotts, Billingford, and Dickleburgh, and decided to help by delivering what she could. After riding around Thorpe Abbotts, meeting a few locals and explaining why Hilda was not on her rounds, Alice pedalled to the other village on the other side of the airbase, then onto Billingford. With legs that felt they did not belong to her but happy the postal sack was empty, she climbed off her bike, leaned it against the post office wall and went inside and explained about Hilda.

'Good gracious, I trust Hettie is with her and that Hilda is comfortable. Send our best wishes,' the postmistress said.

'I will. Do you have anyone else to collect and deliver?' Alice asked. 'Aunt Hilda was quite agitated about it and it will be good for me to reassure her.'

'That's the thing. I only have Hilda. It is a small area to serve. I will probably get someone by the end of the week. They'll have quite a few to post by then, but it is what it is. Hilda did not throw herself down the stairs on purpose, and if I know her she won't be in the best of moods.'

Folding the postal sack and listening to what the woman had said, Alice knew what she had to do.

'She certainly is not; she is angry with herself. Aunt Hettie is with her at the moment. I've been thinking … I can help you. I could collect and deliver post until the replacement arrives. It will help me find my way around,' offered Alice. 'If that's allowed?'

The postmistress thought a moment. 'That I am not sure about, dear. This is the royal postal service we are talking about. There are rules. Bear with me,' she said, and went through a door leading into what Alice assumed was her home. She heard the mumble of voices, and while she waited she selected a postcard with pictures of Norwich on the front, a place where she had been happy for a short time. She placed it on the counter just as the postmistress came back into the shop.

'I have just spoken with my husband – he is disabled, thanks to polio, which means he cannot help – and he said it can't hurt if we take you up on your offer temporarily. You've proven you are trustworthy – unless the letters are in a ditch.' She gave a laugh. 'Try it tomorrow and see how you go, it will help me out a great deal. Thank you, Alice.'

'I will try and do my best, I will see you in the morning, Mrs ... um...'

The postmistress gave a chuckle. 'Durrent. Gladys and Bill Durrent.'

On the way home, Alice was grateful she had only the chickens to tend to, and it was her night to enjoy a bath. Inside, the house was quiet, three plates of cold meat and salad sat on the table nestled under tea cloths, and a note from Hettie instructing the airmen she was tending to her injured sister, and Alice was not to be disturbed. Hettie had a way of protecting Alice around the men when they were home. She was grateful, sometimes she wanted to hear their news, but tonight she suspected she would not stay awake long enough to listen.

Dear Diary

Today, I met Pete Turner again, He is the nicest boy - man, of my age group I have come across. Not that I have met many in my life. I hope I see him again. He is a bookworm like me! It will be nice to have a friend. I am not keen on large groups of friends. I never was in the orphanage. In fact, I think Pete is probably the first person I have exchanged book conversations with, apart from Gran.

I am exhausted from a day delivering letters and have offered my help while Hilda recovers from her nasty accident. Being a temporary postie is better than ironing, any day! I met many different people, some with an opinion about me not being a fully-fledged postwoman, but they were still grateful to receive their letters.

I am glad I never returned to Sheringham to try and go back to my old life at the orphanage. Hettie has suggested we take a trip one day, with a suitcase of clothes for the children. A way of me repaying for their kindness. I was one of the fortunate ones. Apparently, not all orphanages are caring and supportive. At least my parents did something right for me by leaving me at that one. Did they know? Did they care in some way? I think I would like to return, but not quite yet. I am attempting to put the past behind me.

PS: Today, I noticed a little side glance between Hettie and James, the resident airman. I get the impression a friendship is deepening between them. This is not the first time he has blushed when I have disturbed the pair of them chatting in the kitchen.

Chapter Nine

S itting down to rest her tired legs, Alice reached for her personal stack of letters.

Rereading the letter from Gabrielle, some of the words resonated with her again, and an idea formed. She decided to speak about it with Gladys later that afternoon. When Gabrielle's letter first arrived, Alice had felt a rush of excitement and a warm flush of joy that Gabrielle had taken the time to still write.

Dear Alice,

I hope this letter finds you well. Thank you so much for writing to me. During such dreadful times, it is wonderful to see that a letter has made its way across the waters from England. I like to think this letter will bring you a sense of companionship from Canada.

The sound of news about the American forces heading to Britain has been spreading, and we have recently received word that another contingent of our Canadian troops will also depart soon. Our farm has suffered with the lack of men, and the government wants us to increase our crops and hogs to help with overseas supplies. I wish I was not such a burden with my crippled leg, but I do my best. Life will never be the same for anyone, be it the winners or losers of the battles.

Thank you for sharing a snippet of your life since losing your grandmother. How sad you had to find another home, but I am impressed by your determination and the trust you have put into Hettie and Hilda. I guess you are already a loyal friend to them, too. Like you, I am a bookworm. My current read is The History of Emily Montague by Frances Brooke. It was published in the 1700s, I believe, and is a story told in a collection of letters, leaning heavily towards romance. I do not think my mother, or my aunt will enjoy it, but we will see.

What are you reading now? I can picture you sitting by the window, reading and gazing out at the vast fields. Your dream of owning a bookshop (we call them bookstores) is a wonderful dream to have. Picture yourself surrounded by the sights of colourful book covers, and the sounds of customers flipping through pages, and it will come true. I bet you are a regular visitor to your library, exploring the shelves filled with endless worlds and losing yourself in the soft rustle of turning pages. Your tales of cycling around the villages delivering post make me smile, and I can almost feel the breeze on my face as I imagine you pedalling through the countryside, exchanging books as you go. Alice's Traveling Library, a delightful adventure awaits!

I sat on our back porch yesterday, basking in the winter's warm sun for less than a few minutes, it is extremely cold here, several degrees below freezing point. I am writing this by a warm fire, my chores are done, and I have four new books waiting to be explored. We received them as a gift from my mother's friend.

Take care over there and write back soon.

Your friend from afar,

Gabrielle

Dear Diary

Gabrielle does not know what a joy it is to receive her letters. I tell her when I write, but I wish she could feel my joy and truly understand what they mean to me. She must be the kindest Canadian to still take time to write to the granddaughter of a woman she barely knew. What she has given me is something personal. Her letters are mine and mine alone. I do not think she realises how much pleasure I get when placing them into my new memory box. They are rebuilding my worldly goods. I now have personal belongings directly attached to me, and not belonging to someone else.

I will always be grateful.

After wheeling her bicycle through the gate, Alice patiently waited, showing her identification papers to the guard as vehicles slowly made their way through the narrow street, and slowly manoeuvred through the main gate. Her eyes scanned the fields, and the absence of the large khaki tents that had previously occupied the space immediately struck her. The rumbling of the vehicles caught her attention, and she couldn't help but notice the neat stacks of khaki tarpaulins on the open-backed trucks. The sight of so many trucks carrying equipment caught her attention. As did the new flag flying above the gate.

Alice moved through the exit and headed to the post office. When she propped her bicycle against the wall she looked over at the windmill where a cluster of people were standing chatting.

'Morning,' she called out and waved.

One of the women beckoned her over. 'Alice, did your friend Pete say anything about the Americans coming to the camp?' she asked.

All eyes were on Alice. As the temporary postie, like the milkman and others serving the community, she was expected to know all gossip relating to the villages.

She shook her head. 'No, but there is a lot of movement with trucks and equipment going through the gates today. My penfriend in Canada mentioned something in her last letter.'

'Dougie here said the Americans are coming to East Anglia and moving in where our lads moved out,' the woman replied, pointing to one of the mill workers.

'With them on our side, we will win this ruddy war!' the man, Dougie, said and punched the air. Everyone around them gave a resounding noise of agreement. Alice smiled at them. 'I think you might be right,' she said. 'I wonder what it will be like for them over here.'

'Wet, with a fleeting moment of sunshine,' someone said, and the group burst into laughter as they walked away.

Alice walked back across the road and went inside the post office. Gladys greeted her with a smile.

'How are you today, Alice?' she asked.

'There's a lot of excitement out there,' Alice said, pointing at the shop window.

'The American forces are going to be a boost for Britain,' Gladys said.

'It is chaos out there, and the lorries are enormous. Some are wider than the roads. It may be bone shaking but I am better off riding through the woods,' Alice replied.

'Can we have a chat about an idea I have – well, my Canadian penfriend gave me the idea. It's about a small library delivery service,' Alice said, and Gladys beckoned her to go through into her private part of the house.

'It sounds an interesting idea, tell me more,' she said.

'Hettie, Hettie,' Alice called out, as she pushed open the kitchen door and ran down the hallway to the sewing room. She flung open the door and startled Hettie who was bent over her sewing machine.

'Is it Hilda, is she hurt again?' Hettie asked with concern.

Alice caught her breath and shook her head. 'No, no, it's not Hilda, it's the Americans. They are coming here, to the airbase,' she said in a rush.

'Slow down. Americans?' Hettie asked.

Nodding her head, Alice smiled. 'Yes. Gladys's husband said more will arrive when new runways are built, and the Americans will help us win the war. The rest of the British air force are leaving and a few of the Americans are rolling in down the back lanes,' she said.

Hettie pulled a face. 'No doubt my guests will leave, too. Shame,' she said and turned away busying herself with folding clothes.

'Yes, I will miss them, and I know you will miss them, too. Do you think you will be asked to take in Americans, will they be billeted here?' Alice asked.

Hettie handed Alice a pile of clothes.

'Heaven knows. We will see when the time comes. Take these fresh clothes with you and tell Hilda I will visit tomorrow and cook her a meal. I am sure she enjoys your salads, but a meat stew will heal her bones quicker. You are a good girl for staying with her, she is not an easy patient, I know,' Hettie said, guiding Alice down the hallway and out of the door.

'Go and see to Hilda and take care with the lorries. You are a godsend, Alice, thank you.'

As she cycled back to Hilda's Alice thought Hettie would be more excited about visitors from across the world coming to their small corner of Norfolk, but she seemed upset about something, and it puzzled Alice.

The following afternoon she had her answer.

———

'Miss Carmichael!'

Alice clambered off her bike and watched Edward and James stride her way.

'Hello, you two. Are you leaving soon, as well?' she asked, pointing across at the airmen scurrying around and the planes taking off.

'We are, and James here wanted to say goodbye to Hettie, but she's not home. I saw her this morning and said my farewells,' Edward said.

'She's at Aunt Hilda's, cooking her a meal. Apparently, my salads are not bone healing enough,' Alice said with a laugh.

'Darn,' said James. 'I have to leave ASAP. Tell her I will write. Do that for me, Alice?' he asked, his voice almost pleading.

Noting the swift glance between him and Edward, Alice got the feeling there was a strong bond between James and Hettie.

'She will be sad she missed you,' she said. 'I'll tell her, and I am sure she will be pleased to hear from you, James. Take care of yourselves. Stay safe.'

Both saluted her and smiled, then walked away.

Alice watched until they were out of sight before cycling to Hilda's, wondering how Hettie would react when she delivered James's message.

Dear Diary

Poor Hettie's face when I gave her James's message. Crestfallen is a new word I learned recently, and appropriate for this entry. James looked down in the mouth when he and Edward left. I will miss them.

If the Americans arrive as rumoured, I wonder what difference they will make around here, or whether things will remain the same. I do not know much about America or the people who live there. It will be interesting to find out about them.

I am waiting to hear about my library idea. Gladys seemed to like it.

I have started reading rather a fun novel at the moment. It is a children's book, but for someone who has never lived in a family, let alone known one with seven children who are all related, I am finding it amusing. The Family from One End Street have so many adventures and scrapes. I wonder if the author, Eve Garnett, led a similar life, if not, she has a wonderful imagination!

I spent two hours cleaning today but every second was worth the effort. The old hut I came across is now spotless and smells of carbolic soap. It will make a useful rain shelter, or even a safe place for someone if the siren goes.

Chapter Ten

June at the airbase was a frantic month of dodging endless streams of the enormous trucks through the lanes for Alice.

She kept to the edges of the boundary whenever she moved from Hettie's to Hilda's so she could see the runways forming, fascinated at the speed in which the workforce moved.

Life for Alice was exceedingly busy, spent helping both Hilda and Hettie. Repaying them both for their kindness in whatever way she could. Hilda struggled with her leg and as Gladys Durrent had had no joy in finding a temporary replacement for her, she surprised Alice by announcing she had applied for and received permission to keep Alice on the delivery round.

Determined to do her duty, Alice learned from Hilda about each household she delivered to, she had met and befriended most, but some were reluctant to chat with a young girl, often asking when Hilda would be back at work.

Although some days were sad, with the task of delivering a telegram of life lost or someone missing in action, Alice never baulked from cycling to each home and offering her condolences. In a short while, she learned that the community she served was one large family, and they had embraced her into the heart of it because she had shown respect and compassion to those who were in need.

Discussing her future with Hettie and Alice that morning, Hilda confided she was not ready to slow down but was happy to enjoy more time with her sister. As she spoke, she rubbed her hand across her forehead and pushed her wayward grey hair from her eyes.

'At my last appointment over at the general hospital, the doctor said my cycling days are over and my walking is unstable. I must use a stick. Apparently, I am not as young as I once was – can you believe it?' Hilda said with a light laugh.

Alice noticed the pain – not physical, but that of regret – in her eyes.

'I will get to see more of Hettie now that I have formally retired, but I will miss the job – our mother took it on during the Great War, when the postmaster and postman were called up.' Hilda looked at the floor then up at Alice. 'Sadly, they never returned,' she said. 'Our father became postie when he was demobbed out of the army.' She paused. 'I spoke with Gladys about your training and she said it is all in hand. You would be a fool to ignore the offer I am certain will come your way. It is an important job, close to home, and it pays a wage. And you're faster than me on the bike so you'll get the round finished in good time.'

Alice grinned. 'I love the job, and cycling, so combined it isn't a hardship, at all. Even giving out the telegrams is getting easier,' she said.

'Gladys and I also spoke about the library project Gabrielle suggested. She has agreed! I am to become the local librarian on wheels,' Alice said, following through with a laugh.

Hilda sat back in the chair. 'What a grand idea! Put my name down for a good read. I need a bit of escapism. There are boxes of old books in the back room I packed up for the pulp collection, some might come in useful for your library. Help yourself to as many as you want. I think it will be popular,' she said.

'I can cycle to selected villages, and if there is post for the area it will make it even easier. And even if you return as the postie, Hilda, Gladys says she has a bike I can use. She is very keen to be a part of the project. It will give me something else to fill my time,' Alice said with a laugh.

'When I am better, you will have more time on your hands,' Hilda said. 'How is Hettie? Has she come out of her sewing room yet? She was fond of James, I could tell.'

'She is coming to terms with it, and I think she will write to him soon. I've told her not to give up on the friendship. I still write to Pete, Private Tucker, who was always good to talk to. Friendships should not be forgotten just because the war has stepped in and messed things up,' Alice said with passion.

By the time Alice climbed into bed, she and Hilda had unpacked four boxes and found all the books with limited damage to their covers, which amounted to two large boxes.

At the table, Hilda wrote a list of villages to visit and who to approach, and between them they set out a list of the books, giving them codes. Hilda found an unused ledger for Alice to keep track of who she had lent books to and their return date. When Alice slid beneath the blankets that night, she felt a sense of purpose. Even if she could not visit all the villages, she hoped one or two would welcome the idea of a visiting library.

Dear Diary
My library is four days old and proving to be
extremely popular. I have six villages to visit once a

week! Thank goodness the area is flat and there are few hills to pedal up. The thundery storms we are experiencing are a bit of a problem, but I cope. Hilda reminded me not to shelter beneath the trees if lightning flashes. She has a way of scaring me even more, but I won't forget her reminders in a hurry! She is the best teacher and instructor of all things relating to the countryside and weather - and about being a postwoman. Her stories are fascinating.

Thanks to encouragement from Hilda, Gladys wrote to her superiors and asked about me having the postal round permanently, and today I received the official letter confirming my post.

I have a home, a job, dear friends, and soon I will be earning more money. I will ask Hettie to help me open a bank account and start saving for my future. Sadly, I realise that both Hettie and Hilda will not live for ever, and I need to think ahead. Being homeless and penniless is not something I want to go through again.

'Don't move,' mumbled Hettie with pins poking out from her teeth. Alice's uniform had arrived and required a few alterations due to her petite figure. Hettie rose to the challenge, and the final stage of hem-turning meant that the following day Alice would ride around in full uniform showing her official status as the local postwoman. Although it was a sad moment for Hilda, she embraced Alice's enthusiasm by formally handing over her leather satchel.

'It's a family heirloom,' she said with a grin, 'and it has been earned by the newest member.'

Alice saw the look of surprise on Hettie's face as she stared at her sister. Hilda was not one for showing her affection, but her words were always said with conviction.

Unable to move and offend Hettie's pins to the point of stabbing her calves, Alice gave Hilda a grateful smile.

'I'll get you with a hug later,' she said laughing.

Hilda waved her away gruffly, then rose to her feet and shuffled with her walking stick towards the door.

'That's me off to the garden,' she said and both Alice and Hettie giggled.

'It won't bite. One hug.' Hettie called out after her sister.

Once Hilda had left the room, Alice looked down at the top of Hettie's head as she knelt, putting the last pin into the hemline.

'How come you are both so different, Hettie? One mention of a hug and she practically ran out of the door, but you would have rushed over to receive one,' Alice asked.

Easing herself back onto her heels with the assistance of the arm of a chair, Hettie stood upright, stretching her back.

'Hilda used to be very affectionate,' she said, 'but she lost her fiancé to a dreadful farm accident when he went to work the summer in Kent, and it changed her in that way.'

Alice shook her head. 'I didn't realise. That is so sad.'

Hettie nodded in agreement. 'Not only did she lose him, but then she found out he had another family: a wife and child.'

Alice gasped. 'What a dreadful thing to find out. Poor Hilda!'

Hettie was quiet for a few seconds. Alice could see a sadness in her eyes.

'It hardened Hilda,' she continued. 'She shut her emotions away, but then she tried to end her life by walking into the sea.'

Alice stared at Hettie wide-eyed, unable to believe Hilda would do such a thing.

Hettie gave a soft sigh. 'Once she realised she did not want to die, she came home. I tried to help her, but sadly she was never the same Hilda. Then, when my Sarah died, she struggled to console me, and left the county for several weeks.' Hettie's voice trembled with emotion as she looked at Alice. 'You have brought some of Hilda's spark back, especially now you are to replace her on the round. She is very proud of you and her words today speak volumes. You are part of our family now – whether you want it or not.'

Jumping down from the chair she stood on, Alice grabbed a startled Hettie and held her tight. She inhaled the lavender fragrance from Hettie's clothing, a sweet reminder of her grandmother.

'I want it with all my heart!' she whispered. 'And one day I hope you will be Mother of the Bride and stand beside me on my big day.'

Hettie squeezed her tightly, and Alice heard a small sob. A mother-daughter bond had been created and Alice's heart swelled with happiness.

———

Dear Diary

My postwoman's uniform now fits me. What an emotional day I have had. Hilda gave me a leather satchel, which was her father's and then hers. I will treasure it for ever. To be given a family heirloom is an honour.

Hettie is so clever with a needle, she said she inherited sewing skills from her mother, and Hilda inherited gardening and cycling from their father.

I have tried hard to think if I have something I might have inherited, and I realise it is the love of books. My grandmother and grandfather loved them, my mother read a lot and married a man determined to become a published author, and between them all their enthusiasm for the written word has bled into my veins. It pleases me to know I have something which I may be able to pass on to a child one day. I do hope I have a child who loves reading, there is nothing better than being transported into another world created by a different set of eyes.

Hettie and I have a strong relationship. She is definitely my mother figure. In such a short time, I cannot imagine life without her, and after what I have experienced, it unnerves me a little, but I will not let it sit on my shoulders and burden me. A dear woman with the fragrance of lavender will always be in my heart. She had a daughter but has enough space in her heart to allow me to experience her love, too. If the world was filled with Hettie Saltfields, what a wonderful place it would be!

Chapter Eleven

'Post!' Alice called out as she entered Hettie's kitchen a week later.

Hilda had chosen to return home a few days before, coping with regular visits from Hettie, and Alice had moved back to Hettie's where she felt more comfortable. It was home.

Hettie came in. 'I thought I heard you call,' she said.

'I've a letter for you, and I've come to collect my lunch, too. I am going out on the library run and will sit by the river in this gorgeous weather,' Alice said waggling a letter in front of Hettie.

Alice loved delivering post to Hettie, one particular postmark always brought a smile to her friend's face. James wrote as he promised. The exchange of their letters became more and more frequent.

'I wonder who this is from,' Alice said, teasing.

Hettie laughed. 'Give it here, you little minx. It is from James as well you know. My *friend*, James,' she said.

'He's a keen friend. Don't forget, I know exactly how many letters he's written to you – and you to him,' Alice said, giving Hettie a wink and handing over the letter.

The envelope in Alice's hand, addressed to Miss A. Carmichael, begged to be unread. Once opened it promised Alice unrest and sadness.

The only letters she had received from this postmark were from Pete, but this time it was not Pete's scrawling, unruly handwriting, the return name and address on the back was that of his mother, which meant the moment Alice slit the off-white envelope open her world would tilt and yet again bring down a curtain to announce the finale of something real.

Was this a telegram moment?

She slit open the top of the envelope.

When she opened out the paper to read what Pete's mother had penned, Hitler and his followers were crawling across the paper, marching forward stamping out their message loud and clear. Through eyes blurred with tears, Alice read the words again.

Peter died when the plane he was travelling in was
hit by enemy fire and burned out.

Alice did not want to mourn again. Squaring her shoulders and straightening her back she tried to compose herself. There was something wrong with her, life had decided she was tainted.

'My touch must be poison. I'm evil. My parents must have known and that's why they left me. Anyone important in my life dies. I am no good,' Alice said and burst into tears as she flapped the letter at Hettie. 'Now I have lost my only friend. I need to leave. To keep you safe.'

Hettie didn't reply. She took Alice by the arm and lead her back inside the cottage.

Settling her into a seat, she kissed the top of Alice's head.

'You are far from evil. It is the war that killed him. Mourn him and learn to live your life when he can't. It is all we can do. Write to his mother with our condolences and let her know what a fine young man he was and what a privilege it was for us to have met him. It will give her comfort. But please, do not think of yourself as a poison. It is life and we cannot control what happens.'

Hettie's soothing tone calmed Alice and the tears stopped flowing. They hugged for a few moments before Alice broke away to write and post her letter.

Dear Diary

My newest, and only friend my age, is dead.

I cannot describe the sadness and anger I feel. Sad for the loss of Pete. Angry because he was so young and protecting people like me. Angry at myself for no longer writing to him. For thinking the worst of him - that he was ignoring me for a girlfriend, when all along he had died.

I lead a privileged life compared to so many, and for that I am grateful. Hettie said I suffered more than most in my younger years and deserve to live a comfortable one now. Poor Pete's mum, to lose a son so young. Hettie understood what she was going through, but I cannot imagine. I only know the sadness of losing my grandmother so soon after us getting to know one another. That was bad enough.

I feel a little better for writing down my words, and after Hettie reassuring me that I do not have a poison running through my veins that kills everyone

I meet, I will try and settle my mind by reading before bedtime. I am reading more books than ever now. The supply from the donated books is varied and I have set aside a large pile which have captured my attention and which I can recommend or warn readers about.

I am reading Rebecca by Daphne du Maurier, and the newly wed Rebecca is about to enter Manderley, Maxim de Winter's home. Oh, where would I be without my books! Poor Pete, he will never read another one again - or will he, I don't know what happens after death. I will imagine him sitting in a comfortable room, a room like my grandmother's library, enjoying a pipe and a good book, with his children sitting at his feet. I like to think he would have married, had a large family. I always imagined him as a family man.

On another note, I am a little jealous of Hettie. She is so happy when she reads letters from James. How I would love to have a love letter arrive in the post, what a thrill it must be! I enjoy Gabrielle's letters, but to have one from a man writing romantic things and declaring his love - which I am sure James is doing to Hettie in his own sweet way, must be wonderful.

Chapter Twelve

June ended with the 100th Bomb Group, part of the United States of America Airforce settling into the reconstructed Thorpe Abbotts base.

Alice had great pleasure in informing residents of the surrounding villages of the activities and stories which came with the arrival of the Americans. Everything around her sparked excitement for the residents of Dickleburgh, Brockdish and the other hamlets and villages nearby.

New runways buzzed with machine noises and loud, confident voices. Music styles she had not heard before drifted across the fields and Alice spent a lot of time with her bedroom window open to listen.

She worked her routes, often struggling to avoid whistles and cheers as she walked the boundary. The American men strolled in a confident manner and never held back with friendly banter. Their personalities were bolder than the British men she had met.

She wondered what the American women were like in real life. She had only experienced one connection with a Red Cross girl delivering doughnuts and coffee, who was also outward going and confident, as well as extremely attractive. Alice decided all Americans were good-lookers and promised herself to learn more about the country, just as she was discovering about Canada via Gabrielle.

Walking to the bus stop, the engine sound of aeroplanes thundered around her and added to the pounding in her head. She whispered a few words of luck and thanks to the pilots taking off from the runways and disappearing into the sky above her. From the first few days of arriving here the men had been flying into enemy territory.

Like everyone around her, Alice counted each plane crew out and mourned those who never returned. Day after day, there were losses. Heavy losses. She considered how much the Americans must suffer when a plane never comes back, and how thankful the British residents were for their support. Knowing that these young men were risking their lives to help the country made them seem like part of the Great Britain family. They earned that respect.

Amidst the chaos of war, Alice found solace in the simplicity of a small café tucked away from the bustling streets of Ipswich town. The hour-and-a-half journey there took her through pretty villages. Once in town, she browsed the sparse shop windows, purchased a new set of underwear and a headband, then an unexpected shower of rain caught shoppers unaware, and she ducked into the café.

She sat alone at a corner table, her gaze drifting to the window where rain tapped rhythmically against the glass. Lost in thought, she absentmindedly twirled her teacup, her mind consumed by Pete's death, haunted by the loss of a young man with such personality and life plans. Although they had not been linked romantically, they had been connected by books and humour, by friendship. They had enjoyed several chats over a pot of tea, and Alice missed his conversation.

Suddenly, the tinkling of the café bell drew her attention away from her thoughts, and she watched a handsome American enter, his uniform soaked from the rain. Brushing the raindrops from his jacket, he scanned the room with a charming smile at anyone looking his way. His manner begged for him to be looked at and studied, but it was not an arrogance, it seemed to come naturally to him. As Alice snuck another glimpse at him, his eyes locked onto hers and he approached her table. She felt her cheeks flush with embarrassment at having been caught staring. Flustered and slightly starstruck, like the character Georgiana Wade when she first saw Mr Jefferson in *Under the Country Sky* by Grace S. Richmond.

'Mind if I join you, miss? The other tables are full,' he asked quietly, his voice warm and inviting.

Unsure what to do as a room full of eyes stared at them, she gave a soft smile as if she already knew the man in front of her.

'Of course, please do,' she replied, gesturing to the empty seat opposite her.

'I hope you don't mind me saying, but you look like you could use some company on a dreary day like this,' the man remarked, his gaze soft with concern.

'I suppose I do,' Alice admitted, not sure of how to react. She nervously tucked a loose strand of hair behind her ear. 'It has been a tough time recently.'

'Tell me about it,' the man replied, his eyes sparkling with mischief. 'I feel like I've been chasing my own shadow in this British weather.'

As he settled into the chair, he smiled and extended his hand. 'Blake Hardesty, but friends call me Hardy.'

Alice returned the smile and shook his hand. It was large, and warm. She felt a flutter in her stomach. 'Nice to meet you, Mr Hardesty,' she said in a formal manner, not sure on how she should address an American airman, 'I am Alice Carmichael.'

'Hardy, please. It's what my friends call me, and it is my good fortune it rained today as I found a friend with a seat at her table.'

Alice chuckled softly, grateful for the distraction.

'Welcome to the British weather. By this evening, we will be basking in a heatwave, it is July after all,' she said, and Hardy's laugh boomed around the café causing, once again, all eyes to linger on their table.

When the waitress came to get Hardy's order Alice looked out into the street. People rushed past, some with their worries etched across their faces. She tried to feel guilty about sitting with a stranger, but nothing happened. Something had shifted in her small universe, and she relaxed.

'I look forward to the basking. I understand summer in Britain is short-lived. In Dayton, Ohio, where I come from, we have seasons: cold winters, hot Julys,' Hardy said, and Alice turned back to him with a smile.

'It is best not to blink during the next eight weeks, or you will miss your first British summer – but then it might decide to be a long autumn from tomorrow, instead. Who knows,' she said with a giggle.

He gave her a wide grin as their eyes met, and for a moment, time seemed to stand still as she and Hardy shared an unspoken connection. But soon the silence between them was broken by the rumble of thunder outside, reminding them of the world beyond the café walls.

'Your tough time … did you lose someone?' Hardy asked, with genuine compassion.

Alice gave a nod. 'My friend, Pete. He was in the RAF; his mother sent a letter telling me he was dead.'

Hardy reached out and touched the back of her hand. 'He was a lucky man to be your friend, and I am sure sorry for your loss, Alice. Tell me about him.'

With a soft sigh and without wanting to cause offence, Alice slowly slid her hand from beneath his.

'He was a kind person; he had a cheeky humour. Quiet, yet not shy. We shared a love of books. I miss his company. I'm fairly new to the area and we made friends – then became pen pals. When his letters stopped, I thought he had a girlfriend, so I stopped writing back, too.' Alice sat back and looked at Hardy, who was patiently listening.

She shook her head. 'Tell me about yourself,' she said, giving him an encouraging smile.

Hardy smiled, as though sensing her boundaries. 'First, can I tempt you to join me in a pot of tea? I had never tried it until I arrived in England. Coffee is my drink. It keeps me awake. But I will be British this afternoon, considering the company and weather. What could be better than tea with an English rose during a rainstorm.'

Alice laughed and nodded. 'I would like that, thank you,' she said.

After Hardy had ordered and the waitress had delivered their fresh cups and a teapot, Alice asked, 'Are you a pilot?'

'No. I work on the planes. Repairing them. Keeping them in the best shape I can. Ground crew.'

'That must be hard work. I see them flying day in and day out,' Alice said.

'It is, and some days I wish I had never stepped foot in this country. My best friend from school days lost his life here on his first flight over Europe. His plane limped home and struggled to find the runway. I was helpless as it hit a field behind and all I could see was a ball of flames. One of my toughest days so far.' Hardy frowned. 'Forgive me, Alice. I had intended to cheer you up, but here I am talking about…'

She waved her hand slightly in front of him. 'No apologies

necessary, I am glad you felt able to confide in me, and I am sorry you suffered such a dreadful loss.'

'Time to change the topic,' Hardy said with a grin. 'What do you do for fun, Alice Carmichael – do you like to dance the night away?'

Smiling back, Alice looked at him.

'There is not a day goes by when my nose is not buried amongst the pages of a good read. It blocks out the war. I prefer a walk over a dance. Boring, I'm afraid,' she replied.

'You are far from boring, believe me. I am not one for dancing, either. I do enjoy a good walk. A lot of our guys read; I prefer to fix things,' Hardy replied.

'Did you learn when you joined up – how to fix planes and things?' Alice asked.

'There is nothing they can teach me. My pops first let me loose in his workshop when I was six. He fixed engines and anything mechanical, I fell in love with it, so my hobby became my job. Then I became the instructor, too,' Hardy said.

Alice relaxed deeper into their conversations and the laughter as they exchanged stories of their own countries, of life before wartime; not their personal lives but that of their individual country and town. Alice never mentioned the orphanage, and the dark days afterwards, apart from her telling him about Pete. She leaned towards the season changes and British traditions, while Hardy only spoke of family gatherings and missing them all. She found herself drawn to Hardy's easy charm and infectious laughter and was bemused by her situation. What would Hettie say about her sitting chatting with a stranger, five years older and from another country. Hettie had already taken her to one side and spoken to her about not getting too involved with the young men so far away from home. She decided the best thing to do was not to mention anything to Hettie, as she did not want to dismiss the protective advice offered with no other intention than to keep Alice safe.

Slowly, the rain subsided, and a calm atmosphere settled over the café. The afternoon sun peeked through the clouds and people ventured back out onto the streets. Eventually, Hardy rose from his seat, a regretful smile tugging at his lips.

'Well, I should get back to the base,' he said, his tone tinged with disappointment.

Alice also stood up. 'And I must catch my bus home. I've enjoyed your company, Hardy. Thank you for cheering me up, and for the tea,' she said.

Hardy walked around to her seat and helped her on with her coat.

'It was my pleasure, Alice. If I have brightened up your day with my incessant American chatter, then my duty over here is done,' he said, and Alice could feel the warmth of his breath on the back of her head. It sent shivers of pleasure down her body.

They walked to the end of the high street and then Hardy stopped and turned to her. Although Alice was disappointed their meeting was at an end, she was also grateful for their time together. In a world where a bomb could cause destruction in seconds, every encounter with another human being with a thoughtful nature was precious. Hardy had noticed her sadness, and although she never realised it, he had also recognised the need for her to sit in the company of someone who understood the pain of loss. He had obviously wanted to relay his distress to someone, too. Fate had brought them together for three hours.

'Good luck for the future, Alice. Thank you for allowing me to sit at your table and for listening,' he said and shook her hand, before turning it over and kissing it. 'For my good luck.'

'Take it with you and keep safe, Hardy. Oh, and enjoy the sunshine when it appears,' Alice said, making the moment more light-hearted for them both before turning to walk to the bus stop.

Dear Diary

I met an American airman today. A handsome man called Hardy. We had tea. He made me laugh with his English-gentleman act. Pete came to me in a dream and told me to live my life, a life he cannot, it was strange at the time, but him or my guardian angel (because I am convinced I have one after surviving the bombing) sent Blake Hardesty (Hardy) my way. It was a cheerful three hours well spent. Hardy made my skin tingle and when his breath touched my neck it felt – I don't know how to describe the feeling, but it was more than just pleasant. His voice fascinates me, though I do not think my Norfolk accent could fascinate anyone. Today was a happy day.

Chapter Thirteen

A sudden noise caught the attention of both Alice and Hettie, causing them to turn their gazes back towards the horizon.

The day was slowly drawing to a close and the sun had begun its descent, casting a stunning, radiant orange hue across the entire sky. Its warm glow enveloped the soft, cotton-like threads of the clouds below, creating a captivating scene. Amidst this picturesque setting, the noise grew louder as a B-17 plane emerged. It was obviously struggling on its journey home through the skies as it rumbled and swayed from side to side with wild and ruthless red-gold flames eating into its left wing and rear.

What looked like a helpless situation sent shivers down Alice's spine.

Was this how Pete died? Why hadn't the men jumped from the plane – or were there only two left in the cockpit? Questions rampaged through her head as the sun glinted off the metal wings. Black smoke trailed behind its tail and Alice closed her eyes begging the machine to keep the crew safe.

Holding hands, she and Hettie watched the pilot attempt to land, with the ground crew desperately waving the plane over onto the grass area, away from the runway and buildings. Eventually, it landed and everyone willing it home safely let out a collective sigh of relief.

'They are so brave,' Alice said in awe as they watched the crew stumble from the plane.

'And young,' Hettie said. 'Far too young. They shouldn't be put through the horrors of another war.'

A team of medics lifted the injured from the plane, and the ground crew patted the pilot and others on the back. Each man embraced the other, expressing their relief. Even from a distance Alice could see the slumped shoulders of the men watching the sky again for another plane to return, but the body language across the field told Alice and Hettie that the plane they had seen landing was the last one home.

Firemen doused the flames as the ground crew walked around inspecting the damage. Suddenly, the activity around the airfield grew into a well-organised recovery programme as men clambered on and around the damaged planes.

'It fascinates me how they put the planes back together again. I've seen a few come in with only one or half a wing, and the following day they are whole and flying again,' Alice said, as she and Hettie walked towards home from the boundary fence. She resisted the urge to tell Hettie about Blake Hardesty.

'It must be a lot of responsibility on the engineers' shoulders, too. Every plane is needed to be fit to fly within hours. Brave men. All of them. Young Pete was brave, but you wouldn't get me up in a plane,' Hettie said and linked arms with Alice.

'After the war, I would like to travel in one to enjoy a visit, maybe to Canada or America,' Alice said.

'Well, you will never get me keeping you company. A train and bus, the occasional car ride, but not up there,' Hettie said, pointing skyward. 'You'll never get me up there.'

'I think I will save up and go when it's all over. Try and be as brave as they are,' Alice replied.

'Let's go home and be grateful for the heroes out there fighting for our freedom, and work out how many years it will be before you can afford such a trip,' Hettie said with a light laugh.

The loud honk of the truck's horn reached Alice's ears just before it swerved around her. It was fortunate that the recent weather conditions had caused the ditch she was lying in to dry out completely. As she attempted to move, she groaned. Her bike was beneath her, and the handlebars and her legs had become entangled.

The post bag and her box of books ended up scattered across the road and into the opposite ditch, which she knew was not dry, having had a near miss with another truck the previous day.

'Are you okay, ma'am?' a male voice called out.

'I'm stuck!' Alice yelled, her temper at its peak. It was the third time that week she had experienced a near miss with the American drivers, and she had rearranged her route to exclude the busier parts of the outskirts of the base, but today she had a delivery and book exchange nearby.

'Why do you drive so fast around here?' she shouted as the airman slid down the embankment towards her.

'Not me. Ern. He's the lamebrain of the unit,' he replied.

Assisting Alice to her feet and back onto the road, the airman went back to the ditch to retrieve her bicycle while Alice picked up her post bag and the books.

'Mighty sorry about this,' the driver said as he walked towards them.

'You took your time,' Alice said with the intention of being rude.

'Easy, sweetheart, I'm here now,' the man she assumed was the lamebrained Ern said.

Inspecting the bike-chain oil on the end of her torn jacket sleeve, and the tear in her woollen stockings, Alice was in no mood for him.

'I am *not*, your sweetheart, and I think it best you walk back to your truck and keep moving. You've ruined my uniform; my books, and you have the manners of a pig!' she yelled at him.

Ern gave a whistle. 'Don't blow your wig, honey,' he said, and walked away.

His companion laughed. 'Apologies again, miss. If you will allow me to take your jacket to our laundry, we can get it cleaned and repaired,' he said.

'I do not find this funny at all, and my aunt is a seamstress, so she will repair my clothes. The ruined books are for my mobile library, but they'll go for the pulp collection now. I think you need to just leave me before I shout some more,' Alice said and loaded her bike basket with her belongings before wheeling it away. 'Oh, and be more careful driving around here next time. Idiots!' she shouted over her shoulder.

Back home Alice's temper was still on the warmer side of hot and Hettie's grin at her telling of her accident did nothing to help.

'It's no laughing matter, Hettie. It is dangerous, the driver was a fool!' Alice said in an injured tone.

'Then get changed and after lunch take another book to Miss Dikes. She will understand why it is different to the one she asked for, it isn't your fault after all,' Hettie said. 'And then, take yourself to the airbase and report the driver. We do not need dangerous fools driving us off our narrow roads.'

Eating her lunch, Alice thought about Hettie's words and, still fired up from the incident, decided to see if she could speak to someone about the problem. She knew of others who had complained about men intent on driving like maniacs – the milkman's horse had shied nearly creating a major problem. It was the second time the same truck had frightened the horse.

'Good idea, Hettie. I'll head to Clara Dikes, and then across to the base,' she said.

Clara Dikes looked at the book Alice offered her. The young woman was film star attractive, dressed in a green tweed suit and a cream blouse. Her red lipstick suited her pale skin, and her red nails complemented her slender hands. Alice had a flash of envy over Clara's blonde, front and side curls, which were large with not one hair out of place. Clara was the most glamorous secretary Alice had ever encountered.

'What happened to the other books?' she asked Alice, her voice a velvet-toned upper-class English one.

'They will be pulped, the covers are torn, some of the pages ripped in most of them. It was a disaster,' Alice replied.

'Such a shame. I was telling my friend about you, and he wondered if you would consider extending your library services into Great Ryburgh. He used to like exchanging books with me, but has only recently come back home – injured you see. He only likes specific types of books – a bit of a stick in the mud, is Richard – but I can give you the books if you would take them and return them for me. Sadly, they were my father's, which means I am reluctant for everyone to read them, or I would lend them to you for the library. Richard is not able to use the bus, and at the moment he refuses to see me. We had a falling out,' she said, then gave a sigh.

Alice listened to Clara wondering if Richard was more than a friend, and decided the journey would be under two hours there and back. If it helped Clara reconnect with him, then Alice wanted to help, being forever the hopeless romantic, much like many of the heroines she had encountered in books.

'I can try for you until he is well again,' she said.

Clara smiled.

'He is rather odd, and a stickler about time, so it would have to be the same day and time each week. Is that acceptable?' she asked.

With a nod, Alice smiled back. 'I have a few hours spare on a Tuesday afternoon. Twelve until three would suit me,' she said.

'That's wonderful, thank you so much, Alice. I will send this book with a letter introducing you. Come in while I write to him, it won't take me long,' said Clara.

Alice stood in the hallway of the stone cottage. It smelled of lavender and other floral fragrances she couldn't name, although it did not have the homely feel of Hettie's cottage.

'Here we are, and please take this ten-shilling note to cover any bus fares you might have to pay,' Clara said, holding out the book now wrapped in brown paper. Alice assumed the letter was inside.

She shook her head at the money. 'There is really no need to pay me. I cycle everywhere. If I need to take a bus, then it is only a few shillings, and if I am in uniform the drivers often let me on free, but thank you, anyway. I will take this tomorrow,' she said.

Cycling towards the main entrance of the airbase, Alice reminded herself she was angry; Clara's calm personality had taken the edge off her annoyance with the airman, Ern.

Gaining clearance with the guard, after she explained her reason for the visit, he suggested she try first to speak with the master sergeant in charge of the ground crew and to aim for the domed hut.

She tapped on the door of the building and a voice called out a blunt, 'Enter!'

Alice opened the door and looked over at the man sitting at the desk, a cigarette in his mouth and his eyes focused on paperwork in front of him. He had several grease marks on his hands. After a couple of seconds, he raised his head and stared at her.

'Alice?' he said, stubbing out his cigarette into a large glass ashtray nearby.

'Hardy?' she said, as surprised as he was. 'Are you based here?'

'Dickleburgh, Thorpe Abbotts, yes,' he replied, then rushed over to lift out a chair from the corner of what Alice assumed was his office.

'Sit, Alice. What brings you here? Private dick – er, detective work, tracking me down?' Hardy said with an awkward laugh.

Offering him a wide smile, Alice said, 'No. I am certainly not clever enough to work out that an American airman in an Ipswich café might have moved just around the corner from me.' She laughed. 'I am here on what I consider a serious matter, but it might be trivial to you or nothing to do with you—' She broke off, her nerves having taken over.

'In which case, I will wash my hands and…' Hardy looked down at his shirt, 'find my jacket, then you can give me the low down on your problem.' He smiled at her. 'I'll be just a minute.'

While Hardy went into another room to change, Alice sat down and waited, disappointed that she would no longer be able to admire his broad chest and muscular arms. On the desk was a photograph of a woman holding a child in her arms. Her heart sank with disappointment. Hardy had a wife and child.

Just as she was thinking about how many women around the world had experienced their loved ones not only leaving to fight a war, but doing so thousands of miles away, Hardy came back into the room. He wore his uniform well, and Alice tried to hide her admiration as he sat down in the chair opposite her.

'This serious matter … tell me about it, Alice, and we'll go from there.'

Clutching her hands together, Alice wished the anger she had felt before would flare into a small flame again, but seeing Hardy's friendly smile had dampened down the reason she was at the airbase. Now she only felt slightly foolish, but knew she had to speak out regardless.

'One of your drivers knocked me off my bike this morning,' she said. 'It appears the same one, *Ern*, almost caused an accident with the milkman's horse. Our roads are small, too small for your trucks, if you ask me, but anyway, he is reckless. And uncaring, and extremely rude and thoughtless. His colleague helped me out of the ditch, but sadly, several of the books for my mobile library were ruined. Luckily, the King's mail was not, but my uniform is undergoing repairs.' Alice finished with more pomp than was necessary, but seeing Hardy had really thrown her into a quandary.

She felt like a small girl tittle-tattling out of school. Was her complaint warranted in such a place when the men were fighting for her freedom?

'Ern, you say?' Hardy wrote something down on a sheet of paper.

Alice nodded. 'That's what his colleague called him. That and a lamebrain, which I assume is an insult,' she said with a slight grin.

Hardy burst out laughing. 'Yup. That's about right. Ern is a hothead, but he's ace at anything mechanical. I'll speak with him – he won't drive around here again; I cannot have the King's post girl injured in a ditch. Your library books … will the library charge you for them?' he said.

Alice shook her head. 'Firstly, thank you for understanding the driving situation. I won't be charged as the books are mine; I have set up a private library delivery service to surrounding villages. The books were given to me by my aunt, Hilda, to help set me up.'

'That's a swell idea. When we met in the café, I knew you were more than the girl who helped her aunt with chores like you told me. A postie and a mobile librarian, the townsfolk are truly lucky.' Hardy smiled, then rose to his feet. 'I left my manners at the door, I haven't offered you a drink,' he said, and moved towards a small kitchenette area. Alice gave him a slight dismissive wave of her hand.

'Oh, I'm fine, thank you. I won't take up any more of your time, but thank you for listening.' She stood up and held out her hand. Hardy took it, but did not shake it in a formal manner, instead he held it for a few seconds. Alice's body reacted with pleasurable warmth, and excitement shimmied around her veins. She tried to concentrate.

'Where do you live, Alice? I will speak with my chief about the books. We will replace them. Write out a list of titles and I will see what I can do,' he said.

'Thank you, but please don't put yourself out. Your job must be tough enough. Just get Ern under control before the milkman delivers in the morning, because I like a cup of tea before I go on duty,' she said and gave him a cheeky grin.

He grinned back at her. 'I insist,' he said. 'We can replace a few books for your trouble.' Colour crept into his face, and Alice wondered if it was not just about the books. Then she scolded herself for even thinking he was interested in a girl her age. He was a mature man, had flown across the world to fight a war. Women would be his temptation, not a girl barely out of childhood.

'That's very kind,' she said, and gave him her address. New books would be helpful, after all.

'Billingford. I didn't make the connection to here when we were in the café,' Hardy said looking at what she had written.

'We never talked about which airbase you were at, either, so I assumed it was one near Ipswich town. What a coincidence you're here. Perhaps we'll bump into one another again,' Alice said.

'Sure we will ... see you around, Alice.' Hardy's voice was warm and calm. Alice wished she could sit all day and listen to him; his voice soothed her.

When she stepped outside into the warm air she took a few breaths of air. She realised her heart had not stopped pounding since she'd first seen Hardy look up at her from his desk

---

Dear Diary

Blake Hardesty - Hardy - is here! At Station 139. He really is extremely handsome, with his dark hair and the hint of stubble that gives him a rugged look. A handsome hero from a romantic novel. I confess, I prefer the rugged look to the clean-shaven face he had in the café. I tried not to, but could not help myself when I stared at him. I just had to look into those large brown eyes with their long black lashes again. But sadly I saw a photograph of his wife and child on his desk, so he is not for me. The thought of him married is disappointing, but I am foolish to even think Hardy would be interested in a young village girl even if he was single. His wife is a lucky woman, but his family must be worried about him being so far away from home.

Nonetheless, I have been shown I can smile again and enjoy the company of another man. I will settle my mind and lead a good life, and maybe one day I will have a family of my own, with a good man at my side. Who knows, maybe one of the American pilots might take a shine to a countryside postie.

Over and out.

Chapter Fourteen

Cycling along the road towards Great Ryburgh, Alice tried hard not to look at the sky above her. The deafening sound of aeroplane engines reverberated through the air, signalling that multiple airbases were sending their personnel on important missions into Europe.

Ever since the American forces had arrived, the missions had become more intense, with activity happening around the clock. It played havoc with her sleep, so Alice dealt with the insomnia by working her way through her book stash, making use of the intermittent searchlights or sometimes a candle or torch, but there was something comforting about reading by her windowsill, with the light flickering across the sky protecting her.

Alice got off her bike and paused briefly to tidy her hair outside the small, terraced house owned by Clara Dike's friend. The planes, which were once easily seen by the naked eye, had transformed into minuscule black dots on the distant horizon. As she stood there, she couldn't help but wonder how many more years she would spend observing them.

As she stood outside number 23, Alice could hear someone

shuffling about inside and she knocked on the door, patiently waiting for them to answer. The front door creaked open, revealing a man in his early thirties with a pale face, anxiously peering out at her. Noticing the walking stick in his hand, Alice deduced he must be the injured Richard.

'Richard? Clara Dike's friend?' she asked.

The sandy-haired man gave a nod.

'Who is asking?' he said, his voice feeble and slow, and Alice saw a nervous twitch move beneath his right eye.

'I am Alice Carmichael, the postwoman at Billingford, and I recently set up a mobile library, well, it is me and my trusty steed over there.'

She gestured over her shoulder at her bicycle but noticed he did not put his head out to look at it.

'Anyway, Clara thought you might like me to deliver and collect a book of her choosing.' Alice smiled. 'Anyone who loves reading deserves to be on my delivery list… It would be this time and day each week?' she said as he took the package from her. 'Clara has sent this one with a note explaining.'

Richard gave such a slight nod of his head that Alice was not sure it was one, so she waited for more of a response.

'Yes. Put me on your list. Same day and time. Please,' he said and eased the door shut.

Alice stared at the paint-chipped door for a few seconds.

'Goodbye, then. See you same time next Tuesday,' she said quietly, and with some sarcasm, before she walked back to her bicycle and headed home.

———

As Alice was busy selecting another pile of books for her regular readers, she noticed a slip of paper that fell from one of the books.

The paper's strange markings, instead of words, immediately caught her attention.

As she slipped the note into her pocket, she quickly glanced at the book title, just in case anyone happened to ask her if she had found it, and then proceeded to prepare her basket for her weekly library round. Prompted by the sound of voices, she directed her gaze towards the window of Hettie's sewing room as well as the makeshift book storage space.

'There's a truck outside. American,' she said to Hettie, who was altering a pair of navy wool trousers for Alice to wear in the winter months.

Hettie laid down her work and joined Alice at the window.

'They are unloading boxes. I am not due to have the billeted men for another week. It's a good job I am ahead of schedule,' Hettie said and went to the front door. 'Two men, as with our British men, that's all I have agreed. Do not let me cave into the demands for more, Alice.'

Alice laughed. 'You are a soft touch, but I don't think I will be any good as your bodyguard,' she said, and stood behind Hettie at the now open door.

'Good morning, gentlemen, what can we do for you?' Hettie said, and Alice smiled at her aunt's exaggerated British accent and folded arms. She definitely did not need a bodyguard.

'Delivery for a Miss Alice Carmichael,' a voice called out from the back of the truck.

Hettie turned and looked at Alice then back at three men, who placed two boxes each on the pathway.

'For me?' Alice said and moved to inspect the boxes.

Lifting the lid she saw the spines of books facing her.

'Books. A lot of books,' she said, turning to Hettie.

'Compliments of Master Sergeant Hardesty. And,' the voice called, 'an apology from me.'

Alice stared, bemused, as a man jumped down from the back of the truck, holding a large bunch of flowers and a small bag.

It was Ern, the infamous lamebrain.

'The boss gave me a grilling for running you down. I am working my punishment, but this is my sorry,' he said holding out the gifts and the bouquet.

Alice took the small bag and handed the flowers to Hettie.

'Thank you, but since Hettie repaired my uniform, I think she should have the flowers,' she said.

Ern's face flushed red.

'Again, I apologise. My ma would be ashamed of me.'

One of the other men sniggered and Hettie glared at them.

'I think she would be proud of you now, facing up to your mistake. A lesson has been learned. Now if you will forgive us, Alice has a lot of cataloguing to do, by the look of those boxes, so if you could bring them inside for us and thank Master Sergeant Hardesty for being thoughtful.'

Hettie turned heel and went inside, leaving Alice looking at the men only a few years older than her.

'She's small, but don't be fooled, Aunt Hettie has a bite to follow through with her bark,' she said with a laugh and pointed to the boxes. 'She'll tell you where they need to go. I must get to work.'

Ern, who had two boxes in his arms, could not look any keener on getting back to base.

'Thank you, Ern. The soap and chocolate are a treat we have not had for a very long time.'

Clara Dikes greeted her with a wave of her gardening gloves. Her large, floppy hat bounced as she walked towards Alice, who could not help but admire the woman's sashaying stride.

'Alice, where does the week go?' said Clara, as she opened the gate.

Beneath the hat, Alice saw a large black and purple bruise on Clara's cheek.

'That looks painful,' said Alice.

Clara put her hand to the bruise.

'A gardening accident. Silly me,' she said. 'Bring the books this way. I will choose Richard's.'

Alice followed with her basket.

'After my accident, the American master sergeant in charge of the ground crew sent me four boxes of books. Thirty new ones and twenty-five used. Hettie is working around them in her sewing room at the moment. Once they are recorded in my notebook, I will write out a list of them all and you can choose the next read for Richard in advance,' Alice said, though not sure Clara had heard her as she had disappeared indoors.

When Clara came back out she handed Alice the selected book, again wrapped in brown paper, and gave back the ones she did not choose.

'I've written to him again, and it is inside the book, so don't give it to anyone else by mistake or it could be embarrassing,' Clara said, with a tinkle of a laugh, which Alice wasn't convinced was genuine. There was something awkward about Clara's manner with her and it made Alice wonder if there was a romantic past between Clara and Richard.

Was this her opportunity to play the role of Emma Woodhouse from Jane Austen's novel *Emma*?

Alice placed the package in the bottom of the basket and placed the other books on top.

'Hidden and safe,' she said, adding, 'Richard seemed very shy when I met him.'

Clara pulled a sad face.

'Traumatised. He has seen more than any person should see

and has suffered injuries which will be with him for ever,' she said. 'The books will be a good distraction, and even opening his front door is a reconnection with the world, which is a good thing.'

'Hello, again, Richard. How are you?' Alice asked when Richard peered around the front door in response to her knock.

'Library book day. Clara has chosen something for me?' Richard asked, his words stilted. By the marks on his face Alice guessed she had disturbed him from a deep sleep.

'It is and she has,' she replied.

Shuffling backwards, Richard held the door open wider.

'Stand in the hall and I will get the one from last week,' he said.

Alice did as instructed and waited. She could smell the lingering aroma of cooked fish, and noted that like Clara's, the hallway was free of clutter and personal items.

After what seemed an age, Richard returned with the previous book wrapped in the paper and tied with the string Clara had used.

'I've sent her a note of thanks. It's inside,' he said. His face bore no expression as he handed it to Alice.

With a nod, Alice smiled. 'I will see she gets it tomorrow,' she said.

A fleeting flash of panic whipped across Richard's face and beneath his eye a twitch set in. 'Today. Could you always get the book back to her today. She reads it after me, always.'

Startled by his reaction and request, Alice took a moment to think. Clara had never mentioned or asked Alice if she could have the book after Richard, or for any responding note to be delivered on the same day. But since it was not an inconvenience to her – she rode past Clara's place on the way home, and she had a record of the book under Richard's name so could easily transfer it to Clara's – she decided to fulfil his request.

'Don't worry, I will drop it off on my way home. If she's not there I will leave it on her back doorstep, it is not going to rain,' she said, and was relieved to see the panic ease from Richard's face. Whatever trauma he'd experienced, she suspected it was war related, and if she was five minutes later home, but he was content, then it was worth the effort.

'Thank you, Alice,' Richard said, and slowly moved towards the door to indicate his time with the librarian was over.

Tapping on Clara's door, Alice hoped Richard's request would be well received. If there was friction between the two, then Clara might not be willing to read the book, it might be an irritating request. While Alice pondered their relationship, Clara opened the door and looked at Alice with surprise.

'Alice, is there something wrong – with Richard?' she asked, and Alice heard the anxiety in her voice.

Alice held out the book. 'Richard seemed well enough, but he did get a little concerned when I said I would see you tomorrow. He wants you to read the book, too, and said he has put a note inside. He wrapped it up then almost begged that I bring it to you today, on my way home – every week,' she said.

Clara raised her eyebrows as a statement of understanding.

'Of course he does. I should have mentioned he would ask you to return the book to me, I am sorry, Alice. Can we keep that routine, or will it inconvenience you in any way?' Clara asked.

Although the situation seemed strange to her, Clara was obviously aware of Richard's mental state. To refuse would mean

Alice was being selfish, because there was no reason why she could not help the two of them with such a simple thing.

'I don't know what he has been through, Clara, but it is obviously something dreadful. If this arrangement makes life a little better for him, then I will return to you on the same day,' she said.

'Thank you. Sometimes I have to go into London for two to three days. And if that is the case, I will leave him a note in the shed for you to take with you. I will also leave you to choose him a book if you are willing to do that for me?' Clara said. 'It is a lot to ask of you, and I wouldn't only I...' She sighed and gave a soft smile.

Alice smiled in return. 'It will be my pleasure to help. And I can create a list for you to choose from,' she said.

The relief across Clara's face was reward enough. Alice suspected that she and Richard had very few friends or family nearby to help them through whatever problem they were experiencing, and Alice understood the importance of receiving help during a traumatic time. And even though she was busy helping Hettie much of time, what harm would it do to help others when she could?

Chapter Fifteen

S lipping on her new, Hettie-fashioned, sundress, Alice felt refreshed after a sweltering ride delivering the post. A larger batch than usual had recently arrived, and it meant she cycled further and longer than on most days.

The lemon-yellow dress sat neatly around her waist and hung in neat pleats to just above her knees. Small shoulder pads and short, slightly ballooned sleeves sat neat, complementing the white lace-trimmed collar. Hettie had spoiled her with the design, it was flattering, and her loose dark hair set it off well, without the need of ribbons or a hat.

Although it was late afternoon Alice was hoping to visit Hardy and thank him in person for the books.

'Looking swell,' Hettie said with a booming laugh when Alice had walked into the kitchen earlier.

Alice had returned the laugh. 'Listen to you, speaking American,' she quipped.

Hettie smiled at her. 'The new boarders come out with words and expressions that either confuse me or make me want to use them all day long. *Okay*?'

'*Okay*,' Alice replied, and giggled as she carefully pulled on a pair of delicate, white cotton lace gloves and slipped her feet into her polished black shoes. Although she longed for a pair of white shoes, she knew that the dirt and mud of the lanes and woods would quickly ruin them.

'I will be over at Hilda's when you get back,' Hettie said, wiping her floured hands down her pinafore. 'You'll need to get your own supper; the men are eating over at their mess hall tonight.'

Since the two American airmen had moved into the house, Hettie's mood although cheerful, held a hint of missing James. Both Alice and Hilda had suggested Hettie arrange to go on a trip to see him, but they regretted this when Hettie had stormed out of the room. Alice soon learned not to speak about James too much.

The warmth on her face now was pleasant and Alice put it down to the new face powder she wore, which absorbed any beads of sweat. Riding her bike in the summer months had tanned her, enhancing the olive skin tone she'd inherited from her father. Alice knew she was looking very pretty this summer, and she was enjoying still being a teenager.

Three girls she knew in the surrounding villages and towns, who were around her age, were either getting married or already married and pregnant, but Alice was not ready to think along those lines. Instead, she decided to enjoy the flattering remarks thrown her way, and lean into her natural flirtatiousness.

In the time she spent riding or walking past the open spaces of the airbase, Alice had caught sight of quite a few of the men taking a break, lying on the grass with their shirts off. Observing them, she had daydreamed about her future husband, who was handsome and had a velvet-soft voice like Hardy's, as well as his eyes, and his physique.

This fantasy was still in her head when Alice tapped on the door of the same domed hut she'd come to when she'd reported

Ern and the driving incident. This time, no one called out for her to enter and Alice's mood slumped in disappointment.

She turned to see the battered planes in the distance, waiting for attention from the ground crew. Music was playing from buildings around the base and the smell of burning rubber, wood, and doughnuts hung in the air on this perfect August afternoon. Alice watched as men walked out of one building, touching their heads before replacing their caps, and she guessed it was the barber's shop. Some women sat outside a large Nissen hut smoking cigarettes, and Alice thought they must be part of the local Women's Royal Voluntary Service and working in the laundry. One woman was sipping from a bottle, which, thanks to the generosity of Hettie's boarders, Alice now knew contained a fizzy drink called Coca-Cola.

Across in the distance was the control tower and Alice could see the outlines of men moving around. The place fascinated her, it was like a town rather than the barracks of a foreign air force.

'Alice?' came a voice behind her, and her stomach rolled in recognition as she turned towards it.

'Hardy, hello,' she said and gave him her best smile. 'I was just about to go home. I popped by to say thank you so much for the books. They were a wonderful surprise.'

'Ah, that's why you're here. I thought you had come early for the dance?' Hardy grinned, pointing to her dress. He looked down at his own grease-covered clothes and hands and laughed. 'I guess, I am not quite ready, myself.'

Alice laughed, too. 'As I said in the café, I don't really go to dances,' she said, then gestured at his hands. 'I thought you were too senior in rank to get your hands dirty.' She gave him a teasing grin.

'Some guys of my rank wouldn't,' Hardy said. 'But I'm pretty hands-on, especially when we're short on the ground.' He paused. 'Too many ships are taking a beating right now.'

Alice saw a fleeting flash of pain in his eyes. The bomb group were suffering damage and losses of both planes and men, it inevitably took its toll on those trying to keep them safe. Their friends and colleagues.

'Well, I'll leave you to it, you look exhausted,' she said soberly. 'I just wanted to thank you for the books.'

'No problem at all,' said Hardy with a smile. 'Did Ern show his face?'

'He did, and he brought flowers, chocolate, and soap, which I shared with Hettie,' she said. 'And I accepted his apology.'

'I'm glad,' said Hardy, then the two of them fell into silence, until Alice broke it.

'Anyway, take care. You know where I am if you need a good read,' she said.

'Hey, let me clean up and I'll walk you to the gate,' said Hardy. 'I need a break. And this has been the brightest part of my day.'

Alice couldn't help the flush of pleasure that crept up her neck.

'That will be very nice, thank you,' she said, and meant it.

Hardy's offer to walk her to the gate turned into an easy-going amble along the lanes and the still clean-and-fresh hideaway hut. She was grateful for it during rainstorms, or whenever she wanted a quiet moment alone if Hettie's tenants were home with friends. Alice didn't begrudge them one moment of happiness, but when a group of them together played a game of cards, it was a noisy place to be and for the sake of a short walk, Alice would grab a flask of tea, a candle, and a good book, and take an hour of peace during the light evenings.

'How did you find this place?' Hardy asked as he peered into the hut.

'I came across it during a horrible storm one day,' she said stepping inside with Hardy following her. 'It stank – and I won't tell you what I cleaned out of it once I had permission to use it from the farmer...' They shared a chuckle. 'But if ever you need a bolt hole, you're welcome here ... just, please, keep it to yourself. I am sure someone else will stumble across it one day, but for now it is my sanctuary.'

'I'm honoured to be granted entry,' Hardy said, with a grin. 'Thank you.'

'If you look over there,' she said, pointing across the field, 'that's the roof of my home, Hettie's house. Just down the lane beside the trees.'

'Will you let me walk you there – walk you home?' Hardy said.

Alice could think of nothing better than a few more minutes in his company, then she noticed how tired he looked.

'Don't you need to rest?' she said.

Stepping outside and holding open the door for her, Hardy smiled at her. 'I will when I know there isn't an Ern out there ready to run you down.'

When they reached the house everywhere was silent.

'A rare event to walk up here and not hear voices nowadays,' Alice said, as they walked around to the back of the property.

'What a quaint place.' Hardy whistled. 'Nice.'

'It is, and I am extremely lucky to live here. Hettie saved me—' Alice blurted out the truth before she could stop herself.

'Saved you?' Hardy asked.

'She gave me a home when I had lost everything and everyone. She's not my real aunt. We met several months ago or so, at her front door. It's long story. My life story, really, when I think about it...' Alice said. 'I will tell you about it one day, but for now, thank you for walking me home. Please, go and get some sleep. I hear the planes in the night, I know how hard you work.'

But Hardy stood looking at her for a while, his eyes scanning hers and Alice could not move, until she recalled the photograph on his desk and dropped her gaze.

'Well,' he said. 'I sure am ready to sleep on my feet, but it was great to chat to you. If only you delivered our mail we could do it more often.' He turned and walked to the gate. 'Night, Alice, see you around.'

After Hardy had left, Alice stood wondering what to do next. Her emotions had caught her by surprise, and she sensed his had, too. She wondered if they would meet again, though her reason for seeing him was over, she had thanked him and taken up more of his time than she had intended. She thought about the age difference between them, and decided that five years was not much at all.

Dear Diary

I took a walk with Hardy today, and if I do not find out if he is married soon, I will go crazy. He has never said a word about a wife, I am sure of it. And when I think back he's mentioned other members of his close-knit family, but never a word about a wife and child.

If he is available, I would love to build a deeper friendship with him. Walk with him more often. But if he is married, then I won't push myself closer. It is not right nor fair.

If he is single, though, all I can do is hope he will notice me more than just a young woman who speaks with him now and then. I think I want more than a passing wartime friendship from him. Hardy is thoughtful, chatty, but gives me space to speak, too.

Am I wrong to think about a man I have only known for a short while practically twenty-four hours a day!

Am I too young to think about a man his age? Questions, questions!

I see sadness in his eyes, and wonder how much it has to do with his work, the war. Or is it the distance between him and someone he loves that makes him sad?

I dare not look him in the eyes for they draw me into his and my body melts into a weakness I cannot explain. He makes my heart race with a sensation I have never felt before. I do not understand the effect he is having on me. Are they normal feelings?

I do hope we meet again, if we don't, I think I might shrivel up like an old maid. I do not notice other men. I have no desire to be in their company. Blake Hardesty has done something to me and I can't get him out of my head.

Chapter Sixteen

L ibrary day came around fast, and Alice thought about the past few days since she'd walked home with Hardy, and realised her life was all work or the library.

Girls in the villages discussed the lively parties they attended at the airbase and some, although underage, visited pubs outside of the area with groups of the airmen. They regaled her with tales of drunken fights, of how attentive the American men were, how generous with their gifts of nylon stockings and chewing gum.

Hilda called the girls 'flighty' and Hettie thought their mothers ought to have a firm word with them. Alice kept quiet about walking home with Hardy, and knowing she was under scrutiny each time she spoke with one of Hettie's boarders, she slowly withdrew to either her quiet hut or bedroom.

She told herself that work and the library run were what she enjoyed and anything else was a distraction. Her lifestyle was not what some wanted and theirs would not suit her.

Today, she was going to take books to people whose lives she improved just by cycling to their gates and handing over books. Simple but enjoyable for both parties.

As she leaned her bicycle against the wall of a house, the door opened, and a smiling young boy stepped out to greet her. He lived with a couple who had taken him in as an evacuee. His cockney accent always made Alice smile.

'Victor. How are you today?' she asked as she selected two books from her basket.

"Appy to see you, miss. Did you get 'em?' he asked, eagerly hopping up and down, waiting for her to hand over his request.

Alice laughed, just as the woman who, with her husband, had taken Victor in joined them.

'You have a keen reader in this one,' the woman said, ruffling his hair in affection. 'Right little bookworm.'

'He has good taste in books, too. Here you are, Victor, I managed to find both of them for you,' Alice said.

'*The Famous Five*?' the woman said looking at one of the books. 'I remember this one about the group on a treasure island. Enid Blyton is a good choice.'

'And I've got this one,' Alice said. '*The Tower Treasure*.'

'It's a Hardy Boys book,' Victor said, with the pride of an avid reader. He turned to the woman. 'Alice recommended Franklin W. Dixon – that's the author.'

Alice and the woman smiled at each other over his bent head examining the books.

'Well. I will leave them with you for two weeks, Victor. They are a longer read for you this time.' Alice smiled, realising she was no longer of interest to the boy studying the back of the books so intently.

'Thank you,' the woman said and she and Alice stepped away. 'They help Victor through his nightmares,' she added quietly.

'That I understand. He is a pleasure to find books for, although when I am looking for books for him I often find more for my own reading pile,' Alice said, smiling over at him, before returning to her bicycle.

'Bye, miss. Thanks ever so much!' Victor called out as she cycled away, and Alice waved goodbye.

Alice finished her round early as she wanted to speak to Clara about a partially written letter she had found inside the book Clara had returned the previous week. It puzzled Alice and she needed to address the contents. She had shown it to no one, although she had been tempted to ask Hilda what to do, given it was in an unsealed, stamped addressed envelope, but decided Clara must know a Miss Véronique Tremblay.

> *My dearest Véronique,*
>
> *We are heading for France, to our favourite village. I have a pass for both of us. I will meet you there, my love. In the square, near the fountain. Wear your red hat for me. Do not take the train or go near the bridge or it might blow from your head, and I adore that hat on you. Walk the short distance to the house. Monsieur Rebet will give you food and shelter until I arrive.*
>
> *My love is in our language of romance. Aphrodite. Eros. Freyja.*
>
> *My heart is yours,*
>
> *R.*

Walking to the back of Clara's property, Alice saw her swinging a long, thick stick around her head, and passing it back and forth from hand to hand. She stood quietly watching not daring to disturb her. It was a practised move, almost a dance, and Alice could see Clara kept the rest of her body still, just allowing her arms to control the stick.

Once it was obvious Clara had finished her exercise, Alice made herself known.

'Good afternoon, Clara. I hope I'm not interrupting you. I did knock at the front door,' she said, waving that week's book in front of her.

'Alice, gracious is that the time?' Clara said, looking down at the stick now on the floor, then back to Alice. She frowned and Alice wondered if she was embarrassed at being seen. She quickly stepped in to relieve the awkward moment.

'I confess, I saw a little bit of your exercise routine, or was it dance for theatre?' she asked.

Clara bent down to pick up the stick and laid it on a bench.

'This is a combat weapon that my grandfather used in the Great War, when he lost his gun, and he taught me a few things. You're right, I keep it for exercise,' she said

When Alice looked a little closer at the stick, she saw it was a carved piece of wood, a specific tool of some kind.

'I'll fetch the book,' Clara said, turning to walk towards her home.

Alice took a step forward. 'Actually, Clara, there is something I need to talk to you about. To do with last week's book that you and Richard borrowed.' She released a nervous breath.

Clara stopped walking and Alice saw her hitch her shoulders back. A composure movement.

'The book?' she asked as she turned around, a semi-pout of questioning on her lips.

'It was unwrapped this time, as you know, because Richard had no paper, and there was, um – a letter inside. Opened – well, part of a letter. I am convinced it is some sort of code.' Alice bit on her lip as Clara stared at her. A hard stare.

'Well, if you think it belongs to me, then hand it over. If it is for Richard, then take it to him.' Clara's voice was cool and low, not the usual breezy one Alice was used to, and it unnerved her.

'The thing is, my duty as a postwoman is to not hand over someone else's mail – especially already opened items. It is written to a Miss Véronique Tremblay, at this address, but has no sender details,' she replied.

A deep frown then crossed the brow of Clara's face, and she gave her an ugly glare which caused Alice to shiver slightly. After a few seconds of awkward silence, Clara spoke, her tone softened slightly.

'I will take it and give it to Véronique. I know her well. I let her use this address as her home was bombed out,' she said, holding out her hand and waiting for Alice to give her the letter.

Not wanting to become embroiled in conflict or be intimidated in any way by Clara, Alice hesitated, considering her options. Then she thought about the contents she had read. She guessed Richard had also read the letter. Alice also wondered if he was the R who had written it, and it was personal to him, a coded love letter. Now, with her reservations about Clara and Richard's relationship, and the fact he might be in love with someone else, Alice decided against handing it over to Clara and to discreetly approach Richard instead.

'I'm afraid I have to hand it over to her personally, or find someone in authority to hand it to – not even the postmistress will be allowed to see it. This is my responsibility now. Even if she is your friend, Clara. If Miss Tremblay is using your address, then I assume you know her and know where she lives. Speak to her and I will take it to her. I can be trusted, obviously,' she said.

Clara studied her with an unreadable expression.

'Right. Well, let's get Richard's book to him, or he will fret. And I will speak with Véronique and get in touch with you when I have. Leave the book Richard gives you in the shed, I am away for a couple of days.' Clara ended the conversation by striding over and into her home.

Clearly dismissed, Alice cycled to Richard's with the letter still on her mind.

On her arrival, she gave her usual three knocks on the door. Waiting for Richard to answer, Alice made up her mind to definitively ask him about the letter. He would have seen it, but did not mention it to her at her last visit, and like Clara, had left it inside the book for a reason.

'Good afternoon, Richard,' she said when his face peered around the door. She had the book – packaged as always by Clara, behind her back.

'Hello, Alice,' Richard said.

'Richard, do you know of a Miss Véronique Tremblay?' she asked without waiting to express her usual niceties. 'Only, I have a letter for her.'

To her surprise Richard appeared to stagger to one side and placed his hand on the doorjamb. Like Clara he took a moment of composure, while Alice waited patiently for his answer.

'Richard, are you all right? Can I help?' She asked as he moved into an upright position.

'Give the letter to Clara, she will pass it along,' he said, and Alice noted his speech was not stilted, nor barely a whisper.

'As I explained to Clara, as a postwoman I have responsibilities, and must hand the letter to the recipient – and, considering the letter was open and I looked for a return address, I must ensure it gets back to the rightful owner,' she said. 'I thought I would ask you about it, as well as Clara, and it is clear you both know Miss Tremblay, so I will wait for Clara to get in touch. Anyway, Clara has sent you another good read, so I will return last week's. I take it you enjoyed it?' Alice rushed, no longer wanting to linger on the letter.

Richard did not reply. He turned around and walked down the hallway and Alice noticed his back straightened more than she had seen during previous visits.

When he returned to the door Richard held out the book and Alice gave him a beaming smile.

'Thank you, and I will see you again next week. Enjoy your book,' she said, and walked away before he could say anything else about Clara and Véronique Tremblay. Alice was curious as to why he had never asked why she had approached him about a letter for someone other than Clara – the person they had in common. She decided to add nothing further to a conversation which could become a tug-of-word war.

Chapter Seventeen

When Alice collected her post bag, she noticed letters addressed to her and one for Hettie.

Her personal mail always intrigued her, and it frustrated her that she did not have more time to read it. One was postmarked Canada, so was a reply to her last letter to Gabrielle, and two were local postmarks. By the time she had completed half of her round, Alice decided to take a rest in the woodland hut, and read the local ones. Sometimes she received requests to deliver library books to other villages via formal letter. It made her smile that she was thought of as an authority rather than the postie girl as most elderly people called her.

The first letter surprised her, it was short and to the point from Clara.

Alice,

I arrive home on 15th August and would appreciate you taking the time to visit on the 16th, at 11 a.m.

Regards,

Clara Dikes

The note read as an instruction rather than an invitation, and Alice tucked it away into her diary.

'Come in, Alice. Nice and punctual,' Clara said as she greeted her at the door. Her attitude and manner towards Alice were still frosty, and this felt more like a formal interview, or a meeting of great importance, than a general chat.

'Take a seat,' Clara said as she opened the door to a room at the front of the cottage. 'I've made a fresh pot of tea. Or do you prefer coffee? I understand you have friends from across the pond staying at your aunt's, they drink it by the gallon.'

'Tea will be fine, thank you,' Alice said, as Clara turned away and Alice guessed she wasn't really interested in a response on the American boarders and coffee.

Alice stood by the window looking out onto the small front garden made over to a vegetable patch. A white cabbage butterfly flitted from plant to plant, and a swift sailed through the garden, and a peaceful calm settled in the room.

The rattle of cups and saucers in the hallway broke the serenity, and Alice turned around. The shock hit her first, then the disbelief. In front of her stood Richard holding a tray. He was upright, freshly shaved and dressed in smart clothing. Clara hovered behind him.

'Richard?' Alice said and stared ungraciously at him, not caring that she had been taught it was rude to stare. Richard's recovery was beyond the realms of possible from when she saw him last.

'We can explain.' Clara's clipped voice echoed from behind him.

Placing the tray on the table, Richard gave Alice what she

assumed was some kind of apologetic smile. Clara poured the tea and placed a cup in front of Alice.

'Come and sit down,' Clara said, gesturing at a chair at the table.

Seated around the table, Alice was wary of the atmosphere, the strangeness of the situation, and she debated leaving. But curiosity grounded her into her seat and a wave of courage swept over her.

'I am pleased you have made such a miraculous recovery, Richard,' she said. 'But why am I here, Clara? To discuss reading material, or Véronique Tremblay?'

Richard shifted in his seat and Clara swung him a scathing glance.

'The letter you found, it is important, and it's vital that no one else reads it, so please tell us you have not shown it to your aunt or to the American I saw you walking out with the other day.' Clara's voice was clipped and tense and Alice saw a white tinge above her top lip. Her anger evident.

Inside her chest, Alice could feel her heart pound, beating so fiercely that her ribs ached and her body tensed.

'Did you hear me? Do. You. Understand?' Clara asked.

Her voice snipped and sniped with each projected word. A form of intimidation, Alice knew. But given the circumstances, she was not prepared to hand over the letter or give into these obvious bullying tactics.

'I have not shown it to anyone, but as you say, it is important which tells me you obviously know the contents of the letter. I repeat, I am legally bound not to hand it over to you, only Miss Tremblay. Bearing that in mind, I suggest you ask Miss Tremblay to get in touch with me and I can hand her back her property. No amount of intimidation will make me break the law,' Alice said, with a boldness she hoped would end the meeting.

Richard gave a polite cough.

'Unfortunately, we cannot do that,' he said. 'I foolishly forgot the letter was tucked inside the cover when Clara sent it to me.' Richard rose to his feet and walked without difficulty to sit in a seat facing her. 'Alice, what you have stumbled across is a secret letter. One which has helped us find a way to strengthen our fight against the war in Europe already. I am telling you this because I have the authority to do so, and Clara's safety is in jeopardy if this goes any further.'

He looked at Alice as if she should understand what he had just said, but all she heard was something farcical. Then she thought about it logically, a secret letter, the code language and a woman's French name; a man pretending to be injured. It all had to have something to do with a military operation. The bruise on Clara's face, her trips away, the way she moved with the stick in the garden and the defensive manner in which she was dealing with Alice... Was Richard telling the truth?

Alice turned to Clara.

'Miss Véronique Tremblay. It's you, isn't it?'

Clara hesitated, and Alice watched as Richard stood up again and paced the room. She did not miss the swift frown he gave Clara, nor the slight rise and drop of Clara's chest when she caught her breath. Alice felt she already had her answer, but waited patiently to see the outcome of her question to Clara.

'You are a clever young woman, Alice. Sensible and reliable, too. However, we are in a sticky situation here.' Richard said, still pacing, while Clara remained silent and still.

'How so?' Alice asked.

Clara still kept quiet, but Alice looked at her, at the concern building in lined creases across her brow.

Richard stopped pacing and looked at Alice, and beckoned her to stand up.

'Neither Clara nor I thought the book situation would bring us so much bother,' he replied.

'The book situation? Me bringing you books, how has that brought you so much bother?' Alice asked.

'It has placed you, and us, in a difficult position. We now have a potential threat to Great Britain.'

Although she didn't realise she had inhaled loudly with the shock of his words, Alice knew she had as she slowly exhaled. Her head dizzy as she did so. Looking over at Clara for a response, she felt reassured when Clara's features softened.

'Don't be afraid, Alice. This is a delicate situation. A time of trust. All three of us must trust one another, or the problem becomes more serious down the line,' she said.

Alice shifted from one foot to another. She felt uncomfortable with their talk of trust and threat to the country. She was confused and frightened.

'You are scaring me now. I would like to leave please,' she said her voice cracking again as she spoke.

Richard gave a soft smile, and Clara rose to her feet and looked directly into Alice's face.

'There is nothing to be scared of. You truly are in safe hands, I promise,' she said and looked over at Richard.

'We need you to understand what is going on, and the trust we have in you. Your actions have triggered something which needs to be addressed, and it has also highlighted qualities in you we think could be of benefit to the war effort. I am not at liberty to say more,' he said.

Alice burst out laughing. A nervous laugh, but one which also felt necessary.

'I see, I am your entertainment for the afternoon. Joke over. Although it does not explain the letter, your amusing act got the better of me. Now, I cannot hand over this letter, someone needs to read the contents, and it has to be the woman named on the envelope. Trust. Yes, we have to trust the right thing is done as soon as possible. So, if you have finished teasing me...'

Alice said, and the longer she spoke the more indignant she felt.

Clara held up her hand, palm facing outward.

'Alice. I have spoken with the head of our department, and he would like to meet you – in London. I assure you; it is all true. What we've said, it is the truth.'

Alice glanced from one to the other in question.

'Go to London? On what sounds like a ridiculous secret mission. Honestly, do you two think I am a simpleton?' Alice retorted, a fizz of anger brewing inside her.

'Quite the opposite,' Richard said. 'We think you are very clever and astute, for your age.'

Alice ignored this double-edged compliment.

'So, the trip to London, how do you think I can manage that? What on earth can I say to convince anyone I have a sudden urge to head to London? This is ludicrous. I need to leave.'

She made for the door.

'Stay, please. Just listen to us,' Richard said.

Clara gave her a smile. 'I know it sounds farcical, Alice, but trust us,' she said.

With a shake of her head, Alice reached for the door handle.

'I am so confused. Am I safe to leave?' she asked.

'We will have to ask for the letter,' Richard said.

With a sigh, Alice turned to him.

'You know the answer. If your person in London can prove they are Miss Véronique Tremblay, then I will hand them the letter, but—'

'Clara?' Richard shot her a look, cutting Alice off.

Clara let out a heavy sigh. 'I am Véronique Tremblay, Alice. I am both Véronique and Clara. Now that you know that you must come with us and meet the head of our department.'

Alice stared at her in disbelief.

'It is true. I cannot reveal any more than that, but if you come to London you will have your answer,' Clara said.

'We can tell your aunt I am taking you into the city as a treat, a thank you for helping me with looking out for my brother.'

Alice swung Richard a look.

'Yes, we are brother and sister,' he said sheepishly.

The romantic in Alice was disappointed. Although the letters she'd read appeared to be correspondence between a male and female in love, she realised they were coded, written in a way to disguise that they were really about the security of the country.

'What exactly is it you do?' she asked, then turned to Richard. 'You must be an actor, because you certainly had me fooled!' she snapped, both angry and scared about what she had discovered.

'I'm sorry, Alice, but it's not for us to say. I have to remind you that you are under caution not to say a word to anyone,' Richard said calmly.

'Will you agree to London? I will speak with your aunt, and we can work on Mrs Durrent for a day off that won't inconvenience her,' Clara said, her voice now notches softer and friendlier.

Alice shook her head in disbelief. 'It's all a bit much for me to take in, if I am honest. Am I in danger? Are my aunts, my friends? I am seventeen years old, living in a country at war, but right now I believe I am in more danger in this room, with you both. I need to go home.' Alice snatched up her handbag and gloves from the seat beside her and moved towards the door.

Clara followed her and tried to catch hold of her hand. Her touch was not hostile, but still Alice pulled her hand from Clara's grasp.

'I understand this is confusing for you, but if you will come to London, everything will be explained to you – in such a way that will reassure you. Trust us, Alice. I know it is a hard thing to understand, but please, trust us, we are not your enemy,' Clara pleaded, throwing Richard a glance.

'It is probably worse inside your head than the reality of it,' he said. 'Go to London, let Clara treat you to an adventure. Learn the truth about the letters from the top man, but please, you must trust us.'

Alice hesitated. She didn't know what or who to believe. Richard and Clara, or her own instincts? But something told her if she didn't go to London, she'd never rest again while the war raged on around them. She had to find out the truth.

'I am not sure I have any choice in the matter, do I?' she replied coldly. 'But for now, I would just like to go home.'

Back at Hettie's, she lifted out a letter addressed to herself and read it in the quiet of her room.

The letter made her laugh.

Master Sergeant Blake Hardesty; USAAF.
  Somewhere in the middle of nowhere.
  England.

Dear Miss Carmichael,

My thanks for your letter posted and obviously delivered by yourself. Just a guy's luck I was out of town at the time.

This is my RSVP to your kind invitation to join you for another tour of your neighborhood. I would love to accept.

  Date and time noted.
  Hardy

Alice knew she had taken a risk writing to Hardy. She'd told herself she was offering friendship, when in fact she was being totally selfish. She wanted to find out more about the woman and child in the photograph and if the feelings brewing inside her for Hardy were not just sympathy for a man far away from home and his wife and child. But the truth was that whereas her feelings for Pete had been of platonic love, Hardy provoked different emotions: excitement, attraction. Seeing him gave her goosebumps and made her feel a longing she'd never experienced before.

Even his short letter in response to hers gave her a new release of energy, overpowering the anxious thoughts she had about going to London with Clara.

Dear Diary

Letters have become so significant in my life. One has resulted in a formidable request, and an opportunity that I still know little about, and cannot share with anyone, even when I do know what it entails. The other, an acceptance from Hardy for me to show him around the area, has caused a flurry in my heart, hope and longing, and also the selfishness of desire.

I do not want to walk away from such a handsome man - and though his marriage would mean he is unavailable to me - I am prepared to overlook that just to enjoy a few moments in his company. How wicked of me!

Chapter Eighteen

Much to Alice's disappointment, the journey into London did not offer the excitement she had expected. The train stopped at every station, where more and more passengers boarded, until it became completely packed. With each passing moment, the hot and stuffy carriage intensified her jangled nerves as they steadily approached the city.

Clara had been reassuring, and upbeat with Hettie about Alice's trip, and though Hettie had initially had her doubts, she was convinced by Clara that it would expand Alice's education and experience. Mrs Durrent, too, was agreeable to Alice staying overnight in a London hotel. Clara had promised Hettie she would take care of Alice and ensure she had a good time. She even helped Alice select suitable clothing and reassured her she would not need money for anything, though Alice had found the entire experience of packing and preparation to be surreal, given that she knew only part of the truth behind the journey and was yet to find out what it was really about. As the train trundled along the tracks, she found herself deep in thought, pondering the different aspects of her life. The story of her life was so extraordinary that it could have been the plot of a fascinating novel.

Abandoned by her parents and sent to the orphanage. Finding and losing a grandmother, as well as a great-aunt she'd never met. Orphaned without knowing it for years. Stumbling across two kindly souls, Hettie and Hilda, who'd given her a home, and helped her find a job and a purpose. Finding a pen pal in Gabrielle. Finding and losing a like-minded soul in Pete. Starting a mobile library. Meeting a handsome American who was dangerously capturing her heart. And now, all because of a coded letter, she was on her way to London to be part of something of grave national importance.

'Ridiculous,' Alice muttered to her reflection in the train window.

'Pardon?' Clara asked, as she looked up from the newspaper she was reading.

Shaking her head, Alice turned to her. 'Talking to myself, sorry,' she said. Since the day Clara and Richard had confided their concerns about the letter, when Clara had claimed that she herself was the mysterious Véronique Tremblay, her manner towards Alice had softened.

Remembering the letter from Gabrielle in her bag, she pulled it out to catch up with the news from Canada and distract herself from fresh nerves brewing inside, the closer they got to the city.

Dear Alice,

I hope this letter finds you and your newfound family well. My cousin sent my aunt news from Tunisia, which took her by surprise as she thought he was in Britain and part of the army over there. He has told her he will bring her a camel home!

Thank you for your last letter and a pat on the shoulder for getting the library out into the villages. How exciting for you and for those who get to read during the miserable days. Books are a godsend.

We are hard at work on the farm, with increased quota demands from the government again.

My leg is troubling me with the extra workload, but I still manage, and as you know I sit and read when I can. I have recently finished a book by the author of Anne of Green Gables. *The book is* Anne of Ingleside. *I think I am a fan of L.M. Montgomery's and will seek out more of her books if there are any available.*

Mom is calling for me to help her, and I suspect it will involve a large bucket of unpeeled potatoes. My hands are raw and sore.

Keep the courage over there, and our best and brightest wishes from Canada.

Your friend,

Gabrielle.

The train slowed down and chugged through a dark tunnel, as it finally pulled into the London station and Clara folded her newspaper and picked up her overnight bag. She gestured for Alice to do the same.

'Here we are, at last,' she said. 'I think you will enjoy this trip, Alice. Try to relax and take in a few of the sights.'

Alice smiled, following Clara as she stepped off the train. Together, they pushed their way through the crowds, Clara striding ahead looking confident and glamorous.

A large black car transported them to a hotel, which had every comfort Alice could imagine, and after they'd eaten a light lunch in the restaurant, the car took them to the meeting.

Driving through the city streets, Clara pointed out places and buildings of interest. Some of the bombed-out streets reminded Alice of her old home in Norwich, and her heart went out to the residents.

Finally, the car stopped outside a towering building with a large 'To Let' sign outside.

'We're here,' Clara announced, with a happy lift in her voice. Ever since they'd arrived in London, Clara had become animated and chatty. Alice guessed that she thrived on city life, but Alice herself only felt nerves and intimidation as they approached the building.

'It looks ... empty,' she said with a frown, as Clara directed her to a small dark entrance behind the sign.

'I assure you, it is not, but obviously its disguise works,' Clara said as they walked towards the main door.

Alice's stomach flipped with anxiety as she prepared herself to face strangers. Powerful adults who would probably intimidate and unnerve her, but her duty to the letter and country gave her the tiny bit of courage to keep doing as Clara instructed. Inside, she and Clara moved from floor to floor, with Clara acknowledging people in an easy manner. Alice guessed she was a person of influence given the respect shown to them both. Eventually, they entered a large room with a long, large table in the centre of the room where three men in stiff-looking suits were staring at them both.

'Clara,' one of the men said, half getting to his feet and greeting her with a smile before settling back into his seat. Mutterings of hello came from the other two.

'Good afternoon, gentlemen,' Clara said. 'Let me introduce you to Miss Alice Carmichael. Seventeen years of age, from Norwich and a postwoman. Alice had the foresight to set up a mobile library by cycling around the nearby villages and delivering books once a week.'

A man of sturdy build, donning a handlebar moustache, who occupied the seat at the head of the table, stood up.

'Welcome, Miss Carmichael. Clara has filled me in on the

situation and I commend you for your intelligence and trustworthiness. You have the letter with you I take it?'

Clara's swift introduction and the man's immediate address left Alice with scarcely enough time to process her current situation. She was in what was likely one of the tallest buildings she had ever set foot in, surrounded by a group of individuals involved in secret wartime planning.

'Thank you, sir. I take my job seriously, but I do apologise if I have caused confusion for you all. Although she has claimed she is Miss Véronique Tremblay, my sense of professional conduct meant I could not hand over a coded letter until I was absolutely sure.'

As the men in the room engaged in hushed conversations with each other, Alice observed Clara's graceful movement towards a side unit where there was an assortment of bottles on display. Without hesitation, Clara reached for a crystal decanter and skilfully poured herself a drink. She then poured water into a glass and walked over to Alice.

'Take a seat, dear,' she said, sitting down at the table. 'You are doing well, and you are quite safe. Just listen to what they have to say next.' She tapped a chair beside her.

Alice did as she was told and sipped the water while the men continued to talk. Gradually they finished their hushed conversation, and the man with the handlebar moustache spoke again.

'Alice … I may call you Alice?' he asked, and smiled when Alice nodded. 'Good. Let me start with why we wanted to meet you. When someone so young shows such initiative and loyalty, and proves they are trustworthy, myself and my colleagues at the SOE will draw our attention to them. At the Special Operations Executive, we are what is probably known outside of these walls as a "secret service". Our specialism is sabotage, behind the enemy lines. Winston himself is an admirer of our abilities and encourages us forward into Europe.'

Alice's initial reaction was to remain silent, trusting her intuition. She realised she was seated at the table for a reason other than the letter. A letter the man could have demanded from her, and she would have to have handed it over. Clara and Richard were much more than two new friends she delivered books to each week, and she stared at the people in the room in disbelief when the man said.

'It is a lot to take on board,' the man continued, as though reading her thoughts, 'but Clara has spoken highly of you ... and we want to approach you with a mission.'

Chapter Nineteen

The man's voice rambled on, and Alice could barely take in what he was saying.

'I'm sorry, sir, but did you say you want me on a mission?' she said, then turned to Clara. 'Is that what you do, Clara? Undertake missions?'

'Don't worry, your mission won't be like mine,' Clara said with a smile and casually tapped out a cigarette from a packet on the table. Alice looked at the packet, the wording was French.

'I think I am piecing it together now. You really are Véronique Tremblay, but only when you are in France?' she said. 'She is your French identity.'

Clara beamed over at the two men. 'Didn't I tell you, she's relentless and intelligent,' she said, then put her hand on Alice's arm. 'That's right, Alice. I am Véronique Tremblay when I am in France. I am tasked with assisting the French Resistance and for bringing home news of Hitler's position in Europe.'

'Carry on,' the stout gentleman opposite encouraged Clara. 'Alice might as well understand fully what we want of her – apart from the letter, of course.'

'*Ma mère était française. J'ai une famille éloignée qui appartient à la résistance Française et je me suis porté volontaire pour aider la Grande Bretagne. Je saute des avions et j'ai un bleu de temps en temps, c'est dangereux et parfois j'ai peur, mais vous nous aiderez si vous nous remettez la lettre et écoutez mon idée.*' Clara reeled this off with a teasing smile, as the men around the table laughed.

Alice, wide-eyed, was staring at Clara with admiration.

'I am sorry, I don't have a clue what any of that means, but it sounded beautiful,' she said sensing the anticipation of the others as they noted her reaction.

Clara smiled then blew a final smoke ring before putting out her cigarette. 'I said, my mother was French and I have distant family who work for the Resistance, so I volunteered myself, to help Great Britain. It is dangerous and sometimes frightening, and for me, physically hard work – I jump from planes a fair bit and gain bruises now and then. But you will be helping us, Alice, if you hand over the letter and listen to my idea.'

All at once, Alice felt important. She wanted to trust Clara. If, by handing over the letter and listening to an idea would help the war effort in some way, Alice wanted to be part of it all. Clara was so much more than she thought; she was an extremely courageous woman and Alice would never be anything like as brave, but if those in the room thought she was good enough for something, she would give them her time and listen.

She rummaged inside her handbag and pulled out the letter.

'I have something that belongs to you, Miss Tremblay,' she said and handed it to Clara.

'*Merci*,' Clara said and placed the letter inside a brown file sitting in front of her.

'Can I ask what it said – the code?' Alice asked.

The moustache man coughed loudly, and Clara shook her head.

'I am afraid I can't tell you,' she said.

The one man who had said nothing at all up till then spoke up, his voice crisp with the most upper-class British Alice had ever heard. 'Just know you will have played an important part in helping something vital to our defence. But, you can tell no one – even those you are closest to – is that clear? Treason is not taken lightly.'

Alice shuddered and gave a slight nod of her head.

'Now, if you choose to go ahead and help the cause, you will be asked to sign the Official Secrets Act before we tell you our plan. I understand from Clara that you have an American … friend. I am sure he is every bit as trustworthy as yourself, but under no circumstances must he know what you do.' He leaned closer over the table. 'Your father was Spanish, wasn't he? Do you speak the language?'

'No, I'm sorry.' Alice shook her head. The small amount of information about herself that she had told Clara on the journey to London was clearly much more significant than she'd thought.

'Pity, might have been useful somewhere down the line. Where were we…? Ah, yes. To emphasise. What you hear in this room and what happens next stays with you. If you have questions, Clara and Richard will help. But never speak about your role within the SOE. Now a little bit about what we do.'

Alice's anxiety intensified as she listened to the moustached man discuss the SOE – a highly secretive organisation involved in sabotage and infiltration against the German military. Only those who needed to know were privy to its existence. He told her she would hear the organisation called by various names, but she should always refer to the SOE as 'headquarters' when with Richard or Clara.

As he continued, Alice found herself consumed by thoughts of all the information she had already absorbed, and the overwhelming flood of new knowledge they were sharing with her. Stories of bridge demolitions, strategic attacks on tank and manufacturing facilities; covert alliances with the British and Allied forces to achieve peace and liberation. It all filled her mind, and a sudden fear washed over her as she contemplated the unknown consequences of refusing to proceed without signing the official documents.

'It is all happening so fast … it's a bit bewildering, and serious,' she said, her voice parched. She licked her lips, then took a sip of water.

The man who had just spoken gave what sounded like an impatient sigh. 'War *is* serious, Alice,' he said gravely. 'This work is for the benefit of *your* future. No one will line you up and shoot you if you do this for king and country, no jumping out of a plane, no torture chamber for you. You get the easy job.'

Alice forgave him his bluntness, blaming it on exhaustion on his part, but she could not control her facial expression, which was one of horror.

'Lionel…' The man with the moustache said in a cautionary tone.

'Marvellous. Now she knows my bloody name!' Lionel rose to his feet and went over to the decanter. 'Drink?' he asked the man with a moustache.

Tension filled the room, and Alice couldn't shake the feeling of discomfort as she sat there. Clara sat silently, her eyes darting between the men in the room, but Alice felt the need to disrupt the tense atmosphere that made her uneasy.

'I know Clara, Richard, and now Lionel, but I did not catch your name, sir,' she said, addressing the stout man, who was looking red-faced with annoyance at Lionel.

'Douglas Brown,' he said shortly. 'I am head of this particular department. Lionel heads up another service, but we needed him here today. I apologise for his language and manner. It is easy to forget how young you are. A minor.'

Alice took another sip of water, then cleared her throat.

'I am a minor, yes, but I am also a victim of Hitler's attack on Great Britain. My greatest concern is of the two women who are now my guardians. Will they have the same protection as me – I assume you will be protecting me somehow as a member of the SOE?' she asked, with a confidence that surprised her but which still hid a large amount of anxiety.

The whole situation was like the plot of a novel. It didn't feel real. Alice glanced at Clara who sat quietly sipping her drink. Did Clara truly think Alice could handle something so important? Did she truly care about Alice, or was she saving her own skin and that of Richard's for their mistake with the letter. Was it all a test? Alice needed reassurance from the people in this room that her life and the lives of those linked to her were safe. She could not afford to bring danger to Billingham, especially the airbase.

'We will ensure nothing will affect Hettie and Hilda. We know a great deal about them, and I assure you, they will not be in any danger. We are putting a great deal of trust in you, but both Clara and Richard's reports of you and your family life tell us we are making the right choice for our next stage of action,' Douglas said.

Clara placed her glass on the table.

'You will be safe, Alice. And you will be supporting me. I trusted you from the moment I met you, and you have proved your worth over the letter. Let the SOE create your role, it will give you a platform to build a better life for your future. One I am willing to fly into France for and risk everything. I am not putting pressure on you, Alice, simply making you understand the risk that others are prepared to take for you and our future generations. I promise, I would not put you in danger. We are friends now.'

Alice looked at Clara. Her eyes were misted over, and it was as though her true self was revealed. Clara had a genuine, passionate concern for her country and she was prepared to risk so much to protect it.

'I will sign the Official Secrets Act. You can trust me as I have to learn to trust you. And as you and he said,' she nodded towards Lionel now puffing on an oversized cigar like she had seen Winston Churchill do on the cinema news, 'this involves my future, too.'

Chapter Twenty

C lara made encouraging nods as a nervous Alice took the oath, signed the papers and became tied to the SOE in a way she would never have believed.

Having signed the paper Alice was determined to concentrate on every word spoken in the room, she could not afford to fail. Their reassurances she was doing the right thing were not in ink; no black-and-white promises.

'Brave girl,' Clara whispered as Alice laid down the pen.

Douglas laid his large palm on her shoulder.

'Good. Welcome and thank you for your commitment. Now let's get down to business,' he said.

Everyone present shifted in their seats and Alice sat down again. She looked at the men over the rim of her glass, as they faced Douglas.

'The proposal is this. Your mobile library is ideal, but we want to set up in a central base. A village library, for example...'

Alice gave him a quizzical frown. 'I'm sorry, I am a bit lost. What does my mobile library have with you wanting a village library?

And how is that essential to war work? Secret war work? You asked me to sign the Secrets Act for a library…?' Her bold tone took on a nervous quiver as she tailed off. Was she speaking out of turn?

Douglas didn't bat an eyelid, though, and the third man, Gordon, spoke up.

'We will train you as a librarian via a correspondence course, and Richard will become your mentor. This will be the ideal cover. The core of the library will be a collection and delivery centre for vital information. Things are hotting up in Europe and we have increased the number of runners getting word to and from France. Agents and runners will come and go as if they are using the library, and you will be their connection,' he said, and Alice felt all eyes on her as she listened.

Her mind struggled to comprehend what she had heard. She was to train as a librarian. She would run a library. Her dream job, but with a secret twist. As she understood it, all she had to do was hand over books in a library created just for her. It all seemed so selfish, but if it meant securing her own life and not being a burden to Hettie in any way, she was ready to take up the challenge of a lifetime.

'I see,' she said trying her hardest to not show her excitement, which was now threatening to overpower her nerves. 'Though I do have a few questions.'

Gordon laughed. 'You can certainly keep a straight face; I'll give you that. Fire away, what do you need to know?' he said.

'It is more what I will *need*,' she said, noticing how tired and old he looked. He must be under a lot of pressure, she thought, running such a secretive organisation. 'I will have to give up my post office job. My income,' she continued. 'Will you be paying me? I know it seems rude to ask, but I have no family to support me and am reliant on two ladies who have only known me for months. If something went wrong, I would need funds to lead a life elsewhere.' Alice's heart thumped inside her chest. 'And what happens after the war?'

The men muttered amongst themselves again, while Clara nodded at Alice.

'Fair point, Alice,' she said before addressing the men. 'I think Alice has asked important questions. We have a responsibility for drafting her into the organisation. Gentlemen, we need to consider her request.'

Lionel looked over at Douglas and Gordon, and the three of them nodded at each other.

'We will fund you, Alice. By the time the war is over you will have a qualified career. The library will be granted to the council, and everything will be above board. You are a valuable asset, and we will ensure life for you after the war will not be disrupted by our department,' Douglas promised.

'But … I don't want to give up the mobile service. Sometimes I am the only person those people on my list see during the week, we chat about more than just books. And Gladys, the postmistress will have to request a new postie. Until now, I didn't realise how much of a problem I would create for others,' Alice said, frowning.

'We can find someone for the mobile library – one of Richard's reliable local runners, a friendly girl,' Clara said, and Alice got the impression that it was already decided. 'Richard and I have ensured the area is protected. Only a handful of us know the truth. Runners come and go, but their tasks are innocent looking. They are employed to carry out small delivery tasks and included in that is the book collection.'

Douglas tapped the table. 'Your postmistress will have a fully qualified postie working for her from the day you stop, too. You have my word on that.'

Alice stared at him. He worked like a magician, producing people from nowhere.

Douglas continued. 'We will also ensure that the local council will comply with your library opening hours, too, as these need to be synchronised with London and our receiver – Richard.'

'As long as you give me time off to actually read a book, I am sure the opening times will be fine,' Alice quipped, her nerves fading.

The room erupted with gusty laughs. Lionel's was the loudest.

'Clara, you and Richard did well finding Alice. She should go and negotiate with Hitler; her technique is to be admired,' he said.

Alice giggled.

'I am pinching myself. Someone has just offered me a library to run before I even qualify. There has to be a catch somewhere,' she said.

'As we heard from both Clara and Richard, you are well read, your knowledge of books and genres are enough to convince anyone you are more than capable. We do not select without running background checks. Go and enjoy London with Clara and we will be in touch again soon. It has been a pleasure to meet such a courageous young woman, Alice. Thank you for trusting us,' Gordon said and gave her a warm smile.

'Thank you for trusting me, and I promise to do the best I can for you, our king and country,' Alice replied.

'You handled yourself well, Alice,' said Clara, after they'd eventually left the building and were back in the car.

Alice gave a slight snort in reply.

'It is all a bit far-fetched to me still.' She said.

Clara was silent for a second, but her eyes narrowed at the back of the driver's head.

'We'll have a good chat back at the hotel,' she said then, and turned to both smile at Alice and remind her with her eyes not to say anything else.

Back at the hotel, Alice eventually stopped shaking. She sat in Clara's room holding the small glass of sherry that Clara had insisted on pouring her.

'How do you do it, Clara? How do you keep smiling, look glamorous and then jump out of a plane in France, where Germans must be in their thousands?' Alice asked.

'I do it for freedom, for peace and for family – and friends. Friends like you, Alice,' Clara said.

'I admire you. I don't think I could do it,' Alice said.

'Richard will be pleased you are joining us. He's quite taken with you.' Clara lifted her glass to Alice's and changed the pattern of conversation from herself to her brother.

'Richard is a good actor. He had me feeling sorry for him, but not any more,' Alice said laughing.

Clara laughed, too.

'He will still shuffle around with the stick, and you will see him when he visits the library. Your injured mentor.' Clara said with a wink.

Alice settled herself back in the large bucket chair and curled her legs up beneath her.

'I cannot believe they are going to create a library and convince everyone that I am the new librarian to run it,' she said.

'*You* will convince everyone with your capabilities, Alice. I am proud of how you stood your ground in HQ, and look how you won them all round.'

Alice smiled her thanks.

'I still can't believe it,' she said. 'And I keep thinking about the novel *The Night of the Fog*. The author is female but writes under a male pseudonym, Anthony Gilbert. It is a mystery about a politician who is an amateur detective and joins forces with an ex-secret agent who is threatened through mysterious letters. I think I could write a novel just as mysterious.'

'I know the book,' Clara said with a smile. 'And it is a shame you could never write that novel – our story. You will be too busy cataloguing and reading in your personal library…'

The thought of being surrounded by books inside a bricks-and-mortar library was exciting, and to be asked to help Great Britain keep the defence cogs turning was of the utmost importance to Alice now that she had signed her name on the paperwork.

'But please, Alice,' Clara added, 'remember you cannot even give the slightest hint of what you are doing. Douglas will keep his promise to protect you, but you must keep your promise, too, for king and country. Think of it as a repayment for what happened to your grandmother if you need something to focus upon. What I do, is prevent one side from attacking the other.'

Alice knew that the the hardest thing she had to do now was not say a word about who she really worked for, and to run the library the best she could. Clara and Richard had shown a great deal of faith in her, and she would not let them down.

Dear Diary

You will never believe what has happened! I am to run a library and train as a librarian. My mobile service will still continue and someone else will pedal the villages whilst I watch over the static one. I am also going to live above the library. Books at my fingertips whenever I want them - my dream come true. I have an important task thanks to Clara and Richard.

Clara is not the cold woman I thought she was.

She is smart, funny, and clever. Between them they recommended the village has a library and I am the person best positioned to maintain it, and someone in a government office in London agreed. I visited London with Clara. She treated me and it was wonderful. Sightseeing and treats. There were sad sights where the bombs had destroyed large parts of the city, but other places looked untouched and busy as if there was no war raging around them. I am entering a new chapter of my life with new friends. I am one of the lucky ones, providing Gladys does not moan too much and Hilda is not too upset I am not carrying on the 'family' tradition.

Chapter Twenty-One

'It was incredible, and so busy!' Alice gushed as she shared her trip with Hettie and Hilda, ensuring she chose her words carefully.

'We saw St Paul's cathedral and walked for miles. The hotel was so luxurious, and Clara took good care of me... And ... you'll never guess what...'

'What?' said Hettie and Hilda together, intrigued.

'Clara took me to see some rich friends of hers who are in charge of protecting ancient books and artefacts. Clara had told them about me and my mobile library service, and they were so impressed that they are going to fund a proper library here.' Alice was fired up with excitement as she relayed the story that she and Clara had concocted for her.

Hettie gasped, then clapped her hands with delight.

'That is wonderful news, Alice. But won't you miss running your mobile service?' she asked.

Alice shook her head, 'Clara and I asked for an assistant to keep the mobile service running and they have agreed! Richard, Clara's brother, is going to be my mentor and oversee the library.'

'And your chores for Hettie?' Hilda asked, a hint of wariness in her tone.

It was a reasonable question, but it irked Alice all the same. She had never let Hettie or Hilda down with helping out before she left for work in the mornings and evenings.

'Nothing will change,' she said, keeping her voice light and even and looking from Hilda to Hettie.

'Well, I wish you good luck with it all, but make sure you have fun time, too, Alice. You are still young,' Hettie said with concern in her voice.

Alice gave her a gentle hug. 'Dear Hettie, you know me and books, they are my fun.'

Hilda gave a dry laugh. 'I saw you walking out with that American. I told Hettie, we need to keep an eye on you,' she said, and another tremor of annoyance shimmied through Alice.

'Sergeant Hardesty is the man who gave me the books to replace the damaged ones, as well you know. I met him to thank him. I am not walking out with anyone.' Alice said and looked pointedly at Hilda. She felt like suggesting that if Hilda had nothing to do and needed to exercise her leg, maybe she could show Hardy around one of the villages near her cottage, but Hettie's polite cough sliced through the atmosphere and weakened Alice's indignation.

'Maybe Hilda could help you in the library, too?' Hettie said diplomatically.

Alice dreaded the thought of Hilda's grumpiness creating an atmosphere and distracting her, but thankfully Hilda relieved her of that concern.

'I fill my time perfectly well as it is, and my leg won't allow me to walk far,' Hilda said tersely.

Hettie gave Alice a lifted eyebrow of resignation.

Hettie had previously suggested that her sister sometimes took advantage of her, and Alice now realised Hilda was doing the same to her. Hilda had lost herself after her accident, and the confidence to walk far, so perhaps it was the right thing for Alice to take a step back and force Hilda to do more for herself. She wouldn't like it at first, but Alice was sure she would be grateful in the long run. It had to make Hilda feel better if she had more purpose in her life again, after all.

'I'm happy to take Teddy for his usual walk, Hilda,' she said, more gently now. 'But with the demands of the new library, I don't think I will be able to help out with your garden. I'm sorry.'

'Of course, Alice. Your time at Hilda's will need to be adjusted,' Hettie said carefully as she touched her sister's arm. 'I think it will do your leg good to get more exercise.'

Hilda grumbled under her breath about gratitude, but Alice decided to ignore it. She had already repaid Hilda's kindness for helping her find lodgings with Hettie, and for her job, it was time for her to focus on her own life now.

Hettie smiled at Alice. 'Why don't you go and fetch Teddy for a walk now, while I talk to Hilda about getting someone to help with her garden,' she said.

'Of course.' Alice was wise enough to know Hettie meant she was going to give her sister a good talking to and excused herself.

Arriving at Hilda's, Alice fetched Teddy, who was being fussed over by the billeted men. They gave Alice an idea.

'If any of you have a spare two minutes, I think Hilda would appreciate a hand in the garden. I'm going to be running a new library, so will not be around to pick the vegetables and fruit for her,' she said. 'We'd all be very grateful and Hettie will come and change your bed linen tomorrow,' she added, with a sweet smile of encouragement.

'Sure. We'll have it turned over in no time,' one of the men said and patted a colleague on the shoulder. 'This one used to be a professional gardener back home.'

After a few minutes of banter and profuse thanks, Alice left to walk Teddy around the perimeter of the airbase. He loved the attention when several men stopped to stroke him and confessed they missed their own pets at home. Which gave Alice another idea.

Stopping at the guard house, she asked who she might speak to regarding walking Teddy around the base to let the men pet him. She was directed to a senior officer who, after also fussing over Teddy, gladly granted her permission and wrote out a permit.

Alice continued walking Teddy amongst the clusters of men near the runway and encountered another pilot who had befriended a dog of his own; both dogs enjoyed a romp around the grass areas together.

'Are the boys due back soon?' she asked knowing a large number of planes had flown out that day.

'Not yet,' someone replied.

'Let's pray they all make it,' another chipped in.

'Yes, let's,' Alice said and stood by while the men fussed over Teddy.

When the men moved away to work on the battle-weary planes on hard stands, she stood and watched for a while. They whistled while they worked, and their banter brought about loud batches of laughter. How they managed to function with the same fears every day, Alice found it hard to imagine. She admired each and every one of them. They gave her the determination and reassurance that her place within the SOE was worthwhile and, as Clara told her, the effort she put in would help the men get through the war and home to their families a bit sooner.

'Come on, Teddy, time to go home,' she said and walked towards the far exit of the field, Teddy running alongside her as the men called out their goodbyes. In the distance she saw the distinct figure of Hardy working on a plane wing.

She found herself walking closer, until she was just a few feet away from the plane.

'Can you repair it?' she said and stood back waiting for Hardy to look her way. He grinned when he saw her and jumped down.

'Alice,' he said. 'Out for a walk, I see.' He nodded at Teddy sniffing at the grass.

From her pocket Alice pulled out her permit.

'He's on official business,' she said laughing. 'I'm officially allowed to bring him to cheer the men up.'

Hardy pulled a rag from his pocket and wiped thick grease from his hands. 'How was London?' he asked.

'Eye-opening. And, as you often say, quite something. I met important people who are going to create a static library with yours truly as the librarian,' Alice replied.

Hardy shoved the cloth back into his pocket before grabbing Alice's hand and shaking it.

'Congratulations! A librarian.' Hardy gave a low whistle of approval. 'But don't tell me we lose our postie?' he asked pulling a ridiculous sad face and making Alice giggle.

'Sadly, yes,' she said. 'I know being a librarian is not nearly as important as your job, but it is a place where people can find peace and calm.'

'You really find a book calming? I enjoy a long walk to help my mind settle,' Hardy said.

Alice smiled at him.

'I enjoy that, too, but there is nothing better than turning a page into another world and stepping away from the reality of war.'

'Guess we all need something to distract us and give us hope,' he said, just as someone called out to him, and he turned to acknowledge them.

'Gotta go. It's been a bad one. Bring Teddy to see us again tomorrow afternoon if you can – he'll be a good distraction,' he said, stepping closer to her. For a moment, Alice thought he was going to lean in and kiss her, but then he pulled back.

'See you, then, Alice,' he said and walked away leaving Alice staring after him. His sudden, cool reaction disturbed her, but she chose to shake it off. He obviously had a lot on his plate, that was all. And she still had not broached the question of whether he had a wife and child at home – maybe that was his reason for his sudden mood change – guilt?

Tugging at Teddy's lead, she composed herself.

'Come on Teddy, everyone is busy. You'll see them again tomorrow,' she said, and turned away from Hardy, who was in deep conversation with a group of colleagues.

Dear Diary

I so much wanted to tell Hardy all about going to London. Of how excited but nervous I am, but he came across as distant with me today. I feel a bit deflated, if I am honest. The mystery of whether he is married or not is still chipping away inside of me.

For a second, I thought he was going to kiss me when we were at the airfield, but he pulled back. He confuses me. I get the strangest feeling inside of my body when he is close, and I do not know who to ask for advice about what is happening to my emotions and why I feel this way. I would die of embarrassment trying to express my feelings to Hettie. And Hilda, well she is not approachable at all - especially lately. And to ask her about affairs of the heart would not get a welcome response.

Chapter Twenty-Two

Over the next two weeks, Clara and Alice met each day at Clara's house. Their relationship was blossoming, Clara becoming the trusted friend Alice needed.

One afternoon, they ventured into a conversation about an old boyfriend of Clara's, a Frenchman named Marcel. The conversation was comfortable and free flowing.

'He was so handsome,' Clara said wistfully. 'And he rode a horse with great style.'

'Was he your first love?' Alice asked.

'My first love, but not my first lover,' Clara said with a naughty smile and winked at Alice. 'Does that shock you?'

Shaking her head, Alice gave a soft laugh. 'Honestly, if you were anyone else, the answer would probably be yes, but no. No, I am not shocked. I am certain life in France is very different to here. I have read French men are romantics.'

Clara laughed and shrugged. 'Perhaps,' she said, then eyed Alice intently. 'What about you and your attractive American? I have seen you both together and you make a handsome couple – using my mother's words,' she said.

With such a frank conversation opening up, Alice decided to ask Clara for advice about Hardy.

'I am seeing Hardy for a walk, early evening, but I am worried about something,' she said with caution in her voice.

Clara sat upright in her chair when Alice had finished speaking. Her face etched with concern, she looked directly at Alice.

'In what way, Alice? Speak freely and if I can help, I will,' she said.

Struggling to find the right words, Alice hesitated for a few seconds.

'I … um … when I am near him, I feel different inside. When we are not together I cannot stop thinking about him,' she said in a rush.

Clara took a moment to think, then gave an encouraging smile.

'Firstly, what do you know about Hardy?' she asked.

Alice smiled back.

'I know he is five years older than me,' she said, and frowned. 'And I have seen a photograph of a lady and child on his desk, so I think he is married. He has never said a word about them – as if they are a secret…'

Clara gave a knowing nod of her head.

'You need to take a step back, Alice. If you are correct, and he is married, he will eventually return to them. Think about what they are going through back home, trusting that he will come back to America,' she said, then continued kindly. 'You are young and your excitement about this man will take you along the wrong path if you're not careful. If it goes any further with Hardy, it may leave you pregnant. Do you understand me?'

Alice looked down at her hands in her lap.

'You're right. We have never kissed, just walked and talked. We do not even hold hands, but I want him to touch me and kiss me. Is that so wrong of me?' Alice's voice was barely a whisper and she suddenly felt embarrassed as she twisted her hands together.

Clara sighed.

'My advice is that you remain friends and curb the alone time with him. As a man, he will have urges and you are vulnerable enough to respond. Be extremely careful in his company,' Clara said, firmly.

'But I don't think he would ever hurt me,' Alice said, puzzled.

Clara frowned. 'Has anyone spoken to you about "the birds and bees"?' she said. 'Sex … and romance between a man and a woman? Has Hettie? Or your grandmother? Perhaps the matron at the orphanage?'

Alice felt her embarrassment rising again.

'Nobody has said anything. I read romantic novels. The tender kiss and courtship is all I really know,' she replied, knowing her face was blazing scarlet. She could feel the heat when she moved her hair from her face.

Clara laughed, but softly. 'No wonder you are confused about what is going on inside your body,' she said. 'You and I are going to have a frank chat about it.' She stood and reached out her hand to Alice. 'Come with me, we will walk and talk.'

Dear Diary

What a discovery I made today! Clara opened my eyes to what she called 'the birds and the bees'. Making love and giving yourself to a man is a complicated process. She spoke to me as an adult not a child and told me many secrets to keeping a man happy in the marital bed. She also gave me a warning about being impulsive when it came to having - dare I write it down - sex.

Her words were, 'Think, Alice. Clear your mind before action. Always think first.'

I think I will remember those words and her lesson for the rest of my life!

Clara and Richard met up with Alice two days later outside the post office.

'Alice. How are you feeling today?' Clara asked, her voice upbeat as she kissed Alice on both cheeks.

'More informed and comfortable, thank you,' Alice said shyly as she watched Richard puffing on his pipe and looking the other way.

Their intimate conversation had brought Alice and Clara closer together, and Alice could sense that Clara was now embracing their friendship on a deeper level, as was Alice. A deep bond had formed between them, and she knew she could always count on Clara for her invaluable guidance. That afternoon when they'd spoken, Alice had gone to the airbase and handed a note to the guard, cancelling her walk with Hardy. She needed time to think over all she had learned and how to protect her feelings. Clara had warned her against getting involved with a married man, as once word got around, Alice would be branded with the worst kind of names from those who would disapprove.

'How are you, Richard?' Alice asked.

'Happier for seeing you, my dear,' Richard said affectionately. To Alice's relief, he showed no sign of knowing about the conversation she had with Clara.

'Shall we?' he asked, and ushered Clara and Alice forward.

They walked through a small alleyway before entering the building together.

There was great excitement in the villages when Alice informed people a permanent library was on the horizon. For those who could not visit, she reassured them that nothing would change. A new girl would still deliver them a selection to read from the vast number of books which would be available in the coming months, and also run any errands they required.

Alice's own excitement could not be contained, and she clapped her hands with delight when she was eventually allowed inside the freshly decorated building.

'It is incredible, more than I imagined!' Alice exclaimed.

Nothing was brand new, all furnishings were reclaimed items, but the mismatch gave it a comfortable look, and Alice knew a regular stream of people would enjoy sitting in the quiet, calm space.

The books Hardy and Hilda had given Alice were given their place on the shelves hours after the small building had been cleared and cleaned of all building works. The speed with which the SOE had worked amazed Alice.

Clara walked around the building and then to the desk where Alice had laid out everything she needed. Inside the small office behind the desk was a small selection of old titles and a large ledger.

'A fresh batch of books will arrive this afternoon, but remember, not all are for the general public,' she said.

Alice nodded. She had been informed that the SOE runners would request a specific book and repeat a number against the title on the list to be kept in the office drawer. The number was a code for Alice.

Her job was to give out and accept books to and from the

runners. She was under strict instructions to ensure the books were well wrapped with a message in an envelope corresponding with the book code. Once handed over, Alice was to date and add the time, then both she and the runner both had to sign the ledger. They were not to deviate away from the greeting and request. Alice learned the format off by heart, and also learned not to add niceties or weather observations into her response when Richard and Clara tested her. They reminded her the runners were to walk in and out as swiftly as possible.

Richard was to sit in the library as her mentor and monitor the runners.

'I will be moving into Clara's house,' he told Alice. 'She's going away for a while.' His voice was laden with what Alice guessed was worry.

'Oh, I see,' she replied, then added, 'I can help you move if you like.'

Richard gave her a grin. 'I'll let you pedal my small library home for me.'

Alice held out her hand. 'It's a deal,' she said with a laugh. It pleased her to see Richard grin.

Looking over at Clara, Alice felt a sadness at the thought that a mission requiring Clara's presence was imminent. She would be missed.

'Be careful, Clara. Richard said you are going away. I will miss you,' she said softly.

'And I will miss you. Do not worry about me, *ma petite soeur*,' Clara replied. 'When they arrive, catalogue your books and, Alice, well done for being brave enough to take this on.'

Clara had called her 'my little sister' in French once before, and it gave Alice a sense of belonging. Richard had also softened to her and the three of them had formed a relationship she thought might be what siblings experienced.

'You inspire me, and this is nothing compared to *your* bravery,'

Alice said and gave Clara a hug.

———

Dear Diary

I am worried about Clara, and Richard.

Clara has to travel abroad soon, and the news tells us Europe is unsafe. Clara calls me her little sister, and I now feel part of her life – I see them both as family. The war is dictating where she travels and all I can do is live in hope that she returns safely.

She has helped me understand what it means to become a woman. For that I will always be grateful. I understand the triggers which could take me over boundaries I will never return from if I give into powerful persuasion and natural instincts.

Life at home can be hard sometimes. Hilda is moody and needs constant nagging, poor Hettie struggles with pleasing her.

Gabrielle wrote and said Canada is proud of its forces and their success in Sicily. Another country I must research, as I had not heard of it before.

Chapter Twenty-Three

With Teddy enjoying the fuss and attention during their afternoon walk through the airbase, Alice noticed the men were not their usual jovial selves, and many sat alone.

She also noticed the usual number of planes were not on the ground, and guessed a mission had taken its toll on the crew. Her studies had distracted her from counting the planes home as usual, and now she felt glad and guilty she had not witnessed another battered mission.

Despite cancelling their rendezvous, Alice still hoped to catch a glimpse of Hardy working outdoors, and was not disappointed when she saw him. She waved as he stretched then strode her way. Despite his smile, his face looked tired and drawn, his shoulders slumped.

'Alice, fancy a cola?' he asked looking over at the drinks club to his right.

'I do, but unfortunately Teddy will bark the whole time I am inside,' she replied.

Putting his fingers to his lips, Hardy gave a piercing whistle and made a beckoning sign to a group of men. One came running over to them and saluted.

'Clem, can you take the dog with you while I take a break. I need to speak with Miss Carmichael,' he said and handed over an excited Teddy.

'Sure, boss. He'll be okay with us ma'am,' Clem said, addressing Alice.

Inside the drinks club, Alice looked about and thought about how many men would be drowning their sorrows that evening. She glanced at Hardy, who still appeared subdued and not his chatty self. Something had definitely happened.

Hardy directed her to a seat by a table out of view of the several people milling around the room. She sat and watched him order their drinks, noting he was much taller than many of the men around him. When he sat down she let a silence settle, sensing he needed company not chatter. She took a sip of her drink and Hardy did the same. Eventually he gave a sigh, and leaned back in his chair.

'I'll be glad when this war is over,' he said with feeling.

Alice looked at him and her heart ached knowing he had lost more men, they had not all been counted home. Hardy's whole face was etched in pain.

'Did you lose many?' she asked softly.

Hardy picked up his bottle of cola and took a long drink, before placing it on the table again.

'Enough – too many. Half of them,' he said.

'I am sorry,' Alice said, not really sure what to say next. Sitting drinking with a man like this was alien to her, and though she had sat drinking tea with Hardy before, this time there was something deeper about the moment. Something more intimate, but still with a divide.

'I want to look beyond the war, but today I'm struggling. I feel helpless,' he said, running his finger around the rim of his bottle.

Taken aback by his openness, Alice waited a moment before reaching out for his hand.

'I understand that feeling of helplessness, but cannot stand in your shoes and know the dreadful pain of losing members of your crew every day,' she said. 'Losing my gran left me bewildered and full of anger. And losing a friend like Pete was dreadful, but knowing he died to save people like me from Hitler's rage means he will never be forgotten for his sacrifice. People will remember your brave friends, they won't forget.'

She gave him what she hoped was a comforting smile.

Hardy responded with a slight huff of a sigh. 'They will forget. Life will move on, and the world will forget,' he said. The sadness in his voice seemed like a heavy load to carry.

'I promise, they will not be forgotten. Every one of you will be remembered for your bravery and for supporting our country. As we do the men of the Great War,' she whispered.

Hardy lifted his head and stared at her.

'Will you walk out with me, Alice?' he asked, his face serious and creased with question.

Taken aback, Alice wondered if this was a joke, but soon realised it wasn't. Hardy was serious.

'It would be wrong,' she said with heavy emphasis on the last word. Remembering Clara's advice, Alice knew she was not prepared to simply be Hardy's entertainment while he was in England. Helping him open up over a drink when he was suffering sorrow was one thing, but becoming his girlfriend – or mistress – was another.

Hardy's head jerked back in surprise.

'Wrong? Why? Because I'm a Yank and you're a Brit, or I'm a guy and you're a girl I want to get to know better... What's wrong with that?' he asked.

'Nothing. It's because of your wife and child back in Dayton,' she said with a touch of indignation.

Hardy tilted his head and looked at her in puzzled amusement.

'My what? My wife and child?' he asked, his voice slow and questioning. 'I have a wife and child?'

'Yes. The two people in the photograph on your desk,' she said crisply, 'I am not a fool, Hardy.'

Hardy slid his hand over the top of his head, then stared at her. A kindly stare.

'Hmm, you are definitely no fool, but you have made a mistake, Alice. I promise you I have no wife and child. Where you saw that photograph, that is not my office. Not my desk,' he said.

'But—' Alice began.

'It's my chief's desk. They are *his* family,' Hardy said, with a smile playing across his lips. 'I was pulling papers for a job in his office when you came in.'

Alice felt the flush of embarrassment flare in her cheeks, she resisted the urge to put the cool bottle of cola to them. Hardy's eyes sparkled with amusement, and it felt good to see him perk up from his miserable state.

'So … all this time you have thought I was a married man?'

'I did think you were married, yes. Your age and well, your…' Alice hesitated. 'I mean, why wouldn't you be?' she said.

'Because I have not met the right girl for me yet?' Hardy said then winked. 'Or are you surprised because I'm such a dreamboat of a guy with a great personality, but no one wants me?'

All embarrassment left Alice as she burst into laughter. The relief she felt that Hardy was a single man surprised her. He obviously meant more to her than she realised, even after such a short time.

'I am still a little concerned about your age…' she said, with a teasing grin.

'That's kinda nice,' Hardy said. 'So, does that mean you'll take a chance on me, Alice Carmichael?'

Alice peered at him in a theatrical way and moved her head side to side.

'Hmm, you do look young for your age, so maybe,' she said, and giggled. Flirting with Hardy came easy to her. It felt natural.

Suddenly, Hardy jumped to his feet and rushed around to her side of the table. He pulled her up from her chair and into his arms, and before she could say anything else his lips were on hers. Alice's chest ached with holding her breath as she caved into his bold move. Their kiss brought whistles and cheers from those around them, but Alice did not pull away. She was beyond caring about other people seeing such an intimate moment. This was her first true kiss, and she was not going to deny herself the pleasure by feeling self-conscious.

For longer than she thought possible, Hardy's lips were firm on hers and their warmth brought about a tingle inside her belly. His tongue found its place against hers, and thanks to Clara's educational session, Alice now allowed herself to sink into the moment, but hold back just enough of herself to keep things respectable.

Once Hardy released her he looked away, flushed.

'I'm sorry, Alice. That was wrong of me, I apologise,' he said snatching up his uniform cap. 'I'll walk you home.' He looked down at the floor, embarrassed.

Alice laid down the book on the sideboard and turned, lifting his chin with her fingers so that he could see her face.

'Do I look annoyed?' she asked.

Hardy said nothing, his eyes wide, gazing into hers. A shy smile playing at the corners of his lips. For Alice, everything seemed to slow down, the world outside fading away until there was just the two of them, suspended in time.

'It was my first kiss and I think you deserve a response,' Alice said and placed her lips on his. The warmth of his face close to hers and the heat of their lips together felt natural.

When they parted for breath, Hardy grabbed her again and then, as if drawn together by an invisible force, their lips met in another soft, hesitant kiss. It was a moment of pure magic as they lost themselves in each other.

Finally, they walked out of the club together, hand in hand, and Alice's heart filled with joy, knowing he was all hers. It no longer mattered who saw them walking out together, they were now a couple. For Alice, it felt as if she had stepped into adulthood and a whole new chapter of life was about to begin.

The walk home was a relatively slow one as neither of them wanted to rush the time together away. Alice held Hardy's hand, her thumb slowing stroking the callouses on his finger.

'I will have to keep them grease- and cut-free from now on,' Hardy joked.

'But then they would not be your hands. The hands of a man putting his life aside to keep others safe,' she said.

Hardy stopped walking and cupped her face in his hands.

'If they were greasy right now you would have a black beard.' He laughed. 'And I might be reluctant to do this,' he said, kissing her with even more passion than before.

Breathless as they pulled apart again, Alice knew she should only encourage him so far, Clara's words mooched around inside her head like a chaperone.

'I think it is best we keep walking, Hardy,' she said.

When they said their goodbyes, he whispered in her ear, 'By the way, although my friends call me Hardy, those who love me call me Blake.'

Dear Diary
He kissed me! Hardy kissed me and I kissed

him back. Carla told me it would be a natural instinct, and it was. My legs felt like jelly and my head was filled with so many happy thoughts it made me realise I had not experienced true happiness - I have now! He said those who loved him called him Blake, and I think there is a deep fondness for him in my heart which could grow into whatever love is supposed to feel like. Am I feeling it now, or does it become more intense? It was a public kiss, and I was not embarrassed at all! The war needs to end soon so we can relax and enjoy life together. From now on I think I will call him Blake; it will be me showing him he means a lot to me without me being obvious with words. It is early days.

Chapter Twenty-Four

Dear Gabrielle,

I hope this letter finds you in good spirits. My life has taken a turn for the better. If you recall, I met an American airman, Hardy, though his real name is Blake. We are now walking out together.

He is charming and kind, nothing like Mark out of How Could You Jennifer! *That character was mean and shallow. I have taken to reading more Mills and Boon books. I think the romantic in me has been ignited. I also think Blake is the only person who has ever laughed at my jokes. He is five years older than me, but he has never made me feel young and unsophisticated, he treats me like his equal. Unlike me, Blake is not an avid reader, but he knows a lot about geography, which is wonderful as he tells me so much about countries I have never heard of, and will probably never visit. He knows about the stars, too, their names and what they mean, and we sit near the hut I told you about and look up at them.*

Hettie and Hilda are learning to cope with Hilda's retirement and, I must admit, her moods. They drive me to sit in my hut and read! She can be quite beastly at times, but I do realise it is because her life has altered so much. She has never had a husband and told me she had no intentions as a young woman to be at the beck and call of a man, so chose to be a spinster. I cannot imagine feeling like that, as I look forward to the exciting journey of having a family some day. Hilda says she has no regrets, though, and I believe her. I just wish she would find her more pleasant side again.

How wonderful we have reading in common. I dream of owning a bookshop of my own one day!

What have you read recently? I read your last recommendation by Emily Brontë. However, I do not think **Wuthering Heights** was for me. Don't get me wrong, I enjoyed the plot, but the family – and perhaps this is because I didn't have a true one of my own – troubled me. I wanted a light-hearted moment, but it never came. The author did a grand job in making me think about life, though, and that the likes of Heathcliff are not for me!

I am delighted to hear you are walking out, too. A Scotsman of all people! You said there were a lot of Scottish families living out there, so I am not sure why I am surprised. Enjoy your time together and I hope all goes well when his platoon moves on.

I must finish now as I am meeting Blake at the airbase, then we will enjoy an evening of listening to the dance music. Neither of us a keen on dancing, but we tap our feet and enjoy the music and leave the wild moves to others.

Take care of yourself, regards to your family,

Alice

***

A lice made a special effort with her hair and decided to wear flat shoes and a pretty floral, green-cotton dress. She chose a lightweight swing jacket rather than a cardigan, because although the weather was warm, the mosquitos were active when the damp evening air arrived late evening. Her arms always seemed to be their target, even through the sleeves of a knitted cardigan, so a thicker jacket was her defence. Alice walked quickly to the airbase, eager to be held in Blake's arms once again.

'My beautiful girl,' he said when they met, and Alice threw herself into his arms.

His skin smelled clean and fresh, and his shirt freshly laundered.

'My American hero,' she replied with a giggle, then caved into his eager kisses.

'Let's stay out here. It is pretty hot and noisy inside,' he suggested.

'I am so pleased you said that. I am not one for loud, stuffy rooms,' Alice said.

'Nor me! Stay there, I will grab us some drinks and we'll go over there…' Hardy pointed to the far end of the airbase.

They sat talking for a while then lay back on a blanket beneath the breathtaking expanse of stars. They had supplies of cola, and beer – which Blake dared her to try, but Alice found the drink too bitter, the taste lingering on her tongue, leaving a sharp, unpleasant aftertaste.

The field filled with the gentle melodies of music, creating a soothing atmosphere.

'Look at what everyone inside is missing,' she said, pointing up at the sky where the stars began popping into view. 'I am always thrilled when something real reminds me of moments in books.'

'What book does tonight's sky remind you of?' he asked, studying her with interest.

'*Two on a Tower* by Thomas Hardy,' she said. 'Quite fitting for tonight, as one of the characters is an astronomer. The difference between the book's characters and us is that the woman is older than the man,' she added, giggling.

Blake groaned. 'Don't remind me I am older than you, honey.

Tonight, I feel years younger. *You* make me feel young and alive again.'

A silence fell between them, and he reached out for her hand, and Alice's heart skipped a beat as they lay there, with nothing but pleasure running through her. She prayed the sirens would stay silent and the clear sky would not encourage the enemy to destroy a treasured moment.

As the light faded into a soft haze, the sky transformed into a deep navy-blue. Blake pointed out the stars that pilots relied on for navigation when their equipment failed, and Alice felt a wave of contentment. His voice soothed her.

'The stars are tiny sparks of hope,' he said, and Alice rolled onto her side to look at him.

'What beautiful words,' she whispered, her eyes tracing the outline of his silhouette and etching it into her memory for the moments they spent apart. She already knew every inch of Blake's face in the daylight, now she wanted to imagine him in her dreams. His muscular arms holding her. Slowly, Alice was understanding these powerful experiences and their importance when falling in love.

'They are not my words, sadly. They belong to a pilot I know, who sadly never returned from a mission. I will never forget him, or what he said.'

Blake broke the sad moment by pulling her close to him and holding her tightly. Alice relaxed into his arms and embraced his kisses and affectionate whispers with the passion they deserved. She felt his desire to almost engulf her and make her the other half of himself, and she immersed herself in the happiness this gave her.

After a while the sounds of the dancers and drinkers rang out and they pulled apart.

'It is time to go home, honey,' he said easing himself upright.

With reluctance, Alice did the same and looked at all the people filing out of the hut.

'They can't possibly have had such a wonderful night as we have,' she said. 'I will never forget it; you and the stars. It was perfect.'

Dear Diary

I think I am falling in love. It seems so fast, and I doubt myself sometimes, but I have strong feelings for Blake. Such strong emotions rise from inside of me and when he touches me I am rendered helpless. Clara told me about making love and it is something I would like to experience with Blake, but I also know I must not give myself to him unless I am certain of his trust and love. The romantic novels I read still cannot fully describe what I'm feeling - being wanted, to have someone wanting my love and returning it with such affection and passion. My heart races, my mind fills with bright thoughts and my body throbs with desire for the unknown. I think it is love. I am sure it is. If this is not love, then I cannot imagine what true love must feel like and question whether my body and heart would cope!

Chapter Twenty-Five

As Alice unlocked the library door, she noticed a man lingering across the other side of the road, and she was not convinced by his pretence of showing interest in the windmill.

'Morning,' she called out, letting him know she had seen him, but he made no effort to cross over the road. He simply lifted his cigarette in acknowledgement.

From inside the library, Alice stood back so as not to be seen and looked at him through the window. He was of medium height, willowy, and he drew slowly on his cigarette.

She wondered if he was one of the runners and it was his first time visiting. There had been six arrive to date, including two women in their forties or fifties. Richard had not come to library the day before, though Alice was not perturbed by his lack of presence, she knew the routine, and the runner who had come had a pleasant nature. It was unusual for another runner to follow on so soon, though, so she jotted down his description for a just-in-case scenario. Just before lunchtime, having seen the man walk back and forth several times outside, Alice nipped over to the post office to pick up her post from Gladys.

'Hello, Alice. Nice to see the library busy today. Just a few for you today,' Gladys said putting a small pile of letters onto the counter. Alice placed them in her bag.

'Did you see that man hanging around the windmill this morning? He walked by the post office a few times. I thought he was waiting for me to open up, but he didn't come inside,' Alice said.

'Thin fellow?' Gladys asked, and Alice nodded. 'He came in asking for a stamp, but I never saw him again. He's definitely not local.'

'It is probably my imagination,' said Alice. 'But he was very interested in this side of the road. Be careful, Gladys. You never know who is lurking about nowadays.'

***

After lunch, the library was busy and a queue of people formed. Alice focused on them and their choices of reading matter.

'Ooh, I read that last year, Mrs B. It's a very good mystery story. Another author I can recommend is Agatha Christie. Have you read any of hers?' she asked the elderly lady handing over a copy of *Flowers For the Judge* by Margery Allingham.

'No. But I will read this one and you can help me choose next time, dear,' said the lady known as Mrs B by everyone in the village.

'I look forward to it,' Alice said, as she stamped the inside sheet of the book.

***

Richard visited three days later and looked around the library, giving it a nod of approval. It was spotless and people either sat at tables reading or browsed the shelves.

'Hello, stranger.' Alice smiled as he approached the counter.

Richard's nose twitched.

'Perfume, Alice? Not like you,' he said with a smile.

As always she knew her flushed face was giving her away, but Alice simply shrugged.

'A gift,' she said.

'From your American?' Richard asked.

'From Blake. Yes.' For the first time, Alice did not feel shy talking about him. She was proud to be his girlfriend. To walk out on the arm of such a hero was a privilege in Alice's eyes.

'He's a pilot, is he?'

Alice shook her head. 'Ground crew. He and his men fix planes and return them to the sky intact. Another kind of hero. Brave, too.'

Richard lifted his chin in approving acknowledgement.

'Tough job. They are a vital lifeline to the pilots and crew, and as you say, brave. Repairing such damage takes courage; when the planes fly again, lives are in their hands,' he said.

Alice sat, reflecting on his words. Richard was right, it must be a nail-biting moment for the maintenance and repair crew. She glanced around the library. Two women browsed at one end of the room, the milkman sat reading a month-old newspaper by the window, and an elderly couple sat exploring an encyclopaedia. All far enough away for Alice to whisper to Richard.

'Any news on Clara?' she asked.

'Nothing,' Richard said flatly, and Alice gave a sigh.

'You must be out of your mind with worry. I know I would be. It's five days since she should have been home, isn't it?'

Richard nodded. 'Clara is a born fighter, and a deep thinker, she will find a way to keep herself above water,' he said.

'But she's up against an army, and a ruthless one. I'm worried about her, Richard,' Alice said. 'I am fond of her.'

'I'm heading to London; we're planning a search for her and

two others out there,' Richard said. 'But don't worry, you will be safe, just keep doing what you've been taught. Four successful missions have happened because of your work.'

'Really? Four? Gracious, that makes it worthwhile. Before you go, though, I am a bit concerned about a man who has been lingering across the road today. He's not someone I recognise. Nor does Gladys the postmistress.' Alice walked over to the window, looked out and then turned back to Richard. 'He's not there now, but he was there most of the morning,' she said.

Richard tapped his hat back on his head and smiled at her.

'Don't worry. He is taking my place. Just call him Richard and do what you do when I am about the place,' he told her.

A huge wave of relief washed over Alice, his words reassuring her that everyone in London had kept their word about protecting her.

'Go and find out about Clara. Be safe, and promise you'll let me know as soon as there is any news,' she said.

'Promise.' Richard smiled at her. 'See you soon.'

Shortly after he'd left, the tall willowy man walked in and asked for a copy of the previous day's paper. It was the code Richard always used for when a runner was due to pick up a book from the office.

Two hours later a large, smart-looking car pulled up outside and a woman walked through the library doors. Everyone in the room turned to look at her. The milkman focused on the car from the window.

Alice did not recognise the woman and having lived long enough in the area she knew the woman was not local by her clothes. She was fashionable, like Clara, but unlike Clara she wore the outfit locally and not for the city. The woman stood out like a sore thumb. The locals inside all took notice and started whispering amongst themselves.

'I would like to take out the book with this number,' said the woman pushing a piece of paper Alice's way.

She had not used the first formal greeting of 'Good morning' or 'Good afternoon', and Alice stood quietly waiting for this woman looking down her nose at her to recall they had a protocol to follow.

'Well, what are you staring at?' the woman asked, her voice raised and indignant.

Realising the situation was not going to rectify itself, and the transaction could not be completed, Alice rushed around from the counter to the woman and stared at her. As did the rest of the library visitors. The woman had drawn unnecessary attention to them both.

'Evelyn! I didn't recognise you,' said Alice, and noted with relief that all heads lost interest. 'Come into my office.'

She guided the woman into the small room. The fake Richard stared, then quickly looked down at his newspaper. Alice guessed he understood her situation.

She closed the door.

'Code,' she said, almost coldly.

'Seven, thirty-two.'

Alice handed her the book.

'What you need is all there,' she said. 'Oh, and next time, dress like a local and bike in if needs be. Do not draw attention to yourself like that again.'

The woman stared at her and opened her mouth, much like a fish, about to say something.

'Go. This is not a game! You know the rules,' Alice said angrily, and nudged the woman towards the door.

Once the woman had driven off in the car, Alice looked at the new Richard and smiled.

'My friend thinks she is a film star, but she's only a maid to one of the big houses, collecting a book for her employer,' she said in a voice louder than required. 'She told me she was wearing a fur belonging to his wife. A fool to herself that one.'

'She certainly fooled me,' he said. 'She'll not do it again.'

Alice nodded. His words were code. The woman would be reported as unreliable.

'I've given her a letter for a relative, but goodness knows where that will end up,' she said, her voice low, hoping he would realise she did not trust the woman.

Reflecting on the moment, Alice walked back to her office and wrote out a note explaining her concerns. She walked over to Richard the Imposter as she now thought of him.

'Here is the book you asked for, the lady returned it late I am afraid,' she said, handing him a random book. On a piece of paper on the top of it she had written a page number.

'Gosh, it's nearly closing time,' she said loudly, and someone hushed her.

'Sorry,' she called out softly.

She saw Richard the Imposter's face twitch as he tried not to laugh. He screwed up the piece of paper and pushed it into his pocket. 'Thanks,' he said, and walked out of the library.

As she put the key in Hettie's front door Alice took a deep breath. A little pride gave her the shivers. She hoped London would heed her words and remind the runners they were entering rural countryside and to blend in, as local folk were alert and aware, and they were to be respected for their observations of visitors to the area who looked out of place – Americans aside. The world was a dangerous place, and everyone was on their guard.

Chapter Twenty-Six

Turning the 'Open' sign in the library door window always gave Alice a thrill.

She smiled out at the people waiting to enter and stepped to one side allowing them into the warm building.

'Good morning, Mrs B, and how are you today?' she asked as she helped her up the low step leading inside.

'My bunions are paining me, but the rest is still moving,' Mrs B said with a wide toothless grin.

'Well, I am glad you have moved this way, I will come and speak with you just as soon as I have done my duty over there,' Alice said pointing to the counter.

Once she'd finished stamping books in and out, Alice moved to the table where her elderly friend sat.

'What did you think?' Alice asked as she picked up the book *Unnatural Death* that she had recommended to Mrs B.

'I think Dorothy L. Sayers is a new favourite author. Lord Peter Wimsey, what a character he is, I could almost hear his posh voice,' Mrs B replied.

Alice giggled quietly. 'I know what you mean, he stands out on the page as a London gentleman, all top hat and tails. I think it is his title which helps.'

'What are you reading this week?' Mrs B asked.

'Ah, I am page deep into *Shirley*, a story about strong and capable young women in the eighteen hundreds, and it has two love stories on the go. Charlotte Brontëwrote it, but it was originally published under the name Currer Bell. I learned that through my librarian studies,' Alice replied.

Mrs B listened to Alice then patted the back of her hand.

'And now I know, thanks to my librarian. You are the highlight of my week, Alice. Strong women and love stories are not only in fiction, but in real life nowadays,' she said.

'That's true,' Alice agreed and returned to her counter to attend to more library visitors. By the end of the day she was to go home satisfied she had happy readers settled in their homes for the evening.

'Calm down, Hilda.'

Hettie's voice echoed through the cottage. It was rare for Alice to hear Hettie raise her voice, and she dropped her bag onto the table and rushed into the front room.

'What has happened? Are you okay?' Alice asked Hilda, who was flapping her arms in agitation at her sister.

'Even she is talking like them now! Are you *okay*?' Hilda said the last part of her sentence in a mocking, American accent.

Alice turned to Hettie for an explanation.

'Hilda's landlord has evicted her. He said he is under pressure to take on more billeted men, and that he has family who can move in when the war is over. So Hilda's days at the cottage are coming to an end,' Hettie said.

Alice looked at Hilda with sympathy. 'I am so sorry,' she said. 'I know how much you loved your home – and the garden. How can I help?'

'Hettie says she will clear out her sewing room for me,' Hilda said, her voice low in mood.

'Then I will help you pack up your things and arrange for them to be brought here. And I will dig out your best plants, and the vegetables; there's plenty of room for them in this garden. Once that's done, we can take a deep breath and think about what's next,' Alice said softly.

Hettie went to her sister and put her arm around her waist.

'Sit down and try not to fret. We will work it out,' she said.

To their surprise, Hilda burst into tears. Alice's heart went out to her.

'Take my room, Hilda. It will be more private for you. I can sleep in Hettie's sewing room on a truckle bed. My books can be boxed up and stored safely in the library, and my clothes can hang in the sewing room. Once one of the airmen leaves, we can swap you into the larger room. It will work,' Alice said, her voice upbeat and smiling at Hettie. 'That way, you can still sew.'

Hettie returned the smile. 'That's thoughtful of you, Alice. We will do that, and I will get friends to help move Hilda.'

'Yes, thank you, Alice,' said Hilda, gruffly but with a small smile.

Working in the library that afternoon, Alice saw the real Richard walk past the window and ran to the door, pulling it open for him, seeing that his face was ashen and his eyes were dull.

'Richard! You're safe, thank goodness,' she said. 'Any news Clara?' she added, anxious to hear his news.

'Later. Not here,' he said. 'Come to the cottage tomorrow

179

wanted to let you know I am back.' He glanced at his stand-in, Richard the Imposter, sitting looking at them both.

'Two days,' Richard said to him, and the man nodded.

'It will be good to have you back in here,' Alice said and Richard nodded.

'My days abroad are over, but I will explain later. In the meantime, keep up the good work,' he told her.

As Alice watched him walk out she thought 'a lost soul' was how she would have described him, if asked.

With Blake's arms wrapped around her, Alice leaned her head against his chest and tuned into the rhythm of his heartbeat.

'Thank you for the treats for Aunt Hilda, Blake. She needed cheering up,' she said, lifting her head from his chest and kissing his cheek.

'It's tough for her, besides, I don't want her resenting us,' he said.

'I worry about her, she's had no passion for life any more, even before the eviction. I asked if she wanted to help in the library, but she dismissed the idea. I cannot help her, and it is so frustrating – worrying, because I know something is really bothering her.'

'She will come around. You'll find something to help her, Alice. You and your big, kind heart,' he said, and kissed the tip of her nose. Then he looked at his watch. 'Gotta go! I can't wait for the day we can spend more time together. Jeez, we need this war to end.'

His lips on hers took Alice to another place in her mind. To a home of her own and a world at peace. She was not so naïve that she didn't know she'd have to let Blake go one day. Their lives were literally oceans apart, but for now she would enjoy his company, his way of making her feel she was the only girl in the world, the passion he brought into her life.

'Be safe,' she said as she kissed him one last time before heading home.

———

As she approached the sentry box, a loud noise near the boundary startled her and made her jump. As a streak of red-gold darted across the sky, the ground beneath her feet quivered. Alice stood completely still, unable to move a muscle. A déjà vu moment flashed in her mind, and she waited for the ground to open up and the darkness to swallow her again, but all she heard were voices shouting. The young guard leapt from the box, his face etched with concern.

'Alice,' he said, touching his cap. 'Hardy's gonna be busy tonight.'

'One of his?' Alice asked, looking at the ball of flames some distance away from the furthest runway.

The guard nodded, and they stood watching the various crews scurry back and forth from buildings and vehicles. Machinery noises and frantic voices echoed around the grounds. Day after day, they pushed through. Blake and his team repaired the planes under his care, and the pilots and crew knowingly took risks. They came home in their beaten and beloved planes, each with a name representing some important part of their lives painted on the nose. Their battle was personal, and when they lost their lives, it became personal to those on the ground they defended.

The guard, murmuring to himself, expressed his dismay as it became increasingly clear that more planes had failed to return home.

With a heavy heart, Alice walked through the gates, unable to bear witness to any more of it. It didn't matter how many times she saw damaged planes and emergency landings; the horror of it all would always remain fresh in her mind. Brave and heroic were words used all the time in this war, but Alice often wondered if there was a stronger one which summed up their courage.

Back home she wrote to Gabrielle in Canada.

Dear Gabrielle,

I hope this letter finds you and your family well. My part of England is filled with American accents, and I know you said your accent is softer but similar, and I can imagine chatting with you over coffee. I now enjoy a drink or two, but my morning cup of tea will never be replaced. My accent is a country one, not upper-class English. If we ever meet you will understand what I mean. I do not talk like the royal family! The new library is thriving, and I am spoiled for choice when it comes to reading matter. I found a book about Canadian animals, and have decided I am not keen on the idea that bears roam free. Do you see them?

We have a fox, which antagonises the chickens, but no free-roaming bears. I think I would cycle much faster through the woods if we did.

It's the survival of the fittest here. Our forces are strong, but long battles can make men weary. I see them return from missions, embattled and bruised, and the exhausted men repair their bullet-riddled planes, only to have to do the same the following day. Some days my heart breaks when we count home less than left the base. The sky fills and we wait nervously for them to filter through the clouds one by one on their return. Some pilots are guiding home flaming planes and wounded men.

Then I hear the music playing and the occasional laugh and I am reminded that life goes on.

Take care and please find enclosed a selection of headscarves made by my aunt, Hettie. She thanks you for the gift of jam which arrived intact. It was hidden away before we had the opportunity to open a jar.

I recently read your recommendation, Villette *by Charlotte Brontë.*
Gracious, I wasn't expecting the ghost of a nun to appear!
As always give my kind regards to your family.
Stay safe, your friend,
Alice

Chapter Twenty-Seven

A September mist rose across the fields, engulfing Alice in a damp, hazy atmosphere.

As she stood outside Clara and Richard's cottage, waiting for the gate to click shut behind her, a rush of memories from her first visit here came flooding back. It had been a stiff and starchy event and Clara's personality had seemed frosty to Alice at first. But that perception changed after their trip to London, where Alice saw a whole new side of the glamorous woman. She missed her mentor immensely and looked forward to when Clara returned home. They had a lot of catching up to do.

She tapped on the door and waited. Richard's voice called out for her to let herself inside. Alice stepped into the kitchen and noticed dirty dishes in the sink and the curtains still closed. The room smelled stale.

'Richard?' she called out.

'In the front room,' came his reply. Along the hallway Alice noticed the window curtains drawn, as they were across the front door. When she stepped inside the front room she saw Richard sitting in the darkness, smoking.

'Are you ill?' she asked, walking over to the curtains and pulling them to one side to let daylight through. She turned back to look in the room and Richard blinked heavily. His eyes were red-rimmed, and he had a dark unshaven shadow around his chin.

Concerned at his dishevelled state, Alice put down her handbag and moved closer to him.

Richard looked up at her.

'She's dead,' he said bluntly.

Unbalanced by his sudden statement, Alice staggered slightly and gasped.

'Clara? Do you mean Clara?' Her breath came fast as she took in his words and she put her hand to her mouth in horror. Clara was dead.

Richard nodded and tossed what looked like whisky into the back of his throat.

'How many of them have you had?' Alice asked, noting the pallor of his skin.

'Not enough.' Richard poured another drink and gulped it back.

'So, when you saw me the other day you knew?' Alice asked, but could not recall him looking so distraught as he did now.

'No. I knew the Germans had moved her to another town, where more S.S. interrogation centres were. Word had it she was beaten but still alive.'

'In that case, are you sure she is dead?' Alice asked Richard in disbelief. 'They have confirmation – London – they know it is fact?'

Alice waited for his reply, but Richard gulped down another drink.

'Richard, has someone confirmed Clara is dead. Have they seen her body?' Alice asked impatiently. She knew he was hurting, but if he could not face London, then she would. 'I can go to

London, get confirmation from Douglas,' she said. 'I'll beg them to find Clara, and bring her home – regardless.' She let the last word hang in the air.

Inside, Alice knew the reality was that they had already tried, but a helplessness kicked in and she felt driven to find her friend.

Richard lowered his head; he did not need words to convey his response.

'If there is any chance I could fly out and find her, take me to London and get them to agree,' she said, almost pleading with him, her feelings bouncing around inside as she tried to manifest something to happen instead of sitting crying.

'Her beaten body is with the rest of the French family who tried to help; her burial will be included with theirs. Our agent did what he could,' Richard said, his shoulders slumped with grief.

'So, she will remain in France?' Alice whispered.

Richard nodded. 'Yes. At least the family of the others that were killed will find out where in France the Germans are going to bury them, so I can find Clara after the war is over,' he said, lighting another cigarette. 'And at least she is in a country she loved.'

'Yes,' Alice said, tearfully. 'We can go together – if you want company, that is, when the time comes.' She lifted her chin. 'Clara's life must not be in vain, Richard, we need to keep focused on our work here, don't we?' At his nod of agreement, she walked over and put her arms around him. 'I'm so sorry. I'll miss her terribly.'

Already, Alice was chiding herself. Poor Richard had lost his beloved sister. This was not the time to talk of Clara as simply an SOE agent who had heroically given her life for peace in Europe, but to remember her as Richard's beloved only sibling.

'Oh, Richard,' she murmured, a mixture of frustration and fondness in her tone. I am sorry for nagging you. It's the shock. She was my friend, but she was your flesh and blood.'

Richard shook his head and smiled weakly at her.

'Clara saw you as a little sister,' he said. 'Someone to guide forward in this war, in our mission, but to care for and protect, too. She was proud of you. She had faith that you would not let her down. And you haven't. I'm proud of you, too.'

Clara helped me so much more than she knew,' Alice said. 'She helped me grow up...' As she spoke, she felt the warmth of a blush in her cheeks at the memory of all that she and Clara had talked about and a pain in her heart at the loss of her friend and mentor.

That there would be no more guidance from the woman, whom she considered stronger than an army of men, deeply saddened her. Without Clara, Alice would never have found her place in helping the country fight against Hitler and his armies.

'What happens now?' she asked Richard.

A few minutes passed, in which they sat in silence, then Richard startled her by suddenly sitting bolt upright in his chair.

'Your housing situation,' he said. 'You can come and live here.'

Alice blinked at him. 'The local gossips would love that,' she said with a light laugh.

With a slight inclination of his head, Richard nodded in understanding. 'Yes, I can imagine. What about your aunt, Hilda, might she want to live here, too?' he asked.

'I doubt it. She won't want to risk moving again, and this week she has not left Hettie's side. The trauma of it all has aged her,' said Alice. 'But I do have an idea...'

Richard chuckled. 'Of course you have. Our clever prodigy, you keep us on our toes,' he said.

'It can wait though. Clara is—'

Richard cut her short. 'Alice, tell me your idea now, give me a reason to wash and dress. Clara would want me to continue looking out for you.'

Alice patted his arm and gave him a swift smile.

'All right, then,' she said. 'It's about the library. There are two upstairs rooms in need of decoration. Downstairs, the small kitchen and the outdoors privy are new.' Alice took a breath and noticed Richard was still listening with interest. 'With a little tidying up, I could turn the upstairs into my living space. One bedroom has a sink, and I can have a bath at Hettie's. Hilda's sofa and table will make the other room comfortable. If you can help me get permission, I could make that place my home, allowing my aunts to have more room for themselves. When the Americans go home, I can move back in again if needs be.'

Richard smiled broadly.

'You always impress me, Alice,' he said. 'You have such a wise head on young shoulders, and you're so resourceful.' He paused, thinking. 'Listen, I can give you the go-ahead for living there, but it is basic, and I am not sure about heating. I do have an electric heater I can give you, though, and it does seem the ideal solution to your living situation. I'm sure Gladys will want to help, too. She has a soft spot for you.'

Alice smiled back at him 'I can pay rent,' she said, excitement mounting at the thought of her own home.

Richard frowned. 'I'd consider it a caretaker position. No payment necessary. Try it and see, you might not like living alone,' he said.

For the rest of the day Alice helped Richard by cleaning and refreshing the cottage. She washed his clothes and heated water for his bath. She tucked the alcohol to the back of the cupboard and opened windows to air the rooms. Once done she cooked him a meal of potatoes and vegetables with a pork chop and sat back in pleasure as he ate and enjoyed his food. By the time she left he had fallen asleep on the sofa, but Alice knew he was in a better place than when she arrived.

Dear Diary

My sadness cannot be described.

Clara is dead. She is in a communal grave somewhere in France which saddens me,. Because Richard has been denied his last goodbye with his sister. I hope he can pay his respects one day. And if possible, I would like to join him.

I will always be grateful to Clara and will live by the wonderful guidance she gave me to the best of my ability. She was a brave woman.

She reminds me of the character Katherine Radford from the book *A Countess from Canada*. The author, Bessie Marchant, created a physically strong, brave young woman who faced danger with enormous courage. I imagine Clara was a Katherine in her younger years, and even braver later on in life.

Richard is grieving heavily, but still insists on helping me. I am going to have a home of my own shortly at the library. It will be basic, but I will be free to study to become a librarian quietly in a larger space than the corner of the sewing room.

Gladys from the post office has made it her mission to watch over me. I fear I will not be able to sneeze without it being reported back to Hettie. I do know I will enjoy time alone with Blake, and out of respect for Clara will heed her words to ensure I have his trust and love before giving myself to him.

Rest in Peace my dear friend - my big sister.
Clara Dikes 1912-1943

Chapter Twenty-Eight

The damp hedges and fuel fumes merged with Blake's soap-scrubbed skin and gave off a fragrance Alice found surprisingly pleasant.

Walking out in the late September evening, she appreciated the hour she had to spend time with him, but not the chill in the air.

They went to sit inside her hut, and she snuggled closer to him. It always amazed her how nobody else had discovered her sanctuary, but she was also pleased as it meant more privacy for her and Blake, away from the prying eyes of everyone on the airbase.

'How are your aunts?' he asked, after they had kissed.

Alice loved how he always so politely asked about Hettie and Hilda after they'd kissed. It was as if he needed to remind himself they were the two women, Alice's guardians, he'd have to deal with if she and Blake were ever found alone in their hideaway.

'They are very well, and busy with their various projects,' she said. 'At the moment, they are clearing out things for me, now they have come around to the idea of me moving above the library.'

Hettie and Hilda had given their approval for her to move in after they'd inspected the living quarters above the library. Although reluctant at first, Hettie eventually accepted that a truckle bed in her sewing room was not suitable for long-term living, and with Hilda moving into her home permanently, the library accommodation was the ideal answer. Hilda offered Alice anything from her own cottage to make her new library home more comfortable.

'Richard reassured them I would be safe,' Alice said. 'Poor thing, I know he is struggling without Clara. I see him when I can, which is most days at the moment.'

'At the library?' Hardy asked.

'Yes, helps me with stacking books and he's been clearing the upstairs of junk before the main cleaning starts, which Hettie insists she supervises,' Alice said and laughed.

She stopped when she noticed Hardy sat quietly inspecting his hands.

'Is something the matter?' she said. 'What is it, Blake?'

He looked up a her. 'Spending so much time alone with Richard… Is that wise?' he asked.

Puzzled, Alice gave a frown.

'I don't understand what you mean. Richard is my mentor, and the man who has secured me accommodation and a wonderful job,' she replied.

'But you are alone with him in the evenings, and, as you said, most days now,' Blake said defensively.

Alice took a moment to think and watched him study his hands.

'Are you jealous?' she asked and gave a light giggle of a laugh.

Blake still hadn't regained his good humour, it seemed.

'I am just concerned about your reputation,' he said.

'My reputation? Well.' Alice reached out to him. 'My reputation is intact. I am walking out with you in public, and those who need to know understand that Richard is a friend, someone I got to know through Clara,' she said, careful not to give away too much. 'Now that Clara is gone… Well, he needs my friendship, and I need his.'

'I just don't like it that Richard is the guy looking out for you, and I can't be,' Blake said. 'I should be the one helping you.'

'It is what it is, and there is nothing we can do about it,' Alice said.

'You're sure you can trust him? I mean, is he who he says he is – Clara's brother?' Blake asked bluntly, and Alice's heart skipped a beat.

'Of course he is genuine.' She paused. 'Clara gave up her career to nurse him when he was wounded. They are definitely siblings… I thought you understood that, Blake.' Alice rushed out her words in fear Blake might push her for more information.

But Hardy just gave her a wry smile. 'I guess I am a little jealous at times,' he said.

'Well, there is no need to be. Now, kiss me before I have to let you go back to work,' Alice said and put her lips to his before he could say another word and spoil their last few moments together.

Dear Diary

I think Blake is a little jealous of Richard. Of course, he has no need to be, but still it worries me that he has become focused on this. Neither Richard nor I can risk the truth coming out, but I also need to make sure Richard is all right, now that Clara is no longer here.

I wonder if the long days of living through

hellish hours of trauma are making Blake's feelings more intense? I will just have to prove to him that he is the one I love.

Between them, Richard, Alice, and Blake cleaned out the rooms and whitewashed the walls.

Alice smiled to herself as both men tried to outdo one another when painting. Neither of them realised the more they did the less she had to do. She was wise enough not to mention their male pride was giving them extra work.

Hettie had altered spare blackout curtains, and Gladys gave Alice a colourful rag rug made by her husband. A chair and sofa in moss green gave the living room a comfortable feel. But the most treasured items were pieces of Clara's bedroom furniture, donated by Richard.

He also generously handed over Clara's clothes to Hettie for her to alter so that others could enjoy wearing them, and he entrusted Alice with his sister's precious jewellery. Despite Alice insisting it was too much of a gift to receive, he said that Clara would have wanted Alice to have them.

Blake arrived with tinned food for her pantry, coffee, and bottles of Coca-Cola, with a promise of more treats to come.

During an awkward conversation with them both, Gladys explained that Hettie had specifically requested that Blake did not visit Alice as a late-evening guest, and that she promised to watch over Alice.

Blake gave Gladys a reassuring nod. 'I am not here to ruin Alice's reputation, ma'am, I promise. I have extended duties, and they are taking up my days and nights. Alice is committed to becoming a librarian, and I would never stand in the way of her studies.'

'That's right,' said Alice. 'Blake will be too busy and besides, we see one another on the base for a brief hello, and there are an awful lot of eyes watching our every move, believe me,' Alice said with a smile.

Neither she nor Blake mentioned the passionate kisses they shared in the small hut hidden away in the woods.

Gladys seemed satisfied with this. 'If you visit and I think you have been here long enough, I will pop round and knock on the door,' she said to Blake.

Both Alice and Blake heard her words and knew they were a gentle warning, and that from now on she would be watching them closely.

Richard arranged for a local man to build an outer shelter from the back door of the library to the privy and outhouse, which saved everyone a soaking on a dreary day. By the end of September, Alice was installed in her new home. Not even the thought of winter trips to the outside lavatory could spoil her excitement, it was a small price to pay.

Richard's commitment and affection towards Alice deeply moved Hettie, which eventually led to him becoming a regular guest at her house for shared meals and friendly chess matches with Hilda. The sight of both Richard and Hilda thriving again brought Alice great pleasure.

In the library, Richard would recount the story of his life alongside Clara prior to the war. As he spoke of places like Montmartre and the Eiffel Tower, Alice listened with fascination to the bohemian life they had enjoyed in France. He also spoke about the destruction and heartbreak the war had brought to the country. The memories had become so painful that the SOE were retiring him from active duty and had given him a senior role interviewing and supervising new agents and runners.

Alice listened to him. She regarded him as the sibling she'd never had, and even though she had no plans to take Clara's place, she vowed to put in every effort to be the best possible friend to him.

Chapter Twenty-Nine

Rain beat against the window as mid-October brought a late autumnal feel, and Alice guessed the weather was set in for the day and that the wet conditions meant not many people would visit the library.

She was not expecting a runner that day, and after cleaning the main library room, and rubbing the tables to a good shine with beeswax, Alice sat down to her studies on how to catalogue and reference classic books.

After a while, the log fire burning bright along the internal wall meant that the room was warm and cosy. The chimney sweep had inspected and cleaned out the chimney the previous afternoon, meaning new warmth drifted upstairs to her flat.

Alice knew her heart was already embedded in the adapted library. It held secrets which saved lives and the increased support from British shores was important to her. For each runner coming through the door, their sense of duty was at its height, they knew their simple task was the start of a chain. A chain strong enough to choke the oppressors of free will, and liberty. They took their books and walked away. Some returned on a regular basis but every time they, and Alice, abided by the rules of no conversation. For Alice it brought about a balance of trust and reassurance.

She looked across at a couple in their late twenties who were coming in, and for a split second she resented their arrival as it meant her peaceful time was over. But since both of them wore forces uniforms, she quickly put her selfish thoughts aside.

'Come in, and enjoy the warmth,' she said as she moved behind the desk.

'Thank you,' the woman acknowledged, her words accompanied by a warm smile, as she navigated her way towards a comfortable seat positioned in the far corner. As he navigated through the library, the man headed towards the history section, where he took two books from the shelves. Positioning himself on the other side of the table, he reached out and presented one book to the woman. They didn't exchange any words, and Alice concluded they were on a fact-finding mission rather than having a romantic meeting.

She settled behind the desk and took out her magazine. The couple sat at the table for over an hour and only spoke to each other a few times before leaving. They were the only visitors to the library that day.

The following day the couple did the same thing, and although the weather was brighter, they still chose to sit away from the windows studying their books and barely speaking.

A young man entered and browsed the bookshelves. Alice looked at him, wondering why he was not in the forces. He was young enough, and his hair was wild, wavy, and too long for someone in the service of his country.

Suddenly a boom sound rang out around the room, and Alice rushed from her small office.

'Sorry,' the young man said, peering from around the end of a shelving unit.'Dropped a book.'

'A large one by the sounds of it, gave us all a shock!' Alice said, smiling at the still serious couple, who both gave a look of disapproval at the young man. Alice waited a moment to ensure all was well, then returned to her office.

Gradually, the library became busier, and Alice had two runners arrive; both worked the routine perfectly and left. The new postwoman dropped by to say hello, then Richard arrived to exchange a batch of books to be stored in the office. Alice greeted him and helped him with the books.

'Don't look now, but there's a couple in uniform sitting far right. They were in yesterday and sat here for hours. They are reading history books and barely talk to one another. At first I thought they were a couple, but if they are they are an odd pair,' she whispered to him. 'And the young man sitting over there on his own dropped an encyclopaedia on the floor and we thought a bomb had exploded. I wonder who he is, and what prevented him from enlisting. He has no uniform and his hair, well that hasn't seen scissors for many years…'

Richard gave a brief nod. 'I saw the couple when I came in and thought they might be studying for promotion on the quiet. They are not connected to the library or SOE, or I would have met them. They are no threat, Alice. Your observations are appreciated, though. And you are right about the young man, that head of hair has not faced scissors for years. I wonder if he has health problems, or perhaps he is a pacifist.'

Alice pulled a face of questioning at the idea; she was not sure she understood how some people could not find one small thing to help with the war effort, even if they did not believe in the cause. Then she reminded herself it was not her place to judge.

A young woman then entered the library.

'Excuse me, are you Alice?' she asked.

'That's me, how can I help?' Alice smiled.

'I am Mrs B's granddaughter. She asked me to return these for her. Her bunions are too painful to walk far at the moment.' The young woman gave Alice an apologetic smile. 'She lives to chat about her bunions, does Gran.'

Alice gave a slight giggle. 'She does suffer with them, bless her.'

Taking the books from the young woman, Alice noted she did not make a move to find more books for her grandmother.

'Does your gran want another book to read?' she asked.

'Yes, please. Only she said I was to ask you to recommend something that I can read to her. I am Sally, by the way. Sally Burrows.'

'Nice to meet you, Sally,' Alice said, pulling out the relevant registration card. 'Let's take a browse through the shelves and find her something different to a murder mystery this week. She is fond of them, but I wonder if a lighter read would be better when read aloud by someone else.'

Twenty minutes later, Sally sat down with Alice as they chatted about the selection of books they had chosen, slowly reducing it down to one – *Private Duty* by Faith Baldwin.

'It's the story of a nurse and her life. I will say no more because there is nothing worse than having the plot of a book told to you before you read it,' Alice said.

'Thank you. Gran was good to me when my little one was born, and I want to help her now she is not so able. She is stubborn, though, so I am limited, but reading to her while she knits is something she loves,' Sally replied.

A twinge of envy flashed through Alice, but she suppressed the feeling.

'That is lovely for both of you. I will keep you in mind with other book recommendations,' Alice said and took a sly glance at the library clock. It was nearly closing time. She selfishly hoped Richard would not wait around for a chat. She was keen to close on time as Blake had sent word for her to join him on the base for an hour.

'My word, time flies when you are enjoying yourself. It has been lovely chatting about what we both enjoy reading. Let's do it again sometime,' she said to Sally.

'I'd love that.' Sally beamed, putting the book in her bag and setting off home.

Before Alice closed up, no sooner had Richard said his goodbyes to her than she rushed upstairs to change. She always made an extra effort with her hair and make-up, not just to impress Blake, but hopefully to brighten up a bad day for him. She could not wait to see him.

Instead of walking, Alice chose to cycle and pedalled as fast as possible. Their time together meant so much to her she did not want to waste a minute of the hour. Blake greeted her at the gate and instructed the guard to watch her bike with care. A lonely bicycle often found itself abandoned outside a pub in another village.

'Are you due any time off soon?' Alice asked him as they settled down at a table.

'This is it, Alice. The minute we repair one plane, the next batch fly in; and just as we are taking a breather, the spare parts arrive for another … and off we go again,' he said with a sigh.

'I hope you get some time for yourself; you are looking tired. I worry about you, Blake,' she said.

'I love hearing you say my name,' he replied, obviously changing the subject.

'It is funny because sometimes I still think of you as Hardy, but when I see you, you are definitely Blake. I have two of you, how lucky am I?' Alice said with a giggle.

'I'll say, a mighty lucky lady,' Blake said emphasising his accent.

'I would be even luckier if I had longer time with you. The next time you have time off, come to mine. Sit in comfort for an hour,' she said.

He smiled. 'Now there's an invitation I will not refuse. An hour in private with the girl who has my heart, it's a deal,' he said and winked at her.

'Let it be soon!' Alice said.

'Are you happy in your apartment?' he asked. 'Not too lonely?'

'My flat? Very happy. It suits me and it is working out better than I thought,' she replied.

'You have enough cash and food?' The concern in his voice touched Alice.

'I still have my wages from the post office, and I'm always coming home with plenty of vegetables and fruit from Hettie. I will receive my salary for my librarian position soon, too. The flat is rent-free as I am also caretaker of the library. Please don't worry about me, take care of yourself. I've got a good life under the circumstances,' she told him.

Blake sat back in his seat and looked at her, a gentle smile playing around his lips. 'You are an amazing girl. Independent, beautiful, and kind. I am a lucky man to have you in my life. I cannot wait to take you home and show you off. My mom will adore you.'

'Home to America?' Alice asked, surprised.

'Sure. America. When this war is over, I promise, I will take you.'

Although Alice had considered the prospect of visiting another country one day, Hardy's mention of going to America with him made her realise it could become a reality.

'It is a long way from England … and I am not sure I am ready to leave Hettie, but if it means a life with you, I'll take the chance. But the war has to end first and after so many years I sometimes feel it never will,' she said.

'We will end it, believe me,' he said and reached out for her

202

hand. 'Time to let you go, I guess. I'll walk as far as the hut with you.'

After they'd collected her bike, they walked to the hut. When he kissed her, Alice felt the depth of his promise to hold onto her for the future and she knew she would not hesitate to go with him.

'This is how I should be spending my Saturday evening, not filling bullet holes in a battered machine,' Blake said, his voice heavy with reluctance to leave.

'What you do is important, and we will have our Saturday evenings one day,' Alice said and kissed his cheek.

As the searchlights flickered across the sky, she sighed.

'What I would give to see normal streetlights and house windows glowing in the dark again and not enemy seekers,' she said. 'I took so much for granted in the past.'

Dear Diary

Another beautiful moment spent with Blake. How I long to hear the end of war announced so that we can start living again during peacetime. I am torn. He has spoken about me living in America with him, and although I went along with the idea, it frightens me. Yes, I want a life with him, but I also want the stability of my new family life here in England. No doubt another girl would take her chances, but what if America doesn't work out and I make things awkward for Hettie over here. My mind is a swirl of positive and negative thoughts at the moment.

Am I being a silly young woman or a sensible one? Has romance taken hold of my brain as well as my heart?

Am I mature enough to deal with whatever life after the war holds for me – I only know how to survive it; I have not yet lived outside of the orphanage in a peaceful world. Blake promises me things and I trust him; Hettie promises me I will never be alone again, and I trust her. But I do not trust fate – not yet. I have struggled through so many years of abandonment, loss, and confusion that sometimes I think it's going to be a permanent state for my mind and future!

My studies are going well. The library is running smoothly. The list of books I have read is growing rapidly. I try different genres and challenge myself, as I think it will make me a better librarian in the long run, and it is a great excuse to sit and read for hours when I have completed my studies. All of this is wonderful, but again I wonder, how long will it last.

Chapter Thirty

During the early hours, a noise broke her sleep and Alice sat up and listened. She wondered if it was a plane overhead that had disturbed her. When she heard nothing else she settled back and slept deeply until the morning.

Hettie had fretted that Alice would not eat properly on her busiest days, so Hilda suggested Alice had breakfast with them once a week on a Sunday when the library was closed for the day.

She chose to walk there, even though the weather threatened rain again. Her old brown coat took a lot of drying out and became heavy when it was wet, so Alice walked briskly trying to avoid a soaking from the black clouds looming her way.

Both Hettie and Hilda were preparing breakfast for the American servicemen when she arrived, and it was the happiest she'd seen them for a long time. It was reassuring. The noise of so many voices inside the cottage made Alice realise she had done the right thing by moving out. Life in her own space was much calmer.

'Sometimes, when they are all home, it's hectic around here,'

Hettie said. 'But I wouldn't want it any other way. Even Hilda enjoys the company.'

'That is good to hear. There's a lot of activity on the airfield this morning, so I suspect they will be grateful for that,' Alice said, pointing at the plates of eggs and bacon. 'I thought you only had two billeted.'

'They doubled up two days ago, according to the square footage I can accommodate more,' Hettie replied.

'Thank goodness my square footage is enough for one, two at a push,' Alice said laughing. 'I've left a bag of veg by the door. I've kept what I want. Do you have an egg to swap?'

'Take four. You know where the basket is. I had better get that lot fed. Yours is there. I've wrapped you some bacon for you to cook for your supper,' Hettie said, nodding towards the plate of scrambled eggs at the end of the table. She planted a kiss on Alice's cheek.

'They are a generous lot, and today's serving is not our ration allowance. Eat up,' Hilda put in, patting Alice on the shoulder.

With a full stomach and the flavour of pleasantly brewed coffee still on her lips, Alice wheeled her bike away from the cottage and wondered if she would ever return to live there. She turned to look back at the building, then her thoughts turned to America, and she wondered what the homes looked like out there and if she would ever live in one. Her heart was pulled in two ways.

Back in her own flat, she walked through the back door into the small kitchen and placed her belongings onto the unit before carrying a large log to top up the fire. As she stepped into the library she noticed mud on the floor. Mud which had not been there after she had swept up the previous afternoon.

'Richard?' she called out.

She went to the back of the library and unlocked her private door leading to the stairs.

'Richard?' she called up the stairs.

As confusion washed over her, she made her way back into the library and inspected the front door. She found the front door locked, which reassured her. She walked behind the desk and then into her office.

Overwhelmed with anxiety, her heart leapt, and she covered her mouth with her hands.

'Oh, no!' she exclaimed and stood taking in the scene before her.

The shelf where the books for the runners were supposed to be displayed was empty. Heaps of paperwork and stationery was scattered across the floor.

Swiftly, Alice stooped down to inspect the area beneath the bench positioned along the back of the small room. Its surface was empty as always, and the stacked items beneath it had been moved, but most were empty or housed books for pulping. Alice located and retrieved a box she had concealed among another series of boxes that were stacked behind one another, forming a wall. Fortunately, the wall of boxes looked untouched and whoever had broken in had possibly decided they were also empty or filled with tattered books and comics.

Seeing her hidden box still there brought about a wave of relief. Alice let out a sigh. One of her security measures had worked.

She knew the removed books were empty of the secret messages, but the thought that the box, which contained a tin with coded envelopes and messages ready to put inside the books, had also gone, caused her to panic. Douglas at the SOE had insisted Alice place the message inside the code-matching book, but she'd always had concerns about the security of this method.

She sniffed the air, smelling a familiar fragrance. Something was not right. She wrote a note for the front door explaining that the library would open an hour late and then cycled over to inform Richard.

As she pedalled, a sea of planes flew overhead and she heard engines fire up on the runways nearby. Plane after plane took off and joined the masses in the clouds. Under normal circumstances, Alice would have stood and counted them out, but her mind was set on something she felt to be equally important. If there was a breach of security, then the SOE would shut down her precious secret library, and her small mission to help her country would finish.

She jumped from her bike and pounded on Richard's door.

'Richard, Richard!' she called urgently and to her relief, she heard movement inside.

When a bleary-eyed Richard opened the door, Alice walked in without waiting for an invitation.

'The office books have disappeared!' As she spoke, she saw his face grow pale.

'Disappeared?' he asked, looking at her bemused and bewildered.

Alice paced the floor.

'Stolen. Someone has broken into the library. There was mud on the floor, and I could smell perfume. Women's perfume.'

Richard guided her into his living room.

'When did this happen?' he asked.

'I woke up to a noise in the night, but assumed it was just a plane. I got up first thing and went straight to Hettie's for breakfast, without looking in the library. I came back about half an hour ago, and that was when I noticed the lingering perfume. It was familiar, but I couldn't place it.'

'They may have entered and waited until you left this morning. The person either had a key or the ability to pick a lock. So much for secret messages. I had better inform HQ,' Richard said. His voice was calm, but Alice guessed he was swearing heavily inside his head. She had inwardly cursed a few times herself when she'd seen the mess in the library.

'I still have the messages!' she said. 'I took care to keep them hidden somewhere else because I didn't think storing them in books was safe, and it looks as if I was right. I have the codes, so the runners can just use the code system, but we can't use any of the books in the library as they have to give the code and the title to receive the message. They know not to accept anything else.'

'How many are due to go out tomorrow?' Richard asked.

'Three,' Alice said, then looked at her watch. 'I had better get back before the first one arrives.'

Richard looked at her. 'I will drop by and watch out for them before they come inside. We will prepare new titles for them today, and I can give them to the runners before they come in. That way everything still runs smoothly.' Richard gave her a reassuring smile.

'Keep your head, say nothing about missing books to anyone. Good thinking about the messages, Alice. Good work.'

The following morning, Alice went straight into the office. She could see Richard smoking a cigarette across the road and soon a steady calm settled around her. That fragrance still hung in the air, though. It was rich and cloying and, unless a man was trying to confuse the situation, it was definitely expensive and belonged to a woman.

The first two runners arrived, and the transactions went smoothly. When the third arrived, Alice noticed that his boots left mud on the floor in a crisscross pattern, much like the one she'd found that morning. The hairs on her neck tingled. She also thought he looked familiar but could not place where she had seen him before.

He gave her the title and code, and stood propped against the reception desk looking out of the window while she fetched the book.

Handing it over, Alice took a chance and spoke to him.

'Someone's been to the barber,' she said, and the man touched his obviously freshly shaved head.

'Yeah,' he said.

'When do you get your uniform? Freshly called-up I assume?' she asked.

'Next week. Off to Portsmouth,' he replied.

'Ah, the navy. I would be no good at sea, I get seasick just watching waves,' Alice said with a laugh and the young man laughed with her. Both turned when Richard walked through the door, as Alice guessed he would. By talking to the man she had drawn out the in-out process and he had made no attempt to follow his instructions of no small talk. He had failed Alice's test, now she had to convey her message to Richard.

'Short hair. Off to join the navy next week,' Alice said, nodding at the young man but addressing Richard.

'Good luck to you,' Richard said and moved over to a table by the window.

'Yes, I had better tidy up, it's closing time.' Alice turned to the runner. 'Good luck, and maybe we will see you again one day,' she said.

Once the man had left the library, she waited a moment then beckoned Richard over.

'The mud on the floor from his boots is the same as I found this morning. He was in here when that couple in uniform came in, remember? Only he had quite wild and bushy hair then, he dropped a large book on the floor and made everyone jump—'

'I remember him,' Richard said quickly, nodding.

'Then talking with him just now,' she went on. 'He did not do as instructed and just walk away, he chatted with me. It was then I remembered where I had seen him before – before he came in last time. He was driving the posh car that the woman, the fur-coated runner arrived in. I clearly remember thinking he looked out of place behind the wheel, and that her sort would insist on a chauffeur with a cap.'

Richard stared at her wide-eyed.

Alice tapped a fingernail on the desk's surface. 'Two runners, both made sure I noticed them. Why?'

'To lull you into thinking they are friendly, or no one to be concerned about, however, they never banked on Alice Carmichael being so observant. You're right, there is something out of place here – a security breach. I will ring HQ. They know which messages the two of them collected and they will take this further. I'll come back this evening and check on you,' Richard said. 'If they know the messages are not in the book, they might risk coming back to find them.'

Alice shuddered at the thought.

Chapter Thirty-One

B y late afternoon, Alice had thought about the situation and decided she did not want to sit around on her own, so she took herself for a walk to the base.

One brief moment with Blake would make the world feel a safer place again. The thought of someone inside the flat while she was sleeping unnerved her. By being with him, she would not have to talk about it – could not talk about it – and his company would be a good distraction.

At the sentry gate Alice showed her ID papers and was waved through. The moment she entered the base she noticed the hardstands were empty of planes, but everywhere she looked there were people, all looking skyward. The planes that had left that morning were due back, and Alice doubted she would get to see Blake after all.

She walked over to where she would often stand and watch him and his crew work when she passed the boundary. The atmosphere around the group of men she approached was tense; they were agitated. Two children were clambering over a jeep and one of the men called for them to go home. His instruction was sharp, and the youngsters looked bewildered. Alice knew the men doted on the local children, so guessed something was wrong. The men were focusing on something more important.

She walked over to the children. The little girl had tears in her eyes and her brother was tormenting her for being a soppy girl.

'Hey, I think the men are tired. Take this Hershey bar and run home. Share it, mind. I would stay away tomorrow, too. Give them a break,' she said softly, and looked at the boy, no older than six, whose eyes were fixated on the chocolate bar she had in her hand. One of Blake's generous gifts. She snapped the bar in half. 'There, equal shares,' she said and handed them both their treasure.

'Thank you, miss,' the boy said and immediately took a bite. The little girl gave her a gap-toothed grin. 'Ta,' she said and took a bite of hers, before Alice watched them both run back towards the farmer's fields.

'You're going to be asking me for another bar.' Blake's voice cut into the moment and Alice turned around.

'I would never ask anything of you, except to get some sleep. You look done in, Blake,' she said, concerned for the exhausted man standing in front of her. Dark circles had formed beneath red-rimmed eyes and his face was drained of colour.

'They've not come home, Alice,' he said, his voice defeated.

'None of them?' she asked. Her heart picked up a rapid beat.

'Not yet, and the control tower reports are not good,' he replied.

His face paled and Alice could see him mentally recalling old friends he had waved off that morning.

'How many?' Alice asked, not sure if she wanted to hear the answer.

'Thirteen, and all out of fuel by now. They'll be down or captured,' he replied and turned his face back up to the sky.

'So many men. Oh, Blake, I am so sorry.'

Alice felt helpless.

A shout went out and Alice looked skyward, too.

'It's one of ours!' Hardy said and rushed towards his crew shouting out orders. Alice chose to step back into the shadows of the large Nissen hut behind and watched as what looked like chaos became a well-oiled solution to all problems. The flak-beaten plane hit the ground and she saw medics and Blake pull two injured crew members free, marvelling as the rest clambered out. Their body language spoke volumes. Not wanting to distract Blake from his duty she took herself home. As she walked, she realised she could no longer hear any planes and guessed there would be a dark shadow over the base that night.

Outside of the library, she saw the lit end of a cigarette move in the darkness.

'Richard!' She called over to him, 'So sorry to keep you waiting, I went to see Blake. Only one plane made it home. It's dreadful, so sad. Twelve lost with their crew. I didn't want to get in the way so I slipped away. Come inside, I have cocoa,' she said.

Once inside Alice embraced the warmth and Richard took off his coat.

'You have made it homely up here. Cosy,' he said.

'Until this morning I was happy here, but now I keep wondering about who is watching me. I had to get out earlier, which is why I went to see Blake. Obviously, I cannot and did not say a word about what has happened, I just wanted his company.'

'You are safe, Alice. The woman and her co-worker have been arrested. We will know more in a few days, but they will be questioned as potential spies. Which leads me to the library.'

Alice held her breath as Richard paused. Was she about to lose the roof over her head and her precious library. It meant so much to her that just the thought of losing it ached in her chest.

'HQ want you to continue.'

Alice stared at him.

'Really?' she said, able to breathe again.

'Yes. Their thinking is, that now the arrests have been made, any interest in the library from enemy sources will disperse. They will automatically think the SOE will pull the plug here, but that is not going to happen. We can keep running the messaging service without fear of disruption,' Richard said, wrapping his hands around the mug of cocoa she had poured him from a flask. 'My concern is how you feel about the situation. Sleeping here alone at night after what happened.'

Alice blew across the lip of her cup to cool her drink.

'It has made me a little nervous, but now they've been caught and what you say sounds feasible, I will be okay,' she said.

'If you find you cannot stay here, then we will swap, and you can live at my house. But, I did say to London you are proving to be a strong young woman with courage. It is not flattery, it is fact, before you arm-flap me away for complimenting you,' Richard said with a laugh.

Alice laughed with him.

'Thank you, Richard. Talking to you has helped already,' she said.

Richard stood up. 'In that case, I will head home. Can't have Gladys accusing us of something improper,' he said, with a light laugh.

Shortly after Richard had left, Alice slipped outside to the privy, and every noise made her twitch a little inside. Once back indoors she pulled the bolt across the top of the door and just as she went to slide the bottom one, someone knocked.

'Alice, it's me,' Blake called out softly.

Sliding back the bolts and ushering him inside before Gladys's curtains twitched again, Alice continued to bolt and lock the door.

'Tight security around here,' he said with a laugh, but his voice was also questioning. It was rare for people to lock their doors and shut their windows in the villages, so his surprise was genuine and not teasing.

'Gladys,' Alice said quickly. 'She lets herself in sometimes, just to check on me. It's a bit too much, but I know she means well. Take the torch and go upstairs. I won't be far behind. I will bring supper, I am starving,' she said, suddenly realising she had not eaten since breakfast.

Giving herself a moment to breathe, Alice gathered bread and cheese, two slices of corned beef, from their storage spaces and filled a bowl with a mix of sweets that Blake had brought on his last visit. She knew she had two bottles of cola, three beers, and a small bottle of brandy and a larger one of whisky upstairs. Richard's stash was hers to use if required.

Entering the small living room it did her heart good to see Blake sitting quietly with only the light of the torch. He had drawn the curtains, so Alice switched on the electric fire and its red glow soon filled the room. Lighting two large candles, she pointed to the torch.

'You can turn the torch off now,' she said.

'Flashlight,' he said with a smile, and handed it to her.

'I love learning American,' she said with a laugh.

Blake gave a sigh, not of impatience but of sadness.

'Only the one come home?' Alice asked, knowing she already knew the answer.

'Uh huh,' he replied.

Pouring him a whisky from Richard's bottle, Alice handed it to him.

'Compliments of Richard. We sit in the library by the fire some evenings and he enjoys a glass. He is lonely now Clara has gone. If ever I imagined having a brother, I think it would be Richard. So his sadness is mine, at times. Drink it down and we will eat.'

'I've eaten. You eat, Alice. Then sit beside me. Have a whisky, and think of our future,' Blake said.

Alice gave a snort of a laugh as she turned her slices of bread into a cheese sandwich. 'I had a sherry in London, thanks to Clara, but never a whisky. I might try a small brandy later to help me sleep,' she said, then bit into her sandwich.

Once she had finished eating her supper, Alice took her dish of sweets and placed them on the coffee table. She then poured a small brandy into one of the crystal glasses Hilda had given her. She topped up Blake's glass and noticed his eyelids drooping.

'To brave men,' she said and chinked her glass against his. As she moved her arm the light of a candle flagged up something glistening on his face, and Alice realised he was crying. She took a large sip of her drink, allowing the burning sensation to slide down her throat and felt the warming effects move through her body.

'Drink up,' she whispered and wiped away his tears, but more followed. Alice had always heard Matron say to the boys in the orphanage, boys and men do not cry, it was not the done thing, but Alice could never understand why they were not allowed to. Tears came naturally to her, and she could never understand what was different between men and women in that area. Now, she witnessed one of the most capable and physically strong men she knew sobbing his heart out and knew she did not want him to stop. She understood grief and the power of crying out the pain. She touched his glass again. 'Drink, then come and lie down. You can stay here, get some sleep,' she said.

Blake lifted the glass to his mouth and downed the drink. Alice did the same to hers, then she took a candle and put it into her bedroom. When she returned to the living room, she turned out the fire and blew out the remaining candle. Blake followed her into her room.

He removed his boots and jacket, then lay on top of the covers.

'Just like home,' he said, his voice cracking with emotion.

'Well it's my home, and you are welcome here anytime,' she

said, easing off her dress and stockings. She climbed onto the bed and kissed his cheek. 'Sleep. Cuddle up and rest, Blake,' she said, nuzzling her face into his neck and folding her arms around him, before slowly pulling the outer eiderdown over them both. She blew out the candle and lay in the dark listening to an owl hoot outside and Blake's gentle snores beside her. All her fears of being alone left her the minute she closed her eyes in contentment.

Chapter Thirty-Two

Several hours later, daylight peeped around the edges of the curtains. Alice stirred in the bed and stretched her arms.

She looked over to where Blake had slept until two o'clock when he'd kissed her with such a deep passion, she thought she would suffocate and die happy.

They'd explored boundaries they had never done before. Alice had allowed his hands to touch her wherever he wanted and was ready for where their embraces would lead, but eventually Blake had been the one to pull away.

'We'd better slow the train there, Alice,' he said and stroked her hair away from her face. 'You are a temptress, but I would not forgive myself. Unlike some, I have morals.'

Alice had given a soft sigh, she knew he was doing the right and honourable thing, but her body cried out for his touch.

'Don't stop, I don't mind,' she'd said shyly.

'You are so young, Alice. After yesterday, I know I want you in my life. You gave me hope for a future, but it has to be the right time. I am going to go now, back to my crew,' he'd said and rose from the bed. Alice had laid in bed listening to him pull on his boots and jacket, before she'd grabbed her dressing gown and pushed her feet into her slippers.

'I will lock the door behind you,' she said, 'and don't wake Gladys. Go out of the garden through the rear gate, it will take you onto the back road.'

They quickly kissed goodbye, and Alice closed the door behind him. The atmosphere inside her home had altered, it no longer felt threatening but like a place filled with love and hope.

On the days following his overnight stay, Blake visited Alice more often and she blossomed with his attention. She had witnessed the whole of the airbase slip into a dark pit of sadness, the power of the men's loss was palpable. She did not see hopelessness, what she did see were men mourning friends, then forging forward with fire in their bellies, men ready to avenge their deaths. She saw their pain. Their tears, which seeped into the soil of Thorpe Abbotts, with no shame.

Alice had read about heroes in books, and felt a deep-seated sense of privilege to have met so many in real life. She wanted to help them in some way, to take away their pain, but she knew it was not a task anyone could undertake. The survivors at Thorpe Abbotts would return to America and live with their horrors tucked away, as many others around the country would also do. Her own experience of being bombed out and losing her grandmother in such a devastating way was nestled beneath the good she found. Alice tried hard to smother the memories. She could not live in the past, but it was early days for the men at the airbase. As she took Teddy for his usual walks, Alice hoped his wagging tail would bring comfort.

Hettie confided that she thought Hilda was experiencing dark moods; her sister was starting to need encouragement to bathe and change her clothes.

'I wish I could help you more,' Alice said, feeling guilty about the extra workload Hettie had to deal with.

'You do enough. Walking Teddy and keeping him at the library is a great help. Hilda seems to have forgotten she owns a dog. It is all very strange,' Hettie replied, pressing her iron over some clean bed linen.

Alice continued to fold the rest of the linen for Hettie and thought about the situation.

'I can help with one thing. If Teddy is under your feet, let me take him in, he sits behind my desk when he is with me and is no bother at all. He would be good company in the evenings. It would be one less worry for you. If Hilda realises he is not around and creates a fuss, we can have a rethink,' she said, patting the linen pile. 'Shall I put this in your room?' she asked, and Hettie nodded.

'Check on Hilda while you are up there, she went for a nap,' she said. 'She is truly out of sorts.'

Alice peered into her old room to see Hilda snoring beneath the covers. Outside the window, the noise from the airfield travelled across the field, and Alice had a sudden urge to see Blake. She had not seen him for five days, and with it being her day off she decided she would walk Teddy over there.

Hilda shifted in her bed and Alice slipped out of the room.

'She's sleeping soundly,' Alice told Hettie, who was now sitting enjoying a well-earned cup of tea.

'Lucky for some,' Hettie said with a frown.

'I'll take Teddy now. There's no point in waiting until tomorrow. He can say hello to Blake and friends, then move in with me permanently,' Alice said.

'You and Blake, is it serious?' Hettie asked.

221

'I like to think so, but we rarely get to see one another at the moment. What about James?' Alice replied, not wanting to think about what Blake was going through, and the long hours he worked to get men flying again.

'Still writing letters as long as his arm. According to him he is in fine fettle. The words he uses make me smile. As penfriends go, he is a good one,' Hettie said smiling, and Alice felt for her. Hettie deserved happiness and James clearly made her happy. Under normal circumstances, their paths would never have crossed, so maybe fate had something in store for them. Alice thought about the companionship they would give one another in the latter years of their life, and prayed the war did not take away their hope of being together again. Shaking off these melancholy thoughts, she grinned at Hettie.

'Talking of penfriends, Gabrielle still writes from Canada. It sounds a fascinating country. She has invited me to go out there when the war is over and stay on their farm. What with Blake wanting me to visit America, it makes me smile. Only a short while ago I thought the journey from Norwich to here was a long trek. But I will never go, my home is here,' Alice said, hoping her face did not show regret at this prospect.

Hettie put her cup down on its saucer.

'You know how much you mean to me, Alice. But there's one thing I want you to understand: if I ever thought you were tying yourself to me and Hilda because you are grateful we took you in, I would be heartbroken. Of course, I want you in my life, but when this horrid war is over you must live your life to its fullest. If you feel you have a future with Blake, grab the opportunity to join him in America. If travelling out to Canada is a genuine opportunity, then take it, but please, do not stay because you think you should,' Hettie told her. 'Grab your happiness with both hands and take exciting adventures.'

Teddy trotted through the airbase, drawing smiles from anyone who saw him, and soon Alice lost him to a crew who fussed over him and played ball with him, and four local children. Alice looked south-west towards one of the large hangars, where she knew Blake often worked, and had little doubt that was where she would find him. He had several qualities she admired when she saw him with his crew, and one of them was not walking away from the tough jobs. If she walked to meet him on a planned visit, he often ran out from the hangar and would greet her with a hug and a passionate kiss – ignoring the teasing comments from his colleagues, then apologise as their workload required every spare pair of hands available that day. Although disappointed, Alice learned to accept the situation and be proud of him for his dedication to duty. Those qualities told her a lot about the man she was falling in love with, and a sulking tantrum would not show the best side of her either.

The noise of endless drills and hammers sent tinny echoes out into the area she now entered. Men nodded her way and continued filling in flak holes as the shout for 'Hardy' went out.

With the usual stray streaks of grease on his face and a beaming smile, Blake walked towards her.

'It's been too long, Alice. You okay?' he asked, scooping her into his arms and twirling her around.

'Five days, six hours and goodness knows how many seconds,' Alice replied, 'and I am happy now I am here with you. But, what about you, are you getting rest?'

He took her by the arm and led her outside to a quieter space.

'It's tough but we keep going. I sleep and eat when I can. The boys are so angry and hurt they dive right into repairing and making the aircraft safe.' He tucked a stray strand of hair back behind her ear and stroked her cheek. 'What's your news?' he asked, and studied her face.

'Mine? Well, the studies are going well, and the library is busier than ever. Richard has applied for permission to have a bathroom built for me in the back of the property, which will be a luxury! Oh, and Teddy is coming to live with me, so you have competition.'

'Lucky Teddy, but won't Hilda miss him?' Hardy asked.

Alice scrunched her face. 'I don't know. Hettie seems to think Hilda has given up on life. I helped Hettie with the laundry earlier, and Hilda was still in bed asleep when I left.'

'That must be a worry for the two of you?' Blake said kindly.

'It is,' Alice said sadly. She smiled at Teddy, who was out playing fetch in the field.

'Can I come see you around eight tonight?' said Blake. 'Things should be clear here for me to take some time out.'

Alice kissed his cheek. 'Yes. Yes please!' she replied.

'I will be washed and presentable by then,' he said with a laugh.

'Without your oil and grease streaks I probably wouldn't recognise you nowadays,' Alice said touching his face and laughing. The thought of an evening at home cosied up with Blake had lifted her spirits.

Dear Diary

Life is good in many way. Hettie is in love – but denies it – I am sure James feels the same way. But Hilda is still not her old self, she's lethargic and troubled. I try and help, and have taken Teddy in to live with me, for the time being at least. It will take a bit of burden from Hettie, and he is good company. He will be a good guard dog for the library, too.

Blake is visiting tonight. My body aches to hold him again. He is in my thoughts day and night, though my night-time thoughts cannot be written down - ever - for they are classified as extremely private!

Chapter Thirty-Three

A knock at the door gave Alice an excited tremor. She raced downstairs and unlocked the door tugging Blake inside before Gladys or her husband's face appeared at their window.

'I've missed you so much,' she said grinning at him as she flung her arms around his neck, and they enjoyed their first kiss of the evening.

'Well, I might go back outside and knock again if the greetings are always going to be like this,' he joked when they parted.

'Oh, they always will be – always,' Alice replied.

Following an intimate hour filled with affectionate caresses and sweet kisses, Blake gently disengaged and positioned himself at one end of the sofa facing Alice, creating a sense of distance between them.

'My mom would not be happy with me if she could see me now. We must stop, Alice. Guys are getting girls into trouble every day at the base, and I am not going to be one of them,' he said, running his fingers through his hair slicking it back in place.

Just as Alice went to say something, Teddy gave a bark from downstairs in the kitchen.

'Someone needs the garden,' she said when the barking did not stop. She started to stand up.

'I'll go, cool myself down,' Blake said with a grin and a wink. He pulled on his outer coat and picked up his cigarettes.

Alice listened to him go downstairs and the back door clang shut.

A few minutes later he called her from the bottom of the stairs.

'Alice! A guy outside is saying something about a book. I told him you are closed on a Sunday, but he won't leave.'

Alice's heart skipped a beat. A runner had arrived, and Richard had either forgotten or there was a mix up somewhere.

'I'll be right down,' she called out and rushed to push her feet into her outdoor shoes and pull on her warmest coat.

Once inside the kitchen, she grabbed her torch and stepped outside.

The runner was a middle-aged man and he looked at her puzzled.

'What's going on?' he asked.

Alice gave a slight shake of her head as a warning to say nothing else.

'I am sorry, but we are closed. Try in the morning,' she said crisply, all the while looking down the pathway towards the garden. Blake was standing with his back to them watching Teddy run around.

'An hour. Come back then. Richard is supposed to be on duty tonight. He didn't say a word about you coming,' she whispered quickly.

'Apparently, it's an urgent one... Sorry, got the days mixed up,' the man said loudly, and Blake turned around. Alice gave him a brief wave then turned back to the runner.

'See you tomorrow,' she said and watched as the man limped away.

Teddy ran to her, and she tickled his ears.

'Good boy, did you hear the silly man at the door?' she said in a playful voice.

'Silly man?' Hardy said as he walked in. 'Straight from The Horseshoes after a few mild and bitters, as if he expected the library to be open at nine o'clock at night.'

'It's already nine?' Alice said.

Blake nodded. 'Time flies. I have to leave you, honey. Time for me to head back.'

As much as she did not want Blake to go, she was anxious about the situation and did not want him to get caught into something complicated or compromising. It was probably better he was heading off.

'I hate it when you have to leave,' she said, going to him and holding him. Their kiss heated their bodies and Alice was reluctant for the moment to end.

A tap on the door made them both jump apart.

'He's back already?' Blake frowned and pulled the door open. 'Listen buddy, the library is closed. Oh—'

But it was Richard standing there, and Alice, feeling slightly panicked, pulled the door open wider and beckoned him inside.

'Come in before we get told off for the light,' she said. 'A drunk knocked a few minutes ago asking for a library book and Blake sent him packing, and now you arrive. Gladys will have a field day!' She tried to sound frustrated to Blake while secretly communicating with Richard about the runner's strange appearance.

Richard tapped his leg. 'Darn leg, I can't even walk as fast as a drunk. I came to tell you that that I met that man earlier in the pub and he was singing the praises of the library and wanted to get a new book to read. Everyone told him it was closed, but no, he would not listen. I came to see you were all right.' He nodded at Blake. 'It's a good job you were here,' he told him.

Alice's heartrate slowed down. Thank goodness Richard was quick to latch onto the story and think on his feet so easily.

Blake held out his hand.

'I said to Alice, he's had one too many at the pub. Apologies, but I have to go, take care Richard. Goodbye, Alice.' Blake dropped a kiss on her forehead. 'Come see me in your lunch break tomorrow, if you can.'

Once they heard the last of Blake's footsteps on the stone path, Alice heaved a sigh.

The moments she shared with Blake had only intensified her feelings towards him. She knew he had captured her heart. Each time they met, their emotional bond deepened, making her long for a future where they could spend more than just a few stolen moments together. His leaving, and the runner wasting their precious time together, was irritating, but Alice knew something urgent was happening or the runner would not have called at the library so late.

'What a mad moment that was! Who is the runner? There's not one on record for tonight, I am sure of it,' Alice said and closed the door.

'I'm only just back from London,' said Richard. 'The train was late. I have four messages to go out in the next forty-eight hours.'

'Gladys is going to be suspicious of all this male activity at my door,' Alice said. 'Blake visiting for an hour is one thing, and you mentoring me in the library is another, but strangers turning up at nine on a Sunday night is wrong – even with you here. I had not thought it through properly until tonight. We are jeopardising the mission.' Alice sighed. 'You know how Gladys will report anything out of the ordinary. And quite rightly, too, but I do not want to be put in a position where I am defending my reputation.'

Richard nodded. 'I can open the library on a Sunday when I know a runner is coming, and if anyone says anything we can say I am helping people with form filling and private help with reading and writing. Speak with Gladys, let her know about it, so she will get used to the idea,' he said.

'You're right. Tonight might be hard to explain away, but if she asks I will think of something,' Alice replied.

An hour later, the sound of a firm knock on the door alerted them to the runner's return, and Richard ushered him inside. The book exchange went ahead, and the man and Richard left. With her study books in hand, Alice attempted to block out the evening's distractions and focus her mind.

The following day, Gladys marched into the library. Alice could see her mouth set in a tight line and gave an inward sigh. Gladys or her husband had obviously witnessed some of the goings on the night before.

'Morning, Gladys, I hope Teddy didn't disturb you last night. He is living with me now and the little monkey gave me the slip. Luckily, a chap found him and recognised him as Hilda's, but knew I lived closer. Richard and Blake had been out looking for him,' she said, preemptively concocting a story to quell the haughty reprimand she knew she was coming.

'Ah. Teddy. The dog. So that is why so many men were traipsing down your path,' Gladys said, with the defensive edge of someone who could not fulfil what they had practised prior to arrival.

'Yes. He is in the kitchen sulking. It took up my whole evening,' Alice said, putting exaggerated frustration into her voice.

From the corner of her eye, Alice could see a runner who had picked up a book the previous month waiting by the door, then take a step inside.

Gladys turned around to look at him then back at Alice.

'The library is such a busy place. Faces I don't recognise come and go, quite an idea you had, Alice,' Gladys said and then instead of leaving as Alice had expected, she walked down to the other end of the library and looked out of the window that faced the side of the Post Office.

Just as the runner asked Alice for the coded book, Gladys arrived back at the desk and looked at the man.

'Not from around here, are you?' she said.

Alice gave the runner a brief smile. 'I will just get that for you,' she said, ignoring Gladys's remark. He gave a nod.

'I said, you are not local.' Gladys's voice was slightly raised and in the office Alice gritted her teeth.

'No. I work for Richard,' the man said, and Alice sighed with relief that he had used the standard reply Richard taught all runners.

'Oh, yes. Richard. The man who persuaded the council to open this place. He must have a lot of clout to get this done during wartime,' Gladys went on, just as Alice came out with the book for him.

'Here you are,' she said brightly but calmly. 'See you again.'

'Thanks.' The man was just about to push the book into his coat pocket, when Gladys took it from his hand.

'Are you a Dickens fan?' she asked looking at the cover.

'It's one Richard recommended he try. Never read one, have you?' Alice said, to both put him at ease and let him know she had everything under control and try to hasten his departure.

Gladys handed it back, but as she did, the letter hidden inside flew out and onto the floor.

Both Alice and the runner gave one another a swift glance as Gladys, quick as a flash stooped to the floor to retrieve it.

'What's this?' she said. 'It's not addressed to anyone.' She turned the letter over, looking for a return address.

Before panic could set in, Alice looked at the runner again and then slapped her hand to her forehead.

'I'll forget my name next. I'm sorry, Fred, I should have told you. Richard said he had a list of jobs for the cottage and popped them down in a note for you.' She whipped the letter out of Gladys's hand and passed it to him. 'I put it in the book for safekeeping – that worked out well,' she said, with a false laugh.

'That's great. Thanks.' The runner nodded at her and then at Gladys. 'Goodbye, then.'

When he'd gone, Gladys stood with Alice, who was convinced her face was the colour of beetroot.

'Sorry, Gladys, I forgot all about it. Anyway, how are things next door? Mr Durrent getting over his chill?' she said, forcing the conversation in another direction before Gladys could ask questions.

'He is well enough,' Gladys said, then took a breath and Alice, sensing she was about to launch into a question session about the runner, tried to cut her off at the pass.

'Have you seen Hettie or Hilda lately?' she said. 'Poor Hilda, she has aged and is so distant since her accident. You would never recognise her as your postwoman nowadays. If you have a spare hour at all, I am sure she would love to see you.'

Alice continued, rambling through so many topics in thirty seconds that she was convinced Gladys was going to explode. 'Anyway,' she finished. 'I really must get on, I have an essay on mediaeval literature to write, it has been so lovely to see you. I miss our chats before delivering the post. It seems ages ago now.'

With a strange look on her face Gladys tilted her head.

'Well, now that I know about Teddy, and why so many men were hanging around here last night, I won't worry so much. You know where I am if you need me. Oh, and Richard's handyman, tell him I have a few jobs around the house to be done if he is interested,' she added, and walked away without another glance back.

Alice breathed in and out. She exhaled the tension inside her body, but her mind swirled around at such a pace that a painful headache struck later in the afternoon. Her records showed no runner was expected and by four the library was empty. Alice placed a note on the door stating illness as the cause for it closing early. It frustrated her that for so many months she had coped with carrying out what the SOE expected of her and that one fraught moment with Gladys had brought such doubt and concern.

Dear Diary

If Gladys was a dog she would be a bloodhound! She is definitely a Miss Marple. She knows everybody's business and is a dreadful gossip.

Gabrielle wrote to say her cousin marched into Italy, but they have not heard from him since. How many thousands of families around the world are experiencing the same – it weighs heavy on the heart.

Blake is so close by and yet I cannot see him yet. Planes roar out of the airbase and a few limp home. I am eternally grateful to the crews.

I have studies to return to, so my entry is short. Besides my few notes here, it is war news after war news, and that depresses me!

Chapter Thirty-Four

'... And she was like a dog with a bone. The poor runner looked composed on the outside, but I am sure he was as nervous as me. Gladys is a determined woman and I know she is watching my every move,' Alice breathlessly recounted to Richard on his return from London.

On Sunday afternoon they were sitting in his home, while Teddy ran around the garden chasing leaves. Catching up on official business with him. Alice explained the situation in the library on the Monday.

'Are you worried about Gladys interfering again?' Richard asked.

Alice leaned forward in her chair and squeezed her hands between her knees.

'Every time I close up for the evening, her curtains twitch, so I know she has her husband on guard duty when she's working. I am concerned about her noticing the non-local visitors coming in, she is nosy at the best of times, but now I think she is hoping to find something. I wonder if it is my fault for telling her about the man hanging around the windmill ... but that was at the start of the mission.'

Richard stretched his neck and shoulders, something Alice noticed he did whenever he needed to think. She sat quietly for several minutes while he puffed on an overfilled pipe with sour-smelling tobacco.

'There is another problem,' he said.

Alice's stomach lurched with concern about what he was about to say next.

'I am leaving the area. I have a new post in London.'

A silence hit the room and Alice stared at him in disbelief.

'When?' she asked.

'With immediate effect.'

'What? Oh, Richard! How do you feel about it?'

He shrugged his shoulders.

'We are at full capacity and every one of them has proved themselves reliable,' he said and took another long draw on his pipe. As he expelled the smoke Alice got up from her seat and went to check on Teddy, giving herself a moment to suppress the tears that were threatening.

Satisfied Teddy was still happy scrapping amongst the leaves and shrubs, she returned to face Richard. 'What happens with the runners?' she asked, not daring to think what her future was about to look like. 'And what about the library?' Her voice was tight in her throat.

Richard looked at her.

'Alice. You have impressed HQ, and despite your age they want you to continue on without me. How do you feel about taking charge of twelve runners and receiving the messages to issue?' he asked. You could move in here, which would solve the Gladys problem.'

Alice stared at him in total amazement, too taken aback to

reply, then looked down at her folded hands. She was stunned that HQ thought her capable of taking on an important role.

Clara's voice rang out inside her head. *'Confidence, Alice. Where is your confidence. You know you can do this. Do it for me.'*

She took a breath. Honouring Clara was one thing, handling a team of people was another.

'I am sure I can organise the runners, but how do I receive the messages without drawing attention to myself – and how would they arrive?' she eventually said, looking up at Richard who was now standing, leaning one arm on the mantlepiece with his pipe in his mouth, waiting patiently for her response.

'Put Teddy in the kitchen and come with me,' he said in answer.

As they left the cottage and made their way down the lane, they gradually approached a charming, small house that was nestled away from the pathway. Alice was surprised to see the property, as she had never come across it during her time as a postie. She looked to the end of the lane, and it was a dead end, so perhaps the occupant never had post delivered so it was a route she would never have walked.

'Whatever you decide, what you see here today is top secret,' Richard said firmly.

Alice nodded.

As they stepped into the garden of the cottage, a clutter of garden tools and abandoned wheelbarrows greeted them, while the neatly arranged vegetable plot stood out as the only element providing a sense of order. At the end of the long, slim garden, she saw a row of three ramshackle wooden sheds, pieced together with wooden slats at varying angles. Richard, with a determined expression on his face, leaned over towards a towering walnut tree and firmly grasped hold of a long, taut string.

'Always, and I mean always, ring the bell. Don't be fooled by the sheds. Follow me and learn,' he said.

Giving two brief knocks on one shed door, Richard stood back and waited. Alice heard noises from inside and the click of a bolt sliding.

'I've come for my carrots,' Richard said when the door was opened.

Alice saw the wrinkled face of a man she didn't recognise.

'Awlroight, boy?' The man gave Richard a toothless grin. Alice had heard strong Norfolk accents, she had a slight one, but this was the strongest she had heard. The man must have lived deeper in the county in the past.

'Hu do we 'ave 'ere then,' he said peering round at Alice.

'Ben, this is my replacement. Her name is Alice. Alice, meet Ben.'

'Nice to meet you,' Alice said giving Ben a smile.

'Gettin' younger un younger. How'd do, Alice,' Ben said, and turned around to lead them deeper into the shed. He opened another door and right away Alice knew they were about to step into a pigeon loft by the cooing noises and the smell from the bucket, which Ben obviously used for cleaning out the cages.

'Pigeons?' she asked. 'Why on earth are you showing me pigeons?' She turned to Richard, who grinned back at her. Then with a serious face he explained.

'Ben's homing pigeons are messenger pigeons. Highly skilled and trained at taking important messages back and forth. These beautiful birds work for the SOE and Ben is the most trustworthy man I know. This is where our messages come. Ben receives them and takes them to the cottage, and leaves them in a box in the shed overnight. With no neighbours, it works well for us both.'

Stunned by what she'd learned, Alice looked at the speckled head of the bird bobbing in front of her. 'So, you know the contents of the messages, both of you. And the birds are employed by HQ?'

Both men nodded.

'And I will be expected to read them?' she said. 'Handing them over is a huge responsibility, but this is critical, vital work. How do I communicate with the runners?'

'Each runner has a number and area. They know who to hand their envelope to and the HQ agents tell them when to collect. You keep doing what you are doing. If they have a problem, they will know you are my replacement and will come to the library or the cottage. You go nowhere. You won't have to go to London as I can bring any information for you back with me,' Richard said as they watched Ben removing message capsules from three returning birds.

'One of the jobs is to deliver messages personally to the airbase, if the Americans are involved in the conversation, so to speak, but for you that will be easy, your face is well known at the gate for visiting Blake. I will inform my contact there that it will be you from now on.'

Ben handed Alice a small flat leather bag.

'Yewer carrots, miss,' he said with an eye-wrinkle smile.

Alice burst out laughing.

'I am sorry, Ben. I'm laughing because this is a lot to take in,' she said, then faced Richard, looking him straight in the eyes. 'Do you honestly think I am capable of doing your job?'

Without hesitation Richard gave a strong nod. 'Yes. Yes, I do.'

She thought for just a few seconds before turning to Ben with a smile.

'It looks as if I will be collecting carrots from you soon, Ben. I look forward to it,' she said and stepped out into the fresh air.

Back at the cottage, Alice spent another hour carefully listening to Richard's meticulous instructions on organising the messages in the code system. He showed her the contents of the ones they had collected from Ben, and she discovered the names were actually military code names for top-secret missions and the exact locations of specific battalions in Europe. Both the French Resistance and British spies infiltrated the German intelligence network, exchanging crucial information. The realisation of how essential it was to receive the messages overshadowed Alice's fear. It was her patriotic duty to have a role in the fight against the enemy, even if it meant handling sensitive information.

By the time they'd finished going through everything, they'd agreed that she would move into the cottage, and Richard would use the library flat when he was back in the area. They would tell people that Richard's new job in London meant the cottage would be empty much of the time otherwise, and it was better for Teddy, as the tiny patch of garden at the flat was not large enough for him to run around when Alice was working.

'What am I getting myself into, Richard?' she asked, not really expecting an answer.

'If I didn't think you were up to this, I would not have recommended you to HQ. Clara had faith in you,' he said. She told me from the outset you were intelligent and calm. That, although young, you were sensible and reliable. So trust me, you are able to do this … and we are grateful for your courage.'

Dear Diary

Today, my life turned a corner. One that feels daunting, but I am determined to walk the path and succeed.

Owing to the situation at the library with the break-in, Teddy and I are moving into Richard's cottage. He no longer wishes to live there after Clara's death and needs someone to keep it clean. He will use the flat above the library when he returns from his work in London.

Teddy will be happy running around a garden again, and I will be happy to live in such a pretty cottage. I cannot wait to move in! Apparently, due to Richard's job and position in government, he is exempt from having billeted men stay there, so I will have the whole place to myself!

Exciting times ahead. My library position has moved up a notch, too.

Chapter Thirty-Five

At the library, Richard handed over the keys to his cottage, and Alice slipped into her office.

'I am not going to leave the messages here overnight. I will store them with my study books in this bag,' she said, placing the envelopes into a book in her regular bag. 'I use this all the time, so nothing will look out of place, and I will sleep better at night.'

'How did Gladys take the news?' Richard asked.

'She had questions, but each one was more or less answered with Teddy needing more space. She then brought up the square footage that others had given up for the billeted men, so I told her I would deal with the situation if it arose. I then told her I was considering having Hilda live with me to give Hettie a break, as she was becoming more confused than ever. That seemed to satisfy her ... for now,' Alice replied.

Richard gave a sniff of disapproval. 'That woman wants to know everything about everyone. It will be my turn next for the curtain twitching.'

Alice nodded. 'I don't know. I told her that when you were not in London that she could expect to see you living here, and the library open at odd hours as you were teaching again. She seemed happy enough with that.'

At her new home, the cottage, Alice noticed that several things had been cleared away from the surfaces. Richard said he had made good use of the attic space so she could make the place homely for herself.

Hettie had given Alice a box of items, and along with what ornaments and pictures Hilda had given her, she and Blake soon had it looking nice. Blake had helped her clear out her belongings from the library and transported them in a free truck to the cottage. To her delight, she saw Richard had cleared his books from the large bookshelf, meaning Alice was able to place her grandmother's few in pride of place. She had also taken a selection from the ones Hilda and Hardy gave her at the start of her journey. It warmed her heart to see them, as they were now memory treasures of a past, and any she added would represent her future.

Inside the shed, she found the large box Ben would be using, and saw Clara's large stick, which she now realised represented a weapon Clara probably used in France.

'How're you doing in there, found any spiders?'

Alice turned to see Blake standing looking into the shed.

'Plenty! Ugh. It reminds me of a novel, *Something Nasty in the Woodshed*. It's by Anthony Gilbert, who is really a woman called Lucy Beatrice Malleson. I am a fan, but the woodshed one was scarier than finding a spider inside. At least this cottage is not as creepy.' Alice gave a theatrical shudder.

Blake gave a burst of loud laughs. 'You read the darndest books, Alice.'

'I made a promise to myself to always finish a book for the

author's sake, but some I have read nearly made me break the promise, the woodshed one included!' Alice said, with a wide smile.

She moved the box further back on the shelf and closed the shed door. She knew the next time she entered it would mean action stations for her runners and anyone else connected to the missions secreted away in the library books.

'Moving away from creepy things in the shed. I've put all of Richard's things into this one. The gardening tools are in the small one over there.' Alice pointed to a potting shed at the far end of the garden. 'I won't use this one, there are personal items of Clara's in there, too. So, if ever you fancy working on the garden, the non-creepy shed is over there,' she said gesturing at the smaller shed before walking to the door.

Blake looked up at the sky. 'Looks like more rain tonight,' he said.

'I hope it doesn't linger. I forgot I have to walk to work in the outdoors again,' Alice replied.

'It's getting colder by the day. I hate to say it, but Britain loves a dull day,' Blake said with a laugh, then pointed to the log pile beneath a makeshift roof near the backdoor. 'I'll chop you some more wood while I'm here. At least the weather is against a raid, I have rest time.'

From her vantage point in the kitchen, Alice watched as Teddy gleefully ran after a stick the garden, while Blake focused on chopping wood. The atmosphere was filled with peace and tranquillity. The Luftwaffe had not posed significant difficulties for Hardy and his crew during their latest raid over Germany, so he could enjoy a brief respite with her for a few hours. Despite the presence of his uniform, the scene could have been reminiscent of a time before the war. Alice closed her eyes, wanting to preserve the moment and hoping it would transition into a post-war reality.

Setting up the fire in the fireplace, Alice looked around the room. Crocheted blankets from Hettie and her rug from Hilda gave the room a glow of warmth.

'What a funny life we lead. You, the man who works miracles on planes, and me, the trainee librarian,' Alice said later as she handed Blake a plate of corned beef sandwiches.

'Where will you join up when you are eighteen, if the war continues?' Blake asked between bites.

A sudden flash of guilt scurried around Alice's insides. Her secret mission could not be shared with him, ever, and she was not sure how Richard was going to handle her enlisting situation in the New Year.

'I have given it some thought, and I am hoping for something which will keep me close to home. Although Richard said trained librarians are valuable for protecting books and arts. So, I do feel I am doing war work, but if the government changes its mind, I will have to enlist in something,' she said.

Blake frowned. 'I hate the thought of it. You, getting caught up in this mess of a war. You're my girl, you should be free to browse bookstores, and read without fear of a siren blasting every day.'

'I will ask Richard if I can introduce something else into the library that will contribute something useful towards the war effort,' Alice said. 'I am grateful you are on the ground. A lot of the local girls are keen on snagging a pilot, but I am content with the man who keeps them safe to get back into action.'

Blake raised his cola bottle. 'Here's to us, Alice. Finding our way forward. No looking back,' he said, and Alice raised her own bottle in agreement.

'To us,' she said with conviction. She truly hoped there would be a time in the future for them, a period of getting to know each other on a better level. A full day of happiness, not snatched hours of hope.

Dear Diary

I am settled into my new home and am more relaxed. Watching Blake chop wood was like something from a novel. His muscles and strength are so attractive, seeing him washing dishes is a real pleasure. Today, I saw a glimpse into the future. I do believe Blake and I have a future together. I could not bear it if someone like him duped me into being intimate, and speaking false promises into my ear. He makes my life so much happier.

Chapter Thirty-Six

'What a luxury!' Hilda declared, as she tied her dressing gown belt around her middle. Alice looked up from her book.

'You smell of roses. I am so pleased you can get into the bath again,' she said.

Hettie, also sitting in her nightclothes, burst out laughing.

'I think you mean you are pleased Hilda can enjoy a bath and the soap gift,' she said.

Alice took a moment to think about what she had said and then also laughed.

'Sorry, Hilda. I did not mean you needed to bathe and smell better!'

Hilda gave a grin. 'You are forgiven, young lady.'

Curling her legs beneath her on the sofa and earning a stern look from Hilda, Alice threw a smile her way. 'I know it's not ladylike, but I am so content tonight, I just want to relax.'

Hettie rose from her seat. 'I know what you mean, Alice. Hilda's health is improving, and I think that deserves a treat,' she said, opening a cupboard.

'The treat is us all being together for a change,' Hilda said and both Alice and Hettie stared at her.

'We are often together, Hilda,' Hettie said her voice filled with concern.

Hilda waved her words away.

'I am not brain muddled, don't fret. I meant that we rarely have moments like this any more. When we lived together we had bath nights and brandy – well, the brandy was after Alice had gone to bed,' Hilda added and gave a rare laugh.

'Have you been drinking the bath water, dear sister?' Hettie asked and Alice spluttered out a giggle.

'Open the brandy. I assume we have some, thanks to James and our American friends,' Hilda instructed.

Hettie took down three glasses from the kitchen cupboard, then poured milk into a saucepan.

'Hot brandy milk with what the American boys call cookies and we call biscuits. A perfect treat,' she said.

Alice sat back and listened to the two of them chatter about their past and their brandy nights, the dances they had attended and their sad days. Her heart melted with the warmth of the love in the room.

'I wish I had experienced this sort of night at home. A sister or sibling, chattering about our childhood. You are both so lucky, but if I hadn't had the life I did have, I would not have met you both. So, in reality, I am the lucky one,' she said, the brandy warming her insides.

'You reminded me of our good days tonight, Alice,' said Hilda. 'I am sorry I have been so low, and such a grouch. The war … and all the new romance brewing, I became a little withdrawn. We all have to deal with the bad days and not burden others, but I have been sad.' She took a large gulp of her drink. 'I've been missing special people in our lives, worrying about James taking Hettie from me … and other things caught up with me, too. The pain in my legs hasn't helped.'

'Oh, Hilda. We will always be here for you, for one another, won't we, Alice?' Hettie said.

Alice's split-second hesitation caused Hilda to speak again.

'None of us can make that kind of commitment,' she said. 'We don't know what's around the corner. Let us just live for the moment.'

Alice swallowed, gratitude towards Hilda coming to the fore.

'To the moment!' she said raising her mug.

'Hear, hear!' Hettie said.

The next morning, Alice left the two sisters singing happily in the kitchen, and crossed her fingers that the happier moments would outweigh the bad from now on.

———

At the end of the week, Alice received two messages. Both were related to British and American airmen brought down in France who had escaped capture.

Then a third message, regarding a fresh attack on factories in Germany, was for the urgent attention of the American contingent, and Thorpe Abbotts was one of the airbases mentioned.

Alice set out in the freezing fog, steadying herself on the frozen mounds of soil in the farm field leading to the main entrance. Every person inside the gates looked chilled to the bone.

Whenever she passed through the gates of the airbase, she kept one eye open, always on the lookout for Hardy. Despite not needing any distractions, she had prepared an interesting story about a letter delivery request from Gladys.

Today, Blake spotted her just before she was entering the office of the base commander.

'Alice?' he questioned just as her hand touched the door.

'Blake, are you done for the day?' she asked, hesitating to open the door despite being invited in.

'No, refreshment break,' he said with a wink.

'I will drop this letter Gladys found in with her deliveries into your commander. And then I will come find you for some doughnuts and coffee – your treat,' Alice said with a laugh. 'I need something to keep me warm.'

Blake touched his cap and winked at her. 'You do that,' he said, and to her relief, he walked away.

As the door swung open, she confidently stepped into the room, capturing the attention of the base commander.

'Apologies, sir. Master Sergeant Hardesty stopped to speak – it was an awkward moment,' she said to the man behind the desk.

'You are welcome, Miss Carmichael. You have a message for me?' he asked and held out his hand for the letter she produced.

'Yes. It is urgent and for your eyes only,' Alice said.

The commander tore it open and scanned the words.

'Berlin, eh?'

Alice nodded her head in agreement. 'The RAF, along with all of you here and the other American bases, will take part in this mission. Those at the top were hesitant at first according to my HQ, but then this message arrived, along with other urgent ones for different bases putting you all on notice for standby,' she said with a calm and confident voice.

The commander gave a soft whistle as he read the information again.

'A mission to cripple the enemy once and for all,' he said.

'I do not envy the pilots and crew, but I do admire their bravery,' Alice said with a soft smile.

'You are mighty young to carry this on your shoulders. Brave girl, but sensible. I have heard good things about you from the top. Hardesty is a lucky guy; it must be hard to play the innocent librarian,' the commander said and gave a hearty, husky laugh.

'I look at it this way: I am keeping him – and the rest of you – safe, if I say nothing,' Alice remarked, not sure she liked the commander's tone, which suggested she was a weak link in a long chain.

She watched as his face flushed red. Young she might be, but she reminded him she was also doing something towards the war effort, not playing a game because she was young.

'You are appreciated, excuse my crass remark,' the commander said, and he picked up papers from his desk.

'I will take these and the orders. Our paths will cross again soon, I am sure. Nice to meet you, Miss Carmichael.'

Alice realised she was dismissed. 'Goodbye, sir,' she said, and left the building.

When she went to find Blake again, he jumped from his seat – the front fender of a large jeep – and lifted her onto the bonnet. 'One doughnut and a coffee coming up,' he said and went to collect it. The music from the speakers vibrated out and the atmosphere and Blake's laughter was relaxed and light-hearted.

'So, Gladys and our chief are having a fling?' Blake asked her, after he'd handed her the doughnut and she'd taken a bite. She nearly choked on it.

'I beg your pardon?' she said, when she'd recovered.

'Secret notes delivered by the librarian. A romantic novel in the making there,' Blake said with a booming laugh. Alice got the impression he was fishing around for information.

'I doubt Gladys is his type,' she said, 'but who knows who's writing to him. I do know it's not via military mail. Nor is it female handwriting. No doubt a British airman friend of his – penpals, something like that.' She dabbed her mouth clear of crumbs and sugar, having given Blake enough information and red herrings while protecting the commander's reputation. Just the thought of him and Gladys having an affair was more than a fiction story, it was a fantasy, or even a horror story, and she laughed out loud at the thought.

'Did I say something funny?' Blake asked.

'I can't get the idea of your commander and Gladys out of my head now,' she said, and now they both burst out laughing.

Relieved she had been able to overcome her first tricky moment of questions with Blake, Alice could relax and enjoy their time together. Her newfound love was coffee and doughnuts.

Richard arrived at the library with the news that Alice was required to travel to London as part of the mission. He had come armed with paperwork. In her new upgraded role, now that Richard had left, Alice was getting used to the fact that everything came with fresh paperwork. She had once commented on the amount of paper wasted, if they stopped it would be one less book or magazine pulped.

'Douglas wants you there sooner rather than later,' Richard said. 'I am leaving for London this afternoon. You are to travel tomorrow. Here'—he handed her a piece of paper with the address of a hotel—'everything will be paid for, just book your room and I will deal with the bill on Monday. This is a vital meeting for us both, and there are more documents to sign connected to new briefings, I am afraid.'

'When HQ calls, we have no choice but to go,' she said. 'We both know that Douglas would not risk me attending if it was not important.'

'Will you travel alone – I mean, Clara almost always travelled solo, but I realise you have never visited the city by yourself,' Richard asked.

Alice shrugged.

'I managed to bus and walk all the way here from Great

Yarmouth alone, and I have already been to London, so don't worry about me. I will be fine, Richard. But thank you for thinking of me,' she said.

She put up a notice to say the library was to be closed for maintenance from Friday to Monday, and then went home to pack, marvelling that she was about to embark on another secret meeting and stay in a hotel with all bills paid.

When Blake visited her that evening, he was in a good mood.

'Honey, I have been ordered to take a rest break for forty-eight hours. We will have two whole days together. Close the library – pretend you are ill, and we will shut the door to the world,' he said, scooping her up and hugging her close before kissing her long and hard.

After they broke apart, Alice wished she could have enjoyed the kiss more, but her situation had been playing on her mind the whole way through it. She pulled a sad face.

'Oh, Blake, I wish I'd known sooner. I haven't been able to get a message to you to let you know, but I have to go to London for a two-day lecture and an exam … for my studies,' she said, repeating the story Richard had come up for her.

She felt guilty when she saw the disappointment on Blake's face, but she had to put her feelings aside. London was not something she could put off.

'Hey, I've an idea,' he said, with even more excitement. 'Why don't we travel to London together? You can attend your lecture and take your exam, and then we can use the rest of the time enjoying ourselves in the capital of England.'

Alice could not think of anything she'd like more, but working out how she would manage to get to headquarters without rousing Blake's suspicions was going to be hard. Had the HQ location been a university, it would have been easy enough, but for him to escort her to what presented as an empty building would spark questions she could not answer.

'That's such a lovely idea, but I am not sure it's wise we stay together in London. This exam is so important, and I can't have you distracting me...' she said, teasing him by playing with his shirt buttons.

'Obviously, we'd book two rooms, or Hettie would feed me to Hitler,' Blake quipped.

Alice smiled, feeling her resolve crumble.

'All right, you've twisted my arm,' she said. 'Time in the city with a handsome American. Heads will turn,' she added, laughing.

They'd arranged for Teddy to be cared for by Blake's crew at the airbase, who were only too delighted to make Hilda's dog their mascot. By the time Alice and Blake left, to elbow-nudging and endless winks and whistles, she could not have been happier.

As they strolled along the bustling London streets, the city seemed to pulsate with an energy both vibrant and apprehensive. The war's presence was evident, from the dimly lit blackout windows to the occasional sound of debris clearance slicing through the air. Despite the bustle and activity, the evidence of the intensive bombing still caught them unawares as they walked through the city. But when they turned into a maze of narrow lanes, the scene before them was like stepping back in time. Blake stopped walking to take it in.

'These streets. They are straight out of a Dickens novel,' he said. 'One of the few writers I enjoy, because of his description of a city thousands of miles away from America. And now here I am walking through them,' he said, his enthusiasm infectious.

'Oh, look at this,' said Alice stepping up to the window of a second-hand bookshop, her breath fogging the bomb-protected glass. 'I would love to own a bookshop.'

'I can see you running a quaint bookstore,' Blake said with a smile. 'Flicking the books clean with a feather duster and chatting to customers about the heroes and heroines you've enjoyed reading about. Who knows, maybe one day your dream will come true.' His hand gently rested on the small of her back as they peered through the window, and his touch made Alice shiver with excitement. She could not believe they were on a break together. Deep in the recesses of her mind, she also knew they would not be sleeping in separate beds that night.

The anticipation of the meeting at HQ filled Alice with a combination of excitement and nerves. The prospect of seeing Richard, though, and the important reason she was here, helped her focus. But though she knew she had executed her duty to the best of her ability, putting her heart and soul into her job, still she had questions she wanted to ask.

Were her work efforts meeting the expectations that they had set – if not how could she improve? Did her lack of capability at a certain level contribute to a mission's failure, or near failure, in any way?

Every time she came across a newspaper article detailing a successful mission against the enemy, she couldn't help but let out a sigh of relief. If it was connected to a message that she and Ben had received thanks to his pigeons, she allowed herself to feel a small sense of pride.

Richard was always reassuring and fed back positive reports of her work, but Alice wanted to hear it from Douglas.

Chapter Thirty-Seven

As Alice stepped out onto the desolate streets of bombed-out London, she felt the weight of her mission bearing down on her with the destruction she faced on every corner.

She had slipped out quietly from her room at the hotel and left Blake asleep in his own. They'd chosen not to sleep together after a deep conversation where Alice expressed new nerves and concerns about such a big step. He'd been extremely understanding, for which she was grateful and they'd finally retired to their own rooms after several passionate kisses.

Picking her way through the streets, she saw that the area had obviously suffered more bombs than where she and Blake had walked the previous day. All around her, rubble littered the pathways and the buildings that still stood were scarred and pockmarked by the ravages of war.

Alice continued towards headquarters with determination, driven by a renewed sense of purpose. She stopped to catch her breath at one point as traumatic memories flooded her mind – memories of the fatal night in Great Yarmouth when her own world had crashed around her.

She shivered – the kind of shiver people talk about as like someone walking over their grave. Looking at the street she stood on, a residential area, Alice tried to imagine it in a time before the war, when the streets were alive with laughter and music, when families strolled arm in arm, and children played in the parks. But now each enormous pile of debris spoke volumes, with people picking through their belongings, and those days were long gone, lost to the relentless downpour of violence and destruction.

Her heart now heavy with sorrow and determination, Alice continued on through the city, refusing to lose hope. Then she turned a corner and the scene before her was uplifting.

People chatted and walked, they queued for rations, deep in conversation, children challenged one another to a game, and friendliness came from every doorway. Residents greeted Alice with a cheery good morning, and they gave her a silent reminder of her own resilience. She knew what they needed from her: more courage and ability to help them in the one small way she could, from the depths of a small hamlet in Norfolk – a place they probably didn't know existed.

With cheery waves in return, Alice held her head high and her resolve firm. She was on her way to sign papers that meant she could continue to maintain beacons of hope in a world consumed by darkness.

With her coat collar turned up against the chill, Alice briskly strode through the labyrinth of alleys and passages that criss-crossed the area, remembering Richard's instructions. Although he didn't know she was staying in a different hotel in the city – one Blake had chosen, she'd ensured it was near a tube train station for her return.

Richard had made it clear she was to check she was not followed once in the immediate area of the SOE building. Stopping under the pretence of tying her shoelaces, Alice peered around to check the street was empty.

The building she sought still looked tall and imposing, hidden in plain sight behind its 'To Let' sign still hinting at vacancy. Alice smiled to herself.

Her steps quickened as she neared the entrance, her senses alert for any signs of surveillance or unwanted attention, and once satisfied she slipped behind the large barricades.

'You made it, then,' Richard's voice greeted Alice as she walked down a long corridor. She was pleased to see him; it was daunting standing amongst so many strangers. Alice hitched a breath and turned around.

'I did – are you surprised?' she asked with a confident quip back at him.

'Never. I am never surprised by your bravery, Alice. I know this place is unnerving, and meeting with Douglas again is a request you could do without, but you have to conform with the ins and outs of signing the other commitment papers,' Richard said. He took her by the elbow and guided her towards the large room at the end of the corridor; the room she had previously visited.

'Alice!' Douglas called her over to his group.

'Just breathe, and be yourself, Alice,' Richard encouraged her, as she headed Douglas's way.

'Sir. It's a pleasure to see you again,' she said, shaking his hand.

'Pleasure's all mine. Well done, girl. My word you have surprised me with your courage and quick thinking down there in your little library,' he said. 'Richard's reports sing your praises. Darned shame about our girl, Clara, though. She was very fond of you, and she was quite right to push you forward.'

Alice waited for him to pause and puff on his cigar so she had the opportunity to speak.

'Thank you for your kind words, sir. I am always doubting myself, so it's good to hear you are satisfied with me and my little secret library – Clara's name for it, not mine,' Alice said, and laughed.

'Secret library. Yes, I like it. Very clever,' Douglas said, and the group around them gave polite laughs.

'When Richard broke the news about Clara, I was devastated, but I am determined to see this through in her name. She was my inspiration – *is* my inspiration,' Alice said.

Greetings over, the briefing explained about the intensified air attacks planned on Berlin during November and possibly beyond. Alice listened carefully to the instructions and plans, in awe of the fact she was here, part of it all. And though she was convinced some of the men thought she was Richard's secretary, after the meeting finished, she was drawn into the private discussions as one of the team.

'You know, if you ever want to fill Clara's shoes, you are more than capable,' Douglas said to her.

Taken aback, Alice stared at him.

'Apart from the fact I cannot speak French or jump out of a plane, you mean,' she joked.

Douglas leaned back in his seat.

'Apart from that, yes,' he said laughing.

'Just keep thinking of me as the Norfolk-speaking trainee librarian and neither of us will go wrong, sir,' Alice said, and her words brought raucous laughter into the room.

'Richard. Whatever she wants or needs, she has my approval,' Douglas said and walked away.

Once the formalities were over, Alice and Richard exited the building.

'I have a confession to make,' Alice said, realising she had better come clean about Blake. 'I am not staying at the hotel you booked. Blake caught me out with a surprise. A forty-eight-hour pass to London. He booked two rooms nearer to Liverpool Street.' She crossed her fingers at the slight white lie.

Richard considered. 'That is not a problem for me. But be careful not to... Well, I will walk you to the station.'

He didn't finish what Alice knew would have been a quiet warning to behave herself. 'Well done for coming today,' he added. 'You've handled yourself better than most adults would, caught up in this situation. Clara did well the day she trusted you...' Richard paused. 'Hell, I miss my sister. It would have been her thirty-second birthday today, though she will for ever be thirty-one.' His voice was heavy with emotion and Alice's throat constricted.

'She was so brave, Richard, I will never forget her,' she said, not sure what else to say for fear of upsetting Richard further.

'Hello, you two. Join me for lunch?' Douglas Brown's voice interrupted their conversation. Four other members of the department accompanied him and Alice was surprised they moved around the city together. But then, they looked so much like city gents people would probably just ignore them. She had seen several groups of suited gents in deep conversation around the city.

'I am heading for Surrey, sir. And Alice here is about to meet her friend for lunch. Kind of you to ask us, though.' Richard said, saving Alice from worrying about her duty and doing what was expected of her.

'As you wish.' Douglas nodded at them both, and once he and the other men had walked away, Alice and Richard turned to go their separate ways.

Suddenly Richard turned back to her. 'Turn around,' he whispered. Alice did as instructed and together they faced a deserted shop window. In the window's reflection Alice's attention was caught by someone in uniform, who looked very much like Blake, walking in the opposite direction. She held her breath.

'Wasn't that your American friend, Blake?' Richard asked her, his face etched in concern and flushed with anxiety when he faced her.

Inside her chest, Alice's heart lost its rhythm and skipped several beats. She could not deny the image of the back of the airman walking away was every bit like Blake.

Chapter Thirty-Eight

'I very much doubt it was him,' Alice said calmly. 'Blake is probably still dreaming of being knee deep in rivets and shrapnel back at the hotel.' She was still staring down the road, where the mysterious airman had been heading. 'He is exhausted which is why his chief made him take some time off.'

She noticed that Richard was also still staring down the road, and it made her uncomfortable.

'Besides, Blake doesn't know where I am, and this is a strange part of London for him to come and see the sights, don't you think?' she said, unsure whether she was trying to convince Richard or herself.

What if Blake had followed her – maybe to surprise her after her supposed exam. But if it had been him, why hadn't he made his presence known?

'We all have a doppelganger, I suppose,' Richard said, finally turning his attention back to her, and she tried to smile reassuringly at him.

'Anyway, I don't think that man was as tall as Blake,' she said, determined to get Richard to forget the man. 'Where are you off to now?'

'More meetings, I'm afraid, or I would suggest we lunch somewhere. I will be back in a few weeks,' he replied. 'You know which tube trains you need?'

Alice nodded and pulled out the note she had made for herself. 'All here,' she said then pushed the paper back into her bag.

'Right, I'm off that way.' Richard pointed to his right.

'Take care, Richard. And don't worry about me,' Alice said.

He bent to peck her on the cheek. 'I will always worry.'

'Thank you. I will always worry about you, too,' she said and placed a kiss on his cheek.

After they parted, Alice watched until Richard was out of sight before making her way back to the hotel. Once inside, she asked for her key at reception and noticed Blake's key was not on its hook.

A strange feeling overcame her, and she wondered if it had been him near headquarters, after all.

Had he really followed her that morning?

Was he spying on her or worse, the department?

Was she an excuse to come to London? Did he have a different agenda? After all, he had not created a fuss when she said about them not sleeping in the same room.

Alice's heart flipped and skipped a beat.

Had she jeopardised the SOE building?

The more she allowed her mind to race through different scenarios, the more panicked Alice became. She could not afford to be questioned by Blake if he had seen her with Douglas Brown and his colleagues. Richard, she could get away with, but five city gents was stretching the truth if she said they were librarian examiners.

'Calm down. Think, Alice,' she muttered to herself as she took her key and rushed to her room, where she packed her things into her bag.

She pulled out paper and pen from her bag and wrote Blake a note. She could not afford for him to get caught up in something she had no ability to help him out of, and she also needed to protect her own position.

Back at home, she could spend some time thinking of a story if Blake were to start asking questions. She needed to think, to calm down.

My dearest Blake,

I am truly sorry, but I am catching the next train home.

My meeting went well, and the exam was easy, but I was reminded that staying with a man in London at my age is not appropriate. I love spending time with you, but the thought of Hettie and Hilda – or Gladys, God forbid – finding out I have come here alone with you is too much. I am afraid I will let myself down by getting caught up in the magic of the city and being with you and one thing will inevitably lead to another and then I will be anxious. I don't want to spoil your time here in the city.

Stay here and have fun. See the sights and rest, too. Goodness knows, you deserve it. If you cut short your leave I will feel dreadful. I will see you back home – get in touch when you want to meet again.

When I collect Teddy, I will tell the men at the base that my aunt suddenly became unwell, and that you are staying on for a well-earned break.

With affection,

Alice x

Downstairs, Alice asked for an envelope and sealed it, leaving it with the receptionist to pass to Blake.

After scrambling onto the train, she found herself standing in a cramped corridor, pressing against others, and gazing out of a smudged window at the blur of the passing scenery. The train journey felt like it would never end, leaving Alice feeling both physically and mentally uneasy, as a heavy cloud of negativity hovered over her. Her head throbbed with the weight of her thoughts, each one pounding inside her like a relentless drumbeat, as she realised she might just have destroyed her relationship with Blake.

Her sensible brain told her he would understand her reason for leaving, and there were more important issues at stake. She could not let her logical thoughts be consumed by emotional baggage, but the guilt of leaving him weighed heavily on her.

Impulse and fear had overruled her, but it was too late to turn back. She had to face the consequences if he decided to get in touch or if she found the courage to go and talk to him on his return.

Chapter Thirty-Nine

A s Alice walked through the gates of the base, she couldn't help but feel a sense of awkwardness.

It had been just over two weeks since she had left Blake in London. Neither of them had contacted each other. Alice tried to tell herself it was because they were both busy, but she knew her letter was most probably the culprit. She could not hold back any longer. She had seen the contents of the latest mission correspondence and was not prepared to risk never seeing Blake again. She needed to hear him tell her to walk away, and she would, without argument, but she needed him to say it to her face.

Uncertainty filled her as she wondered about his reaction upon seeing her. She had left Teddy at home as she wanted to speak with Blake without distraction. A local boy, who loved to hang around at the base, suddenly appeared and sprinted towards her, his laughter filling the air.

'Miss, where's Teddy?' he asked.

Alice ruffled his hair. 'He is with my aunt, Ronnie,' she said.

He gave a slight huff of disappointment.

Ronnie was a mischievous young boy, but he had a kind heart, and he was a regular at the library, immersing himself in books on every visit. His curious nature meant Ronnie asked countless questions, which Alice was usually happy to answer. One day, he had surprised her with a wilted bouquet of wildflowers. His sweet nature made her think he was the type of boy she would have liked as a sibling.

'Is Blake … Hardy about?' she asked.

Ronnie pointed to the first of the large hangars. 'He's over there but I would not go inside if I was you,' he said.

'Why?' Alice asked, looking over at the hangar.

'Got a right temper on him today,' Ronnie said, giving a comical smile and putting his hands on his hips much as his mother might do when imparting a titbit of gossip. 'No gum from that chum, if that's what you're after.'

Alice could not help but smile back, yet at the same time it hurt her to think Blake was suffering and she could guess why.

'Ah, I see,' she said. 'In that case, will you be brave for me and give him this note?' She held out a readily prepared note in case this kind of situation arose. 'It is worth thruppence,' she said, handing over the money.

'That'll do,' Ronnie said, grabbing both letter and money, leaving Alice staring after him. She watched the boy slip inside the hangar before turning to walk back home.

Back at the cottage, Alice tried hard to keep her mind on her studies but ended up writing a letter to Gabrielle. Both of them were leading different lives, but caught up in the same war, and Alice wondered if there would ever come a time when their correspondence would have no mention of food shortages, bombed-out cities and towns, and the loss of loved ones.

Even Teddy could not lift her from her grey mood. Until she had communicated with Blake again, Alice felt she could not move forward.

The library was busier than usual, and Alice wondered what would happen if it closed for good. A schoolmistress brought children to sit and read quietly for an hour a day, and Alice smiled as the woman sat with her own book in hand. A crafty way to find an hour's peace.

One afternoon, a runner arrived and stood waiting for Alice to deal with his request. Once he had gone the schoolteacher approached her.

'Please do not think I am being nosy, but when he collects the books, does he bring them back?' she asked, looking at the back of the runner walking past the window. 'Only, I have known Reggie since he was little, he lives in my mother's village – Pulham – and he's an odd lad. He likes to hoard things and I have never known him to be keen on reading.'

Alice's mind went into overload. A young man who liked hoarding things was not what she wanted to hear, but she reminded herself that no one had reported missing messages when she went to London. Richard would have checked Reggie's background and credentials. And who's to say the young man hadn't learned the love of reading after he left school, even though Alice knew he was not reading the books.

'Always, Miss Vincent. Regular as clockwork. I suspect with all that's going on with the war, he has found books a comfort,' she replied with a smile. 'But thank you for warning me.'

The hours drifted into one another and appeared to slow down the closer they got to closing time. As per her usual routine, Alice would normally stay back and let people slowly leave the premises, diligently stamping books long after the library had closed. However, tonight, she was unusually eager to head home. Her note to Blake had given him a date and time to meet to discuss London.

Watching Ben enter the shed, Alice sighed. It was the first time he had arrived at the cottage during daylight. Instead of walking away, he tapped on the door and handed her a bag of vegetables.

'Alroight, gal?' he asked, giving her his gummy smile and, as always, reminding her of a kindly grandfather figure.

'I am, Ben. Thank you for the veg, it is a hot-soup day. I swear it is getting colder by the hour, and this fog is dreadful. How are things with you and your birds?' she asked.

'Busy. Travellin' further nowadays,' he said, and Alice knew that meant across the sea to France.

'They are incredible creatures, I had not given them any thought before, only when the farmer moans and groans about his crops,' she said.

'He can moan, they are not mine. Mine do not eat out, theys well fed at home,' Ben said laughing. 'You got enough wood?'

Alice's heart filled with affection for the man. His story was he had lost both his wife and son during childbirth just after the Great War, and he'd became a recluse. Whenever she met with him, Alice felt she wanted to match him with Hilda. They would make wonderful companions for one another.

'I have plenty, thank you. My friend cut me quite a few logs. Ben, do you know my Aunt Hilda? She was the postie for this area,' she asked, knowing that post might not have come to the cottage, but it was worth asking.

'Seen her bout the village plenty times,' he said. 'Good woman. Fierce tongue on her but loves a garden.' Ben stroked Teddy's head. 'This is her dog. I heard she was injured, but that was a while back.'

'She was, but when she retired and she had to move out of the cottage, she was in a bad way for a while. Her sister Hettie struggled to help her, and everything got on her nerves ... but she's getting better, back to her old self...' Alice smiled and pushed a jar of jam his way. 'Blackberry. Aunt Hettie made a big batch, there's one for you.'

'Yewer a good gal and will make a lucky man happy one day,' Ben said.

Alice sighed. 'I think that ship has sailed, Ben. Love ... well, let's say collecting carrots got in the way,' she said with a wink and wan smile.

Ben's arthritic hand patted hers. 'It will be, if it is right. Don't rush life just because there is a war on,' he said. 'By the way, one message for the commander is in the box.'

Once Ben had departed, Alice ventured into the shed to retrieve the messages. She worked on their coded level of importance and placed three for the library in her bag, and the fourth for the airbase commander sat in front of her ready for despatch.

Blake had not visited after she'd sent the note, and although she kept telling herself he was extremely busy, she also knew he was angry and hurt, and she had destroyed something wonderful.

Ben's words about taking things slow in love during wartime didn't sit right with her. She couldn't shake the feeling that if she had embraced a relationship with Blake in London, she wouldn't be in this state of loneliness and heartbreak. She and Blake would still be on track ready to build a future together.

Gathering her things and Teddy, Alice made her way to the airbase.

The commander greeted her with a grimace of a smile.

'When a pretty girl walks in here I am usually a happy guy. When you arrive I know it is a call to action, and not in the way a man might enjoy,' he said laughing at his own innuendo.

Alice felt her face flush, though she was used to his outgoing banter.

'Maybe one day I will have good news to give,' she said and handed over the message. 'But sadly, not today.'

'Wilhemshaven – yup, this one is a big one,' the commander said as he read it. 'Keeps the boys out of mischief. You off to see Hardesty?' he asked.

Alice, taken aback by his question shook her head.

'No, I am running late for the library. Besides, he is busy,' she said. 'Take care, commander...' she said, with a gentle smile.

The commander gave a nod.

'Take it steady, Alice. And thanks.'

Walking through the base, Alice paid no attention to the large hangar area, completely ignoring the mobile drinks club where men gathered, relishing their coffee, doughnuts, music, and the charming companionship of the Red Cross girls. Choosing a different path, she walked alongside Teddy, retracing their steps back out of the main gates. As she walked beside the boundary fencing, a woman's laughter echoed through the air, catching her attention. She peered through the gaps in the fence to see Blake casually leaning against a hut, engaged in conversation with one of the local girls who delivered freshly ironed clothes for the men.

The flirting was clear on both parts, and Alice felt a nauseating swirl in her stomach, causing her to struggle for a breath for a second.

She had lost him.

Dear Diary

It is over!

Blake has a new woman in his life, and it is all my fault.

I drove him into the arms of someone else with

my behaviour in London. I am a girl when he
wanted a woman to hold in his arms.

Why didn't I stay with him? Did I make him
angry by leading him on?

My other thoughts are - does he know about the
secret library? Is he all I think he is?

Did he follow me? Does he think Richard and I
have a relationship, after all?

Oh, I don't know what to think, I am beside
myself with worry and sadness.

I have so many questions unanswered in my
head. I am not scared about my future, I am
furious at myself for ruining it, and for losing a
man who filled my heart with happiness and love.

Seeing Blake flirt with another woman has made
me realise how much I really love him, and it
breaks my heart to think I let him go.

Chapter Forty

By mid-November Hilda's health had rallied around, and on Stir Up Sunday Alice marked the twenty-first as a major turning point.

James, eager to see Hettie again, had made arrangements to stay nearby and arrived at Hettie's house with a bag filled with ingredients, ready to make a delicious, traditional Christmas pudding. Her aunt had not looked so happy in a long time and bustled about her home with renewed energy.

Laughter filled the kitchen, creating a lively atmosphere, as each person in the house at that moment took their turn to stir the mixture, taking their time and making a wish while doing so. Hilda surprised everyone with her positive change as she teased and joked with her sister.

'It was as if she was in mourning for her old life and is now recovered,' Hettie said to Alice as she looked across the room at Hilda and James playing a game of cards.

'Hilda, would you like to come and stay with Teddy and me for a couple of days,' said Alice. 'You haven't seen my new home, and you can stay home with Teddy while I am at the library, and try to complete some of the jigsaws Richard left for me. A log fire to yourself and a double bed.' Alice looked questioningly at Hilda, expecting a grumpy rejection to her offer.

'Well, I do miss Teddy, and it will be a change of environment,' Hilda pondered. 'So I think I might take you up on your offer.'

The room went quiet, and Hettie looked over at her sister. 'Are you sure, Hilda?'

'If it will stop you fussing over me, I'll pack my bags now,' Hilda replied.

Hettie gave a tut. 'Well, I think it is safe to say my sister has recovered and is her usual blunt self once again, so stand by your beds.' She winked at Alice. 'Take her, you are welcome to her.'

Dear Diary

Today has given me mixed feelings. I tried to laugh in the right places, and made an effort to enjoy moments when I was not thinking about Blake.

I have spent endless tears over him and it is not helping my heart heal. Christmas is getting closer and is supposed to be a happy time. But each day leading up to it is cold and miserable. Literally. The weather is dire and coal is hard to find. We make do with what logs we can find, but cutting down trees in the woods is not allowed.

I am jealous, miserable, and lonely - even in a crowd. James surprised Hettie with a visit, and they are most definitely in love. I am in love but *have no man in my life. I drove him away. I am a fool!*

I will never love another man as I have loved Blake Hardesty - never!

Much to Alice's surprise, Hilda quickly settled into the cottage and whenever Alice left for work, Hilda would hand her a prepared lunch. On her return home Alice would sit down to a hot meal. Hilda's manner softened, too, and although she limped and had the odd ache in her leg, she rarely grumbled about a thing.

One afternoon, Ben arrived at the library door waving Alice over to speak to him. He looked flustered and out of breath.

'Message for you, Alice. I went to the cottage and a woman shooed me away. Realised it was that Hilda, but she won't have me go near the shed when I said I was returning garden tools,' he said.

Alice ushered him inside.

'Oh, gracious, I can imagine. I am sorry, Ben. I forgot to tell you; she is staying with me for a while. I will explain to her you are the gardener and to let you into the sheds.'

'While I was there, I noticed your wood pile was low. I take it your young man has not had time to chop some more.'

Alice gulped at the mention of Blake. *My young man is no longer in my life.* She tried, but could not say the words, it was painful enough as a thought, to hear it out loud would fracture the barrier she had built herself. She simply shook her head.

'Alroight, then. Tell your aunt that Ben the gardener will be over in the morning. Can't have you cold. Worst winter I have known for years,' he said as he clambered onto a bike that had seen better days.

Alice watched him pedal away from her front window and was grateful he did not drive, although driving might be the safer option for him on the pot-holed lane.

Dear Ben, she thought, you are so brave and thoughtful. No one knows what you do and of how dedicated you are to the fight for freedom. Will they ever know?

The following day, Alice mentioned to Hilda that Ben would be visiting to chop some wood.

'Please be gentle with Ben, he is good to me, and all the vegetables in the rack are gifts from him. He is a kind man,' Alice said. 'And he has full use of both sheds.'

'He seemed harmless enough, but we cannot allow any Tom, Dick, or Harry to roam around your door,' Hilda replied with a firm voice.

At the end of the week, Hilda and Ben were seated at the kitchen table when she arrived home from the library. They were planning new vegetable patches for the cottage and fixing a jigsaw together. Alice laughed to herself, Hilda was a dark horse.

Sitting in the quiet of her temporary corner of the sewing room on Christmas Eve, Alice sat wrapping gifts for her small group of family and friends downstairs. She thought about the friendship forming between Ben and Hilda, and in the case of Hettie and James, the one deepening into something serious. All four were sitting enjoying a cup of hot cider after the cold walk home from the St Leonard's church evening service.

'Come for Christmas dinner, Ben,' Alice heard Hettie say.

'My table is groaning with foods from our American guests, and two chickens will complement the vegetables Alice shares with us, which I understand come from your garden. I know you have told Hilda you always have Christmas Day alone, but how about changing the routine and venturing out for the day.'

Hettie's kind heart had no boundaries and Alice waited to hear Ben's reply, but it was Hilda's voice that spoke out first.

'Succulent chicken, a Christmas pudding, peach and apple pie, and my company, what more could you want, Benjamin?'

Alice giggled to herself and placed the last of her packages onto her bed. She touched the book Pete had brought her, what seemed so long ago, which she had kept out to remind herself how lucky she was to have known him, and went downstairs to join the others.

'There's a lot of giggling going on down here, I take it the hot cider is flowing well,' she said, grinning at them all and not letting on what she'd overheard. 'What have I missed?'

'Hettie has invited Ben to eat with us tomorrow,' James said. 'And Hilda has shared the menu, which means I will definitely be there!'

'Ben?' Alice looked at him, his weathered face moving from one person to another. She knew he was not usually sociable, and was already surprised he had agreed to attend the church service with Hilda.

'I'll bring a pail of potatoes,' he said to Hettie. Alice smiled at him, then noticed a smile play across Hilda's face, too.

After everyone had left, Alice washed and wiped the glasses while Teddy ran round the garden for his nightly sniff. Suddenly, he began barking, then stopped. Alice listened with a cocked ear, but she heard nothing untoward. Then Teddy barked again, and she switched off the light and went to the door, it was pitch-black in the garden, with a fog rolling in across the fields. Suddenly a shadow moved along the path.

'Who's there?' she called out.

'Alice. It's me, Richard.'

Alice's heart deflated, part of her had hoped it was Blake.

'Get inside so I can put the light back on,' she said, and walked back into the kitchen.

'Sorry, silly me, I left my key for the library in London,' he said. 'I won't stop it's a filthy night.'

She paused. 'Would you like to come to Hettie's for Christmas Day?' she asked. 'I don't think you should be alone'

'Really?' he said. 'Are you sure?'

'Of course,' she smiled. You'd be very welcome.'

He looked genuinely touched. 'Thank you. In that case, I will see you at your aunt's tomorrow.'

'Wonderful. Now about that key,' said Alice, walking to the drawer where she kept spares. She selected the one she wanted and handed it to him. 'By the way, there's another guest coming tomorrow … Ben.'

'Ben?' Richard lifted his eyebrows in surprise.

'Aunt Hilda and he are getting along rather well, and Hettie invited him. Hilda has gone home with Hettie now, but she is staying here on and off now she is better, and when they met something changed for them both, I think,' Alice said.

'Will Blake be there, too?' Richard asked.

Alice's heart sank, and she gulped back a threatening sob. She had kept her emotions at bay for weeks, but Christmas Day talk made her sad she would not have Blake at her side.

'No. Sadly, we have parted ways. In fact, I saw him recently with another girl much older than me. Probably more suitable considering our age gap,' she said, hoping to sound positive, the sadness she felt not permeating her words. 'And my priority is to help the war effort. This war has to end, and happiness and peace must never be taken from us again.'

'I am sorry, Alice, but don't give up hope. You are young…'

'Not so young that I can't run a secret library to save our country, nor so young that I have not felt the pain of loss through the cruelty of political brutality. My age is a number, my life is a fact. Please never say I am young and there is a life out there for me, because right now, I do not believe it.'

Richard reached out his hand and squeezed hers.

'Understood,' he said.

After Richard had left, Alice curled up on the sofa. The clock chimed out ten o'clock, and although she was weary, she was not tired. Her mind raced with thoughts of her past. With her family gone and her heart broken, her life built on fragments of friendship during a bid for survival, maybe now was the time to take a different road. Her eighteenth birthday was approaching and her health at its peak meant she was able to offer more than receiving and delivering messages.

Dear Diary

Not hearing from Blake and seeing him with another woman is breaking my heart. How does one recover from such pain?

What I would give to turn back the clock, to before London.

Because I cannot see a future without him in it, my life will probably be one where I am a spinster. My heart cannot take another battering, but I do not relish the idea of being alone, either. Maybe I will be like Hilda and Hettie and find companionship later in life.

Am I supposed to throw myself at Blake, beg for him to see me as a grown woman worthy of holding in his arms again, instead of the silly girl who threw away love like a sweet wrapper?

Diary, what am I supposed to do when pain of love lost - so different from that of death loss - overpowers every thought?

I miss him so much, and am not sure I am supposed to after such a short time together. Does love grow that quickly? Is that true love?

Chapter Forty-One

Hettie's home was crammed to the doors with people and food. Alice had never experienced such a vibrant Christmas Day.

Grateful for the hospitality, the American airmen brought with them an abundance of their thanks in the form of bottled beers, soap, and chewing gum; they also brought packages containing tinned peas, evaporated milk, and bags of sugar – which made Hettie squeal with delight – along with other valuable food items not available with a ration book – or even on the shelves of the British shops.

Alice chatted with each person in the room, helped Hettie, and generally focused on the day. The gifts she received were thoughtful, and she had never felt so valued. Ben produced a trinket bowl, which he had carved with her initials, and Richard gave her a leather writing case and a fountain pen. Hilda and Hettie settled a large parcel in her lap, carefully wrapped in brown paper stamped with holly patterns – a lino-cut project the three of them had worked on during the lead up to the day.

Inside the parcel was a worsted woollen coat in emerald-green.

Alice lifted it out and shook it free. It had a pinched waist and large lapel, and was edged with tiny silver studs, which caught the light. The draped skirt was modern and more suited to her age than the old brown one she wore each day. Alice gasped.

'It is beautiful,' she said, holding it close to her chest. A teardrop snaked its way down her cheek.

Hettie passed her a handkerchief.

'No tears. It is about time you had something new and stylish. I do my best with alterations, but as soon as I saw this in Norwich, I knew it was a Christmas and birthday gift for the most precious girl Hilda and I could ever have in our lives. You have given us a reason to smile again and filled a gap in our lives we never realised was missing. To us, you are a daughter, not an adopted niece.'

Hilda gave a slight cough. 'You have also given us someone else to worry about, but that is a good thing – I realise that now.'

Alice frowned. 'Are you saying you were ill because you worried about me?'

Hettie and Hilda both nodded. 'Hilda cannot express her feelings as easily as I can, and she bottled up her worries about you leaving us and going to America with Blake Hardesty.'

Alice laid down her gift and went to Hilda, who, despite the room filled with people, accepted the embrace given her.

'I am going nowhere with anyone. I might travel when the war is over, but it will be a brief visit out of curiosity. This is my home. I am sorry I made you fret.'

Hettie brushed away a tear of her own, and looked at everyone in the room who stood watching the scene in silence.

'Time to sit and eat,' she said and smiled at Alice. 'After you hang your coat up and help me in the kitchen.'

After feasting, they sang carols and told jokes. By the time the afternoon light outside drew to a close, Alice's mood was happier, and she was ready to face a new future. Nearly eighteen years old, she was ready to step up as a woman. Her mother had married at her age, as had Hettie. Although marriage was merely a passing thought, now that she and Blake were no more, Alice had the urge to try something new to fill the adventurous side of her nature.

'When are you going to London again?' she asked Richard when they were drying dishes together in the kitchen.

'Why?'

'I am thinking of applying for Clara's old job,' she said in a low whisper.

Richard caught the edge of the plate he nearly dropped before it hit the floor.

'No!' he said and leaned against the edge of the draining board. 'You are not old enough.'

'I will be eighteen in January,' Alice replied, taken aback by his abrupt reaction.

'Alice. You have no life skills to survive in France. Listen to me. What Clara did was dangerous, and she could speak the language, but this did not stop her getting shot by the enemy. I cannot sign off on sending you to a death sentence,' he said, and his voice was firm and edged with an angry frustration.

'Is it your decision?' Alice challenged him.

Richard laid down the cloth in his hands.

'We need to talk, now, and out of earshot. Walk Teddy with me,' he said. 'Put on that lovely warm coat and get some air.'

Nudging her towards the room from where laughter rang out, Richard walked to the coatstand in the hallway and pulled on his own coat.

After calling for Teddy, they set out to walk through the small streets, the fog thick and damp.

'Let's go to the cottage, talk there,' Alice suggested after a while, her new coat getting damper by the minute.

Inside, she pulled the curtains to and hung up her coat by the

282

fire still glowing from when she'd left that morning. Richard did the same.

'About France and London,' he said. 'You have experienced a great deal, more than most your age, and handled everything with incredible strength, but right now the war is in full flow, and more experience is required. Our handlers cannot afford to take time out to teach and train girls as young as you. And yes, I know you hate to hear it, but it is fact. Plus, I do not want to lose someone I have grown fond of, and you know what *that* feels like.' Richard had hardly paused for breath.

She stood looking at him. Richard had experienced more loss than she realised.

'You lost someone else out there?' she said quietly. 'Not only Clara, but someone else you loved?' She swallowed, not sure she wanted to hear his reply. Hurting Richard was the last thing she wanted to do.

Richard lowered his head in a movement of defeat.

'Sit down. Tell me,' she said.

Richard sighed; pain etched on his face.

'She had just turned nineteen...' he began. 'She was recruited by someone Clara knew—'

Richard stopped speaking and closed his eyes. Alice waited.

'Annette, that was her name, she could speak French and German fluently. She had attended a finishing school in Switzerland, then moved back to Britain when the war began. Her parents moved to France, and despite me begging her not to, Annette joined them. We had fallen in love. Deeply in love. Plans of our wedding day were in black and white, and the date – June bride and all that – was set.'

Richard walked to the fireplace and tapped his pipe against the chimney breast. He refilled it, lit it and took in a sucking breath on the mouthpiece before puffing out the first coil of smoke. Alice dared not say a word, she had to hear what Richard wanted to tell her, to explain to her. She needed to hear a good reason not to take a deeper step into the heart of war.

'Then I found out Annette had chosen to join a different agency, one that opposed the ideals of sabotage in France, which went against my beliefs and Clara's. It was then I had my accident. A bridge-bomb success, but at a cost. Clara went to visit Annette and her parents to tell them, but they told her that Annette died after her group were captured by the Gestapo, and her parents escaped to Switzerland.' Richard swallowed back tears. 'June and September were not good months for me this year. You are the only living person I come home to, and it keeps me going.' He paused. 'So now you know my reasons for asking ... begging you to not take that road.'

Alice digested his words and his heartfelt request.

'I knew when I met you that you had fought a battle,' she said, 'but I did not realise you had lost your fiancée. We are people drawn together for a reason, and I will not be the cause of you reliving nightmares. I do understand your reasons. Always come home to me, Richard. I will be there for you, here, or wherever I end up.'

She went to him and took his hand.

'We need to get back to Hettie's. At least I do. Thank you for letting me see your heart, Richard,' she said.

'There is something you can do for yourself, Alice. If Blake is the man you want as part of your future, then go and get him back,' Richard told her.

She shook her head. 'It is too late. Besides, I have several important reasons to stay in England after the war, and Blake obviously wants to return to America. Hettie, Hilda, and you are not easy to walk away from. You are stuck with me for life, I'm afraid.' She gave him a brief peck on the cheek and walked to the cupboard to get her old coat.

'I think I had better wear this one back – a good reason for our delay. My new coat is airing off thanks to the fog. There's an old one of yours here,' Alice said, grabbing it and tossing it over to him. 'Catch!'

On their walk back to Hettie's, Alice thought about his words and her desire to take over Clara's job. Maybe it was the break-up with Blake that had made her want to run away. Richard's words of advice were valuable, though. And he was valuable to her. So she allowed the idea of approaching Douglas for recruitment to subside and focused on enjoying the rest of a special day with her family and friends.

Dear Diary

What a wonderful Christmas Day. My gifts, oh my goodness, my gifts. Never have I received such beautiful items. I stood looking at the room filled with love, and listened to the laughter. After my talk with Richard, I realise that to put myself in a position of danger would suppress the joy my family and friends have found at last. I cannot be the one to put them through such anxiety. My work within the library is enough. It is important enough.

My sadness came when I saw Hettie and Hilda so happy with their men. Blake is a man of my past now, someone who helped me grow into a woman with desires. I now know the difference between family love and romantic love. I am grateful to have met him, to have enjoyed our cultural differences and experiencing new and exciting things with him.

My focus now is to bring my sights back to Billingford and stop looking beyond its boundaries. My place is here. I am sure of it.

Chapter Forty-Two

Teddy's muddy pawprints across the floor and the lifeless rabbit he had unearthed in the field were evidence of his latest triumph. He had proudly dropped the dead rabbit at her feet.

'Shoo, you scoundrel!' she said, and pushed him outside before clearing up the mess.

After enjoying a late, yet pleasant Christmas evening at Hettie's, Alice had not thought she would spend part of Boxing Day morning scrubbing clean the kitchen floor.

The smell of lathered Sunlight soap on her cloth filled the air, and once she had finished, Alice knew she had to deal with the rabbit.

'All this before my breakfast!' she muttered at Teddy. His tail wagged so fast he created a draught and, as furious as Alice was, she could not be angry with him for long.

Wrapping the rabbit in rags to ward off its ripe smell, Alice grabbed a shovel from the shed and shut the gate on Teddy.

'This is going deep in the ground. Somewhere you won't find

it,' she said and set off into the foggy field to bury the offensive item. When she'd finished, she made her way back home and pushed open the gate and her heart sank when Teddy was nowhere to be found.

'Teddy! Come!' she called, but was greeted with silence. She rushed around the back of the cottage and checked the garden but could not see him anywhere. Suddenly, she heard a bark coming from the smaller shed and ran to let him out.

Teddy leapt out in a hurry, brushing against Alice's shins and raced around her ankles, barking excitedly. Standing perfectly still, she paid no attention to him. She stared at the man in the shed.

'How did you get in...?'

With a serious expression on his face, Blake stood, his eyes locked onto hers, and Alice couldn't help but notice the deepening dark circles beneath his eyes.

'Blake, what are you doing here?' she asked, her voice filled with confusion. 'And why on earth are you hiding with my dog in the shed?'

With a sheepish smile, Blake stepped out onto the lawn.

'I needed to find a way to speak with you without you slamming the door in my face,' he said.

Alice turned heel and walked away.

'You know where the exit is,' she called out pointing over to the gate. 'Come on, Teddy. Breakfast.'

'Okay, Alice, I need you to hear me out. Please, give me a chance to speak – I deserve to be heard, don't ya think?' Blake called after her.

Inside her head, Alice knew he was right. He had received a scribbled note and his girlfriend had walked out on him leaving him alone in a hotel in London.

'If you have come to tell me you've moved on, I know. I saw

you – with her, the laundry girl – a few days after London. Be happy, Blake, she is more your age and can give you the experienced love I cannot. Please go,' she pleaded, and trying to breathe calmly she went to open the back door. Knowing all the while he was behind her, she silently begged him to walk away. Her heart ached with the love she felt for him, but she was not prepared to return to the upset of the previous events.

Just before she managed to turn the handle, Blake's presence enveloped her from behind, his arm draped over her shoulder, his hand gently pressing hers on the door. With no option to turn around and the risk of tumbling into the kitchen if she opened the door, she stayed motionless, feeling his breath against her cheek. The scent of fresh sandalwood soap clung to him.

'What do you want from me?' she whispered, gripping the door handle.

'You. All of you,' he whispered back.

The hairs on Alice's neck sent warning signals to her body, a shiver of want lurched forward. She became overwhelmed, with longing, and with the annoyance she felt about him turning up and playing with her emotions.

He was dangerous and could break the fragile barrier she had put in place. Blake Hardesty had the power to strip her of her senses, to take away the family bond she had built during the course of the previous day, because she knew she would follow him to the ends of the earth. He had tied her heart to his.

Think, Alice. Clear your mind before action. Always think first.

Clara's words rang out inside her head, her message loud and clear. Alice inhaled and released the breath.

You gave him the opportunity to talk, but he ignored you. Found another woman. Think and remember, Alice.

'I can't do this; I cannot give you what you want – there is no future with me,' she said, her throat tight with tension.

'Why? Why do you say that? Because of Richard? I saw you together in London, coming out of that empty building. Is he why you left me there?' Hardy asked.

Alice held her breath, his words lunged at her chest squeezing and suppressing her reply. He *had* seen them, which meant he had followed her.

'Step back, please, let me breathe,' she said abruptly, finding the strength to push back into him in fear of what would happen next.

Blake stepped away and Alice took a second to compose herself before she turned around.

'Trust,' she said when she faced him.

He pulled a face to show he did not understand her meaning.

'There has to be trust in a relationship,' she said.

'But I have not done anything to make you distrust me. I stayed away because I thought that is what you wanted. You saw me talking to the girl who is marrying one of the crew,' he said and shoved his hands into his pockets.

'And ... you saw me talking with Richard in London,' she said slowly.

Giving a huff of a laugh, Blake shrugged his shoulders.

'I saw you kiss him,' he said. 'And then I got your note, so I figured you had made a choice. He won.'

His words stunned Alice. She stared at him. He'd followed her and drawn the wrong conclusion.

'I thought I saw you that day, but I wasn't sure,' she said. 'Why did you follow me?'

In an effort to warm his hands, Blake removed them from his pockets and gently blew on them.

'Can't we continue this conversation indoors?'

'No.' Alice shook her head, despite wanting to take her damp boots off and warm herself by the fire.

'So, this is where I will get answers? Out here in the cold fog, my emotions in tatters while you justify yourself,' he said sadly.

'Why did you follow me, Blake? Richard is not a man I would become romantically involved with. He is the brother I've never had and my mentor for my library course.'

'Yes, but—' Hardy tried to speak but Alice cut in.

'You saw us coming out of the building where I took my exam and made the assumption we were a secret couple? Really, Hardy, you think I am a girl about town?' Alice said crossing her own fingers in her pocket against the lie she had told him.

A lie which protected the SOE and Richard.

'Next you will accuse me of having an affair with your commander because Gladys asks me to deliver the odd letter to him!' she said angrily, annoyed that she had allowed herself to be followed without noticing, angry that it had been the man she loved showing distrust, and hurt that he did not know how much he meant to her.

'I followed you because I care, Alice. Bombed-out London is a frightening thing to see, and I did not want anything to happen if another bomb dropped and you were alone and scared. I waited for you to come out, and when you did, he was with you. You both looked so happy that I guessed it was more than you just having lessons with him. I walked away and when I turned around, I saw you kiss,' Blake said, a heavy sadness in his voice.

'What you saw was Richard giving me a brotherly peck on the cheek when I mentioned he was like a brother to me. You did not see *me* kiss him,' Alice countered.

'So, you really were worried about what would happen if you stayed in London with me? That was the real reason you upped and left?' Hardy asked.

Alice nodded.

'I was going to talk with you about it, but you were out, and now I know where you were, walking the streets trying to catch me out. Not trusting me. You say it was to protect me, so if that was the case why ignore my note asking to meet you. No, Blake, you have lost me. And as for the woman marrying your friend, it looked extremely cosy to me.'

Blake took a step towards her, but Alice gave her head a slight shake and he stopped.

'Please. Can we try again, Alice. I have not slept for days, and it is not all because of my job. That woman flirts with every man she sees. My friend is a fool, but a fool in love. Love makes us do crazy things,' he said, his words urging her to listen.

Alice took a moment to think. The truth was, she thought his story about following her and seeing her with Richard was believable. Thoughtful, even. She knew that if London had come under attack while they were there, she would have felt the same overwhelming sense of dread as Blake. He had walked through a strange city to protect her. She saw it in his face. A face pinched with cold and emotion.

It was time to make her feelings clear and let him know where he stood in her life.

'Come inside, then, before we both freeze. Or do you have to get back to base?' she asked, with her hand on the door handle again.

'The fog is on my side for a change,' he said.

Inside, Alice busied herself with brewing two cups of steaming coffee and slicing thick, crusty bread, on which she spread as much butter as she could, then put the bread onto a plate and placed two knives beside it. Balancing the plate and a toasting fork, she carried it into the cosy sitting room by the now crackling fire.

'Simple, but warming and filling on a cold day,' she said as she poked the fork into one of the slices of bread and held it over the flames.

'I see you have logs chopped ready,' Blake said pointing to the pile beside the fireplace.

'Ben ... the handyman here ... he keeps me well stocked,' Alice improvised, as she passed Blake a piece of grilled bread and put another slice on the fork.

She sat watching him eat and drink, his face pinking from the heat of the fire.

'What did you do yesterday?' she asked.

'Rejigged a shot-up engine,' Blake answered between bites.

'Alone? Surely the rest of your men were enjoying Christmas Day?' she said, and shuddered at the thought of him alone, cold and working on a plane because he was miserable over her.

'They did not need me to dampen their day, the English weather did that well enough. I slept a couple of hours, then went to the officers club for a drink. But honestly, I was lonely and angry at myself. I am a stubborn fool.'

His voice was flat, and Alice took a bite of her toast. There was nothing to say that would change the past. She had to focus on the future.

Once they had eaten and cleared away the dishes, they sat quietly watching the flames flicker in the grate and she felt Blakes' eyes on her. The warmth she felt was inside her heart, and when he looked over at her, Alice knew she, too, was flushed in the face, her inner thoughts fanned by the flames flitting in the fireplace. She wanted Hardy to hold her, to kiss her and make her his. She imagined them lying side by side in bed, but she still had questions and was not prepared to cave into his needs just because he arrived on her doorstep. He had not bothered with her on Christmas Day, he had sulked imagining her with Richard. She needed him to give her straight answers.

He hesitated before he spoke. 'I came here to win you back, Alice, but I realise I've let my head do the work instead of taking action,' he said.

293

Alice stared at him, waiting for more.

Blake stood up and looked down at her.

'I have nothing but respect for you, Alice. Nothing would have happened between us in London – except some fun and happiness together. My mistake was to follow you and not return to the hotel when I knew you were heading back that way. I told myself you were off somewhere with *him*.'

'Richard. His name is Richard, and he is important to me – he is my family now.'

Alice said, her voice letting him know his lack of respect for Richard was affecting her. 'I think you should go, work out your anger against Richard, trust my words are the truth and get over what you think you saw. Think about what I have told you, of what I saw when you were with that woman, and then come back this evening at six o'clock. We will have a cold meat, mash-potato supper,' she said, thinking about the food she'd brought home from Hettie's to eat whilst studying. 'Let's see if we can get our friendship back on track.'

Alice inwardly smiled. She'd borrowed what she and her aunts called the *Gladys tone*. Schoolmarmish and direct.

Dear Diary

My heart aches. I love Blake so very much, but I cannot be watched and followed. He has to learn to trust me. I must not allow my emotions to lead me down a path I cannot walk.

We are good company for one another, we both know that, and in the dark days we need the support and companionship of someone kind, and understanding. Blake has both of those qualities and many more.

I have hope in my heart again. Hope that we can find a way to restore our love, but if it means we no longer remain romantically involved, I hope we can find a way to remain friends.

Chapter Forty-Three

After Blake had left, Alice curled up on the sofa with her latest read, *Little Women*, a book whose characters had captured her attention.

Louisa May Alcott's imagination brought the story to life on each page and Alice decided she might be her favourite author. Alice saw herself in two of the characters. Writing her diary was important to her, hence the writing connection with Jo, and she considered herself quiet, shy, and disliking conflict, like Beth.

Alice promised herself a day off from studies, and hoped, as it was Boxing Day, that no messages would arrive. She knew Hettie and Hilda were spending the day with Ben and James, so she was free to please herself.

After an hour of reading, Alice drew a warm bath and enjoyed the floral fragrance of the dried lavender bags she had made during the summer. She took the time to wash and style her hair before selecting a navy-blue wool dress and thigh-length wool socks, ensuring both warmth and style. Looking around, a deep sense of comfort and contentment overwhelmed Alice. It was as if she had finally found her place of belonging.

Alice now wondered if all she really wanted was a simple life. Experiencing the joys of family life on Christmas Day, her dreams of thrilling adventures seemed to have diminished.

———

Alice knew Blake had arrived when she heard Teddy's excited bark and the sound of him scratching at the door to be let out. Despite having watched the clock for the past half hour, she couldn't help but glance at it one more time. Six o'clock. Her smile grew wider as, knowing how busy and frantic things were on the base, Hardy had shown her how much he valued the opportunity to renew their friendship and start afresh by arriving right on time.

Blake's firm knock on the door caused Teddy to spin in circles chasing his tail. Alice swiftly stepped in, gently guiding him to the side and holding onto his collar. She carefully directed him towards the door, making sure he didn't accidentally collide with her visitor.

Easing the door open, she was met with the sight of Blake's smiling face and her heart bounced as wild as Teddy around the kitchen floor.

'Nice to know someone is happy to see me,' he said, looking over at the bouncing dog.

'We both are,' Alice said, urging him to come in quickly. 'The fog tonight is freezing everything it finds.'

As Blake brushed past her he left a brief kiss on her cheek, and Alice touched the place where his lips had left their warmth.

After they had eaten, Blake excused himself and went to his coat pocket. He returned with a small package and held it out to her.

'I bought this in London. I might be helping to fight the enemy, but I was not brave enough to bring it to you yesterday. Happy Holidays, Alice,' he said with a shy grin.

Alice looked down at the neatly tied gift and then back up at him.

'Open it,' he said with eager impatience.

Alice smiled and undid the cream ribbon, then the flimsy piece of cloth wrapping the gift box. She lifted the lid and inside nestled a gold necklace with a book charm attached. She lifted it out and laid it into the palm of her hand.

'It opens … see…' Hardy lifted the small side latch to reveal a small, folded piece of paper inside.

Alice placed the necklace in Blake's palm and lifted out the piece of paper, slowly unfolding it; she could barely breathe with the anticipation of what it might say.

She looked at the words printed in what looked like Blake's best handwriting.

Alice Carmichael. Will You Be My Girl?

Her eyes filled with misty tears. It was a distraction from her earlier decision to want a simpler life. She could not hurt him, but she needed to explain herself.

'Blake, this is beautiful. Thank you, I adore it, but—'

He put up his hand.

'But you just want to be friends. Okay. It's okay, I get the picture,' he said his voice low, and heavy with resignation.

Alice sighed.

'You are doing it again. Assuming and then getting the wrong picture. *Please*, just listen to my concerns about agreeing to be your girl.'

She took the locket from him and placed the piece of paper inside, clicking the book shut.

'Sit down and hear me out. I need you to understand, Blake; really understand.'

He did as she asked, and she noticed he wiped his palms

across the thigh of his trousers more than once. His nerves were evident. She guessed he also knew that the two of them were on a precipice and could fall at any moment.

'When I met with Richard, we chatted about my life with Hettie and Hilda. They are not my real aunts, they unofficially adopted me when I walked here from Great Yarmouth looking for my only surviving relative – a great-aunt, from whom, according to Hilda, I had a lucky escape, because she had died, unbeknownst to me. Hettie told me she was a vindictive woman whom nobody had liked. So, I had lost the last of my family. I didn't tell you, but I am an orphan. I do not even know my true birth date; an orphanage created it for me by guess work.' Alice paused to hear Blake take a deep breath then release it, allowing her to continue.

'Slowly, the people around me now have become family. They have encouraged me to better myself, trusted me, fed me, and clothed me. I pay my way now and am fortunate to live in this cottage. I have a bright future as a librarian, which is my dream – that, or owning a bookshop, as you know. Yesterday, on Christmas Day, I made a promise to myself to visit Canada and America when funds were available, and the war was well and truly over.'

Blake gave a nod. 'I am so sorry, Alice, for all your losses.'

She smiled her acknowledgement but drew a breath to carry on with what she needed to say.

'But, I also made another decision. I have never had a true home in England, not one where I have felt settled, and I want to find my place in my own country before I travel to another. I want to be part of rebuilding Great Britain when the time comes.'

Blake's deep sigh and the way he ran his fingers through his hair told Alice he understood what she was about to say.

'Which means that if I am your girl, it is for the duration of the war only. I am not ready, nor will I be until I am at least thirty, to leave my new family. Some would call me foolish, but they have not been in my shoes.'

The room fell into a heavy silence apart from the crackle and spit of the fire. Alice's gaze was fixated on the necklace in her hand. As he shifted in his seat, Blake's eyes met hers, reflecting both his hurt and his respect for her. Alice knew she was right in telling him she was not ready to leave her life in Norfolk for him.

'Say something,' she pleaded, knowing this could possibly be the last time they spent in one another's company.

'I hear you, Alice,' he said. 'I understand.'

She gave him a soft smile of thanks.

'I'd rather have you in my life as a friend than not at all,' Blake said. 'I can't pretend I don't want more, that my feelings aren't stronger than friendship. But I care about you and what you want. If this is it, then I respect that.' He smiled sadly. 'Besides, I have the love of a mother with a heart so big it would explode if I never returned. I have roots tough and buried in the soil of my home.'

Alice knew what he said was true, and understood his struggle was much like her own.

Blake rose from his seat.

'Need me to put your necklace on?' he said.

She nodded in response, a bittersweet feeling washing over her. A blend of happiness and a hint of sadness tingled through her body. Although Blake had accepted their friendship, her words had caused him pain.

Taking a moment to compose herself, she closed her eyes and positioned her hair, enabling him to secure the necklace, feeling the warmth of his touch. Once the war ended and he returned home, she would have to move on without Blake. It would be awful, but if she went with him to America, she would make his life there a miserable one because she would never be happy being so far from the life and the people she loved in England.

'We can see out the war as friends,' Blake said. 'And I promise you now, you will be the only girl I will dance with and ask to walk with me.'

When his hands had arranged her hair and he was no longer touching her, it took everything Alice had to control her emotions as she turned to face him.

'Blake, if you meet someone else…'

He put his finger gently on her lips and shook his head.

Alice knew they had said all they could to one another before it became too sad for them to enjoy one another's company.

'I have a present for you, too,' she said. 'I think Richard left a bottle or two of whisky in the sideboard. Help yourself to a drink. I will be right back.'

When she returned to the room Hardy looked more relaxed, sipping whisky from a glass.

She held out her gift.

'I was going to bring it down to you yesterday, but then I lost the nerve. Happy Christmas, Blake.'

It made her smile the way he tugged eagerly like a child at the twine and paper to reveal his present.

'Of course, it is a book that much is obvious,' she said. 'It is one I spotted through the window of the bookshop we looked at in London, and on my way back to the train I just knew it was the perfect gift for you. Well, I hope it is.'

Hardy studied the book front and back then smiled at her.

'*West With the Night* by Beryl Markham. I know of her flying achievements, but nothing about her life in Kenya. Flying the Atlantic solo – incredible. I look forward to reading this, thank you.'

Blake lifted the cover, read her inscription, and smiled.

With my love and respect to Blake Hardesty, Christmas, 1943.
An American in Great Britain.

It is people like you who give others the courage to trust flying high
again during these dark days of war. You are my kind of hero.
Alice x

'This is special. Something I will always treasure,' he said.

'And I mean it. You have my love and respect, always,' Alice said.

Blake folded her in his arms, and they stood together until he moved away.

'I'm going now, but I will be back. Come and see me as you used to, we all need sunshine on a miserable day,' he said pulling on his coat.

'True enough. And yes, I will come and see you soon,' Alice replied.

After Blake had left, Alice encouraged Teddy outside and settled him for the night. Once in bed she allowed herself the tears which she had held back, not wanting Blake to see them for fear her resolve would flounder.

Dear Diary

Inside I have a pain. A knot of pain refusing to move. I think it is my love for Blake. It has not died, it never will; it has simply found a different heart pocket. A place inside of me where I can feel loved when his physical embrace is no longer available.

I need to learn to breathe and live a life without him at my side, but right now I am not sure I am strong enough to do that. My heart is broken; shattered. We made choices and the right ones. We have to live with the consequences now, and the promises we have made to ourselves. We cannot deny ourselves happiness outside of the love we feel for one another. This is the biggest test of my life. How to survive lost love.

The war brought Blake to me, and it will divide us when it is over. Our romantic love is at an end, but we still have friendship. If he finds someone new to share his life in America, I truly hope he will never forget the friend he had in me. I will never replace Blake Hardesty. Never.

Chapter Forty-Four

A few days after Alice turned eighteen, Ben visited with a gift of six eggs, three rashers of bacon, a small loaf of bread, and a small leather handbag with green trimming to match her coat.

'B'lated birthday wishes,' he said. 'Bag mightn't be t'your liking, not brand new, but I thought of yewer Christmas coat.'

Touched, Alice held the bag against her new coat.

'Perfect choice. Thank you so much, Ben. It is very thoughtful of you and an unexpected surprise. I adore it, and the food will keep me going for days,' she said.

'These for you 'n all,' Ben said, handing her several messages for her runners.

'Your poor birds must be freezing in this weather,' she said, taking the messages from him.

'Do me proud, they do. Work for king and country,' Ben replied.

'They deserve a medal. My guess the recent night attacks on London again have stirred things up here, which is why we have so many messages at once. Got time for a hot drink?' Alice asked.

Ben gave a nod. 'Not for me, girl, ta. That aunt o' yours will have me guts for garters if I am late. We are taking a trip to Diss. 'Hilda says I will enjoy meself.' He gave a hearty belly laugh, which triggered Alice into laughing, too.

'You are a brave man, Ben. Give Hilda my love.'

'I see you and that Blake fella are walking out again,' he said with wink.

'We keep each other company when we are free. We cannot be anything else but friends. I won't leave Norfolk when he returns to America. My new family and home are too important to me,' she said.

Ben tapped the side of his nose. 'Love'll decide for you, girl. It has decided I am going shopping in Diss today.'

Alice laughed. 'It is wonderful how you two have found one another. I envy you because there are no obstacles in your way.'

'Only time. We might not have a lot of that left. Lucky that Hettie made us both see sense.'

Alice watched Ben walk away. Hilda had smartened him up, and he looked taller and definitely much happier.

She closed the door and stood pondering Ben's wise words for a while. He had reminded her of how fragile life was, and that time was a gift. Any time spent with Blake was a blessing. Was she wasting it with stubborn ideas of what could not happen instead of enjoying what could?

While she organised the messages into envelopes and code system, she thought about the contents of some of them. So many raids and attacks were being organised and the people around her, aside from the select few, knew nothing about them. She knew that on the twenty-second of the month Operation Shingle would commence. Allied troops would land on the beaches of Anzio in Italy. Fifty-thousand men defending peace, and she could not tell a soul. Her heart often felt heavy with the burden of secret mission knowledge, even though it was a burden she was willing to carry.

Not wanting to think about what was about to take place and bring about a downcast mood, Alice concentrated on her personal mission of the day.

Aware of her damp hair and the absence of her usual curls, she opted to give it a brisk shake and run her fingers through it, fashioning a casual style before entering the airbase.

As she approached, she could make out figures of men moving about through the misty haze outside the main hangars. A sudden, blaring siren filled the air, instantly transforming the place into a bustling hub of activity. Men dashed from every corner, each fulfilling their contribution towards the successful take-off of the planes to protect those who couldn't take to the skies.

Alice's body stiffened, her limbs all at once weighed down by an overwhelming heaviness as she surveyed her surroundings in a daze. She desperately tried to regain some composure as the siren continued to wail, its shrill tone piercing the air, while in the distance, the deep rumble of planes filled the sky.

But Alice felt disoriented, her mind spinning in circles as she struggled to choose a direction until finally gaining focus. Recalling her small hut on the edge of the boundary, she sprinted towards it, navigating through the chaotic paths filled with the loud honking of jeeps and trucks that were converging at the end of the airfield. As the engines fired up and shouts of instruction and encouragement echoed around her, Alice remained steadfast in her decision to not stop and watch the planes leave the ground, nor witness a dogfight overhead. She had seen and felt the weight of death and destruction first-hand. Determined to reach safety, she ran with all her might, the wet mud splattering onto her shoes and clinging to her legs.

Inside the hut with its tired furniture, Alice sank down on a chair to catch her breath. Engines droned and roared overhead, and the ground rumbled beneath her feet. She trembled and clasped her arms around her body, as the air erupted with defensive fire, creating a chorus of pinging sounds that echoed through the area. To her relief, the battle gradually shifted away.

'Poor Teddy, how frightened you must be,' she whispered when she realised the overhead gunfire was near the cottage, and the fear of losing another roof over her head brought about a sensation of nausea.

'Keep Hettie and Hilda safe!' she said aloud. 'Stay safe, Blake, my love.'

When it fell quiet and Alice assumed it was safe to come out, she decided it was best to return home, as Blake would be occupied, with the base in such disarray.

She carefully made her way back to the cottage, and her eyes caught sight of a figure leaning over the gate, appearing to be out of breath, their attention fully focused on the fields in the opposite direction. Alice's heart lurched.

It was Blake. Despite his duty, he had abandoned his post and come to her.

Though her legs felt on the verge of collapse, Alice ran, pushing herself to go faster. Her exasperation grew with the muddy dips, but with determination she made her way over the piles of earth that the tractor had sculpted. With no regard for the boundaries of the field, she fearlessly cut through its middle, well aware that she was out in the open and vulnerable, but also aware that time was precious. The enemy planes could return at any moment.

'Blake! Blake, over here!' she called, struggling to keep her balance as she moved.

He was running towards her, a sense of urgency and longing in his expression, his arms outstretched to embrace her.

'I saw the direction of the gun fire and planes, and knew, just knew it was over your place,' he said as he hugged her.

'I was at the base. I came to see you,' she said doing her best to breathe and talk at the same time, partly due to the anxious walk home and partly down to the bear hug Blake was giving her. 'You need to get back, I am fine now. I'm going to check on Teddy, he will be so frightened.'

'No way am I letting you go alone,' he said. 'I'm coming with you.'

Inside the cottage, Teddy was beside himself with excitement and the need to rush outside and investigate. Alice and Blake watched him sniff his way around the garden.

'He seems happy enough,' Alice said and turned to go back inside.

She picked up a painting that had fallen on the floor due to the vibrations.

'Do you want me to check for more damage?' Blake asked.

'Thank you,' she said. 'I'll make us a drink.'

Busying herself with the kettle and Teddy's food, when Blake came back into the kitchen Alice could not turn around and look at him. Her eyes were stinging with salty tears. She made a discreet move of her arm to wipe them away, when he gently took hold of her elbow and turned her around.

'Alice. You've had a shock, honey. Sit down,' he said, and Alice looked into his tired eyes, at his grimy face and gentle smile.

The feelings flooding inside of her were drowning out her logical thoughts, the ones she had told herself day after day. She and Blake could not be a couple, her place was here in Norfolk, and yet here he was watching over her, worrying about her. His first thought had been of her, he'd come to find her. Her heart ached with the agony of it all, and it took all of her strength to not reach up and kiss him.

'Really. I'm fine now,' she said instead. 'Go back to your men, and thank you for worrying about me.'

'I will never stop worrying about you. Are you working today?' he asked.

Alice nodded. 'I am not opening until two o'clock today. It's cleaning morning. Once a month I work a half day.'

Blake moved away and went to the kettle which was now whistling merrily on the stove.

'Then, as you Brits say, there's always time for tea.' To Alice's surprise he reached out and put on her apron, prepared the teapot, and passed her over the cups and saucers, then laid a cloth over his arm butler style. Alice burst out laughing at his antics.

'Would Madam care for a cuppa?' he asked putting on an English accent and placing the teapot onto the table.

For an hour Hardy entertained her, making her laugh, and he reassured her his crew knew where he was, and he would leave once he could be sure she was over the shock of the attack.

While he talked, Alice's mind went back to their situation: a series of heart-wrenching dilemmas.

Could she really manage to keep Blake at arm's length? Should she simply surrender to her feelings and let their romance bloom? And if the latter, was she brave enough to go with him to America when the time was right for them both?

Their love for one another was undeniable. It was evident that he cared deeply for her by his actions. By binding herself to Hettie and Hilda out of gratitude, was she denying herself the right to happiness? The thought of a life without Blake seemed overwhelming. Her feelings for him were so intense, it was hard to imagine finding that again. He was the missing piece of her puzzle, and without him, her life would always feel unfinished.

Alice felt her chest constrict. There was only one choice to make.

She turned to Blake, her face serious and determined. She also had to make him aware of the consequences her decision would have on their shared future.

'Blake, if I leave a key under the backdoor mat when I am at the library, please come and use the bathroom and rest here – make the spare room yours,' she said.

He grinned. 'Okay, hint taken. I'll make use of your washroom for sure, this greasy look has to go and resting quietly on a soft bed is an offer I can't refuse. Thank you, Alice.'

'If you find you don't need to return to base you can eat with me when I get home. And if you fall asleep and stay the night, that's okay, too,' she said, suddenly feeling shy at her bold offer. 'But only if you want to, please don't think I expect it of you.'

Her cheeks stung with the blush as Blake's eyes held her gaze. He understood her meaning.

'We will go with the bath and meal first. Sleeping over might prove difficult, but it is good to know there is a bed here for me, thank you,' he said, then winked at her and gave a shy grin. 'The nights can be cold. Time in your warm arms is something I dream about.'

Alice walked over to him and put her arms around him.

'Slow and steady,' she whispered.

He kissed her. A kiss sealing a pact of togetherness, and Alice responded. She could no longer deny her love for him.

Dear Diary

I cannot deny the love between Blake and I.
With bombs dropping and the war intensifying, this
might be the only love I will experience. I cannot
write any more words to express my feelings

towards him. I am eighteen years old and feel I have led the life of a woman much older. I am happy at the moment. If the war ends tomorrow, my happiness will be called to question. It will be the day our future together will be torn apart.

Chapter Forty-Five

April 1944

'Keep still,' Hettie said as she pushed a pin through Hilda's hat.

'All this fuss. Wedding finery and food,' Hilda grumbled.

Alice laughed as she checked her victory roll in the mirror and tucked the odd stray hair back into place.

'Your turn, Hettie,' she said and lifted a pearl hatpin from its box. She had bought both the sisters one each.

'You both look lovely. Beautiful,' she said as she made them stand side by side.

Hilda looked a changed woman in her rust-coloured two-piece corduroy skirt suit, adorned with gold buttons. She had her hair tied into a neat bun, complemented by a stylish hat adorned with a rust-coloured fabric flower, gracefully tucked to one side of her head. At first, she'd firmly rejected the idea of wearing a hat, but eventually gave in to Alice's persistent pleas.

Hettie's outfit was a sophisticated two-piece red-tweed suit, accompanied by a red felt hat that was adorned with a lovely bow at the back and a delicate lace trim at the front. Framing her face, her greying curls gently brushed against the rim, adding elegance to her appearance. Both women wore their best flat black shoes, the glossy shine reflecting Ben's meticulous polishing.

With a scalloped collar, Alice's vibrant tomato-red two-piece skirt suit made a bold and stylish statement, her navy shoes and gloves perfectly complementing the ensemble. On her head, she wore a wide-brimmed halo-style hat in navy, adorned with a velvet ribbon and bow.

'You look wonderful, Alice. What a day!' Hettie said, tucking a handkerchief into the small pocket of her skirt.

Hilda gave a huff. 'Roll on when I can take this thing off,' she said touching her hat.

'Stop grumbling, you will spoil the day,' Hettie reprimanded her sister, and tapped Hilda's hand away from her hat.

'Are we ready, ladies?' Alice asked as she picked up two small flower posies and handed them to Hettie and Hilda.

'As ready as we will ever be. Here goes,' Hettie said, and led the way downstairs, with Hilda and Alice following her into the front room, where a table was covered in white tablecloths and a vase of daffodils and tulips.

The three women stood side by side waiting for the honking of a car horn. Once heard they all made their way out to the front, where Richard sat in a car borrowed from a friend.

He jumped out and helped each one of them inside.

'I must say you all look splendid!' he said and jumped back into the driver's seat. 'Saint Leonard's, here we come.'

When they arrived outside the tiny church of Billingford, a fleeting streak of sunshine danced across the rooftop, casting a warm glow on the hilltop perch that overlooked the picturesque

Waveney valley. As she took a deep breath, Alice felt the freshness of the air, intertwined with a subtle, comforting warmth. A soft breeze that blew across it gently rippled the grass, the sound of surrounding birdsong triggering a realisation of where authors found their inspiration for the serene moments they depicted in their books.

'It's time,' she whispered to her two aunts and linked her arms through theirs.

The three of them walked down the aisle, their footsteps echoing through the church. James's friend Edward, and Richard, had both driven the main wedding party and sat behind James's mother. A few local friends were invited, and everyone eagerly looked ahead, waiting for the ceremony to begin.

Kissing Hettie and Hilda on the cheek, Alice settled herself into the pew next to Blake, who returned the gesture with a kiss on her cheek.

Nervousness was clear in the expressions of both Ben and James. However, it was Ben who caught everyone's attention with his sharp attire, exuding confidence in his suit. When someone made a joke about them having a double wedding after both men had proposed to Hilda and Hettie at more or less the same time, they all agreed it would be a delightful and memorable experience for them.

Alice recalled the day Hilda had announced her engagement to Ben when they had arrived home from their trip to Diss. Apparently he'd approached the subject of marriage and companionship after the war, and as they'd sheltered from a sudden flurry of hail stones, Hilda had agreed they were a good match.

James's proposal to Hettie was the trigger for the early wedding. After newly retiring from the army, he'd also inherited a pleasant house in Whitby, near to the North Yorkshire moors. Although Hettie was hesitant at first, her love for James was stronger than she realised and the thought of him no longer fighting in the war and living so far away upset her. Alice and Hilda encouraged her to forget her loyalties to them, and think about herself for once. She was still going to be in England. A train journey away.

Hilda and Ben then purchased Hettie's house and Richard reassured them all that Alice would always have a secure home in his cottage. Hilda suggested that Ben give up his small home, but he, equally stubborn as her, refused, claiming that his pigeons were settled, but promised he would consider the option after the war. Only Alice and Richard knew his true reason. His pigeons knew their way home with vital information and to train them again would disrupt the process and create havoc for the secret service. He told Hilda he would visit his pigeons every day, three times a day and if that did not suit her marriage plans, she could forget the whole idea. He said it in a teasing way, but Alice could hear the heavy truth behind it.

The vows and the end of ceremony moved Alice to tears and Blake held her hand, giving it a comforting squeeze.

After the flurry of throwing flower petals at the newlyweds and driving back to what was now Hilda and Ben's house for the wedding feasts, Hilda and Hettie tearfully said their goodbyes.

Alice lingered discreetly in the background, listening to their voices filled with hope and optimism as they spoke about their reunion in the summer. When Hilda's eyes filled with tears, Ben acted swiftly and produced a handkerchief from his pocket, using it to tenderly wipe them away.

In that precise moment, it became clear to Alice that she no longer had to concern herself with the worries of her aunts and could finally embrace the freedom to live life on her own terms.

Then, with a heavy heart, it was Alice's turn to say her farewell, her voice trembling as she tried to find the right words.

'Be happy, Hettie, and do not worry about me. I will come and see you when I can. Richard has promised to run the library for a week in the summer, so I will plan a visit during that time. I love you, Hettie, as much as any child loves a mother. Thank you for taking me in and showing me life can be good,' she said, hugging Hettie close.

'And I love you, Alice,' said Hettie. She then leaned closer and whispered, 'Take my advice and listen to your heart, not your head. I haven't felt this happy in years, and today I feel alive and full of joy. You are not a foolish girl and I know you will make the right choices in life.'

As Hettie and James set off for their new life in Whitby, the guests waved goodbye and Alice buried her face in Blake's shoulder, tears streaming down her cheeks. As he gently stroked her hair, he whispered comforting words, urging her to find joy in Hettie's and James's happiness.

'It must be tough, but Hilda is still around to turn to, sure she is a bit on the blunt side, but she loves you and wants what is best for you. Don't cry, sweetheart,' he said and Alice let his words soothe her. Once her tears had subsided she dried her eyes and kissed his cheek.

'Thank you for coming today. It meant a lot to me and my aunts. Their wedding cake was a thoughtful gift, and so beautiful. Not a cardboard layer in sight.'

Blake smiled. 'It helps to have an old school friend as cook on base; I called in a favour,' he said

'I'm so glad my aunts found love later in life,' Alice said. 'They're wise not to spend their time deliberating.'

'They sure are,' said Blake, his eyes shining.

With the evening winding down, the guests left one by one, while Alice and Blake stayed behind to ensure the table was tidy and the dishes cleared. They gathered up the leftovers, packing some treats for Teddy, and began their journey back to Alice's.

Once home, Alice slipped upstairs to remove her clothing and brushed her hair free from its pins. Wearing her hair loose to her shoulders, she returned downstairs in a simple floral dress.

Hardy expressed his appreciation with a wolf-whistle.

'You're such a flatterer,' Alice replied with a playful giggle.

With a relaxed posture on the sofa, he gently patted his knee, invitingly. 'Why don't you come and sit with me?'

For a moment, Alice hesitated before remembering Hettie's advice to listen to her heart.

As she nestled herself into his lap, he gently wrapped his arms around her waist, pulling her closer to him and planting a tender kiss on her lips.

They shared a few intense minutes, holding onto each other tightly, before finally breaking apart and meeting each other's gaze.

'I'm not a man of many words, Alice, but I want you to know you are a special girl. The day I walked into that café was the luckiest day of my life, and regardless of what others may say, I firmly believe that it was fate that brought us together. We have tried fighting this dang love thing, but it is a losing battle. I am all in – head, tails, I am in love with you.'

As Alice leaned her head on his shoulder, she could feel the comforting rhythm of his heartbeat and the profound impact of his words seeping into her very being.

'And I love you, too, Blake. I cannot imagine my life without you in it, and that scares me.'

She felt the subtle tightness in his shoulder.

'I understand. I face danger every day, but I never think about it, if I am honest. I do know that I would worry day and night about whether I would see you again. So, I cannot tell you not to be scared, but believe me when I say I want a future with you. I will not play hero and jump inside burning planes with bombs still inside. And I won't let you down. I truly promise,' he said, his voice firm with conviction.

And Alice knew he meant every word.

———————

Dear Diary

What a wonderful day. A double wedding and time spent with Blake. The wedding made us realise we could not fight our love. Hettie and James, Hilda and Ben, they tried fighting their feelings for one another but love eventually overcame all obstacles. Hardy and I will take each day as it comes. We renewed our romance. Promises were made.

Last night was a special one. We held one another in the darkness and fell asleep content in the knowledge that we will overcome our own obstacles when and if they arise.

Chapter Forty-Six

O n the hour, runners would arrive and depart while Alice struggled to catch her breath amidst their constant flow, and that of the regular visitors to the library.

Her heart raced as she watched a distracted runner fumble with a cigarette, book in hand, outside the window. A local woman bent down and picked up a brown envelope that Alice recognised from inside the book. The woman handed it to the runner.

Alice discreetly made her way to the window and observed as the woman walked away. Alice tapped on the glass with her fingers, a frown on her face as she looked disapprovingly at the runner. He had the good grace to look embarrassed. She watched as he put the envelope inside his jacket pocket, the first thing he should have done before lighting the cigarette, as per his training.

Alice made a note of the incident and a mental note to keep a watch on him when he next visited. Today they had averted a problem, and as a regular runner he was reliable. Alice knew his message was of the utmost importance and related to a mission set for the sixth of June – two months away. In the hands of the wrong people it could have proved disastrous. Richard would have her report on the runner the next time he returned from London. Major concerns were reported by courier if Richard was not home. Everything moved in secret and with deep-seated trust.

Dear Diary

June 6th, 1944 – an important day today. Words cannot explain what this means to me. Me, a small cog in a very large wheel.

At three o'clock this morning I heard them leave. The heroes both on the ground and in the air will have a long day ahead. Everything has led to this moment.

The summer was a whirlwind of activity for Alice, Ben, the pigeons, and runners, but amidst the chaos, Alice found time for herself.

Once she had come back from seeing Hettie and James, who were both in good health and in high spirits, Blake was waiting for her at the train station.

Their overwhelming workload and her upcoming trip to Whitby had kept them apart for a gruelling five weeks, heightening their longing for time together. Alice could always tell when he had used the bath and had a sleep, as she would find small love notes waiting on the table, along with the occasional gift of nylons or a bar of chocolate.

In that moment, as Alice felt the softness of his lips against hers, she knew she wanted Blake to stay the night. The passion between them was undeniable.

As they chatted, Blake revealed more of his dreams, expressing a strong desire to pursue a career in car mechanics. He also confessed his admiration for the air force, mentioning that he had at one point contemplated extending his service in the USAAF.

Filled with anticipation for what lay ahead, their discussions of a future together and their intimate caresses pushed them to cross the threshold into the uncharted territory of making love. Blake proved to be a gentle lover. His touch was tender and considerate.

Alice had always expected her first time to be with Blake on their wedding night, but that evening she learned to let go of that expectation and live in the present, savouring each day as it unfolded.

'Are you ready yet?' Blake called up to Alice as he let himself in through the backdoor of her home.

'Coming!' she called out. 'Just a minute.'

She carefully applied a fresh coat of lipstick, taking her time to ensure it was perfect, and then she stood in front of the mirror to admire her reflection. The red spotted dress that she had brought back from Hettie was a perfect fit, accentuating her curves beautifully, and as she walked, the skirt elegantly flowed around her. She felt like she could dance all night long, especially with her navy heels that added an extra spring to her steps, while her hair bounced with every move, managing to stay perfectly in place. Not only had she mastered the art of the victory roll, but she had also dedicated herself to learning numerous other creative styles. This part up with side victory rolls and long curled style was her favourite. Before rushing downstairs, she delicately dabbed a few drops of perfume on her wrists and neck, leaving a trail of sweet fragrance.

'Ta-da!' She twirled around in her polka-dot dress, her voice filled with excitement as she exclaimed, 'I love this dress!'

With wide eyes, Blake stood looking in awe, and Alice could see the appreciation on his face.

'Huh, looks okay, I guess,' he teased, a mischievous grin on his face.

Alice lightly tapped his arm as a reprimand.

'Let's go, chauffeur, the show is about to start,' she exclaimed, feeling a sense of excitement in the air.

Blake had borrowed one of the air force jeeps to pick her up and he helped her into her seat.

As they arrived at the base, the sound of chatter and the sight of endless lines of people waiting to enter the largest hangar filled the air. Blake grabbed her hand, his grip strong and reassuring.

'Follow me,' he instructed, weaving through the queue and leading her to the front of the hangar.

'Evening, sir,' one of the serviceman said at the entrance to the hangar, and he saluted Blake, stepping to one side to let Blake and Alice through.

Alice stood, breathless with excitement, taking in the stage set at the back and marvelling at the complete transformation of a place she had only seen as a workshop a few weeks ago.

Blake handed her a refreshing drink, cold to the touch. She took a sip of the gin and orange, savouring the zesty and aromatic flavours. During their evenings at the local pub, he had gradually introduced her to a variety of alcoholic beverages, but it was gin that had most captured her tastebuds.

'Bottom's up!' she said and clinked her glass against his.

'Excited?' Hardy asked.

'About seeing the Glenn Miller Orchestra playing live? Not at all,' Alice replied with a playfully straight face.

The hangar was teeming with a lively crowd, the atmosphere electric with the buzz of conversation. As Glenn Miller made his grand entrance and his band's music echoed throughout, the space miraculously opened up for dancing, and Alice eagerly joined in.

Apparently, she loved dancing after all!

During an exhausting but exhilarating evening, Blake swept Alice off her feet, and they swayed in one another's arms to the melody of 'Moonlight Serenade' – Alice's favourite. Even though she was new to dance, Blake was such a skilled partner that she quickly moved effortlessly to each step. As the beautiful music filled the air, her heart swelled with an overwhelming sense of love, so powerful that she felt an irresistible urge to proclaim it to the entire world. Instead, she absorbed each tender vibration and allowed the song to filter into her soul, where she tucked it there as one of her most precious moments.

When the evening had finished, they climbed into the jeep and Alice looked up at the stars. The September sky was navy-blue and stars flicked through the thin veil of cloud.

'What an evening. It was wonderful, thank you, Blake,' she said and leaned over to kiss his cheek.

'One of the best,' he replied. 'Brilliant music and a beautiful girl, what more could a guy want in life?'

Dear Diary

Making love with Blake is more than I ever imagined. He sparks a need inside of me and fulfils it every time. This is an extension of our love, not just a part of it, there is more to us than moments beneath the eiderdown, but I treasure our intimate times.

Glenn Miller! What an experience, what a musician. My ears are still ringing. Exhilarating. A night I will always remember.

Chapter Forty-Seven

January 1945

Another New Year and another birthday soon came around for Alice, but she did not feel excessively thrilled.

The night she'd spent with Blake, immersed in the enchanting melodies of Glenn Miller, became an even more extraordinary experience when they realised how fortunate they were to witness his live performance.

The announcement of the musician's death in December had cast Alice into a shadow of sorrow and misery. She had hoped that by the time she turned nineteen, the war would finally be over, allowing her to find more balance in her life and focus on other aspects instead of constantly worrying about ration books and the ongoing conflict. Despite receiving messages showing Germany's struggles, Alice remained sceptical and had her doubts.

On the evening of her birthday, Blake arrived with a large parcel, his face beaming like a child at Christmas.

'What in the world do you have there?' Alice asked as Hardy struggled against the excited Teddy and the back door.

'Wait and see, honey, wait and see!' With a loud and cheerful voice, Blake's excitement was clear as he carefully placed the parcel onto the table. He took a step back to allow her to unwrap and fold the paper. Once she'd finished, he watched her stand there, gazing at the box before her.

Hardy had brought Alice a gramophone player.

'For me?' she asked, overwhelmed.

'And this.' He handed her a slim package.

Alice unwrapped it with care, excited to discover a recording of 'Moonlight Serenade' nestled inside.

'Oh, Blake,' she exclaimed, her voice tinged with a mixture of surprise and delight. How thoughtful! '

She walked over to him and pressed her lips against his, giving him the kiss he deserved.

'Thank you, my love,' she said with a smile.

'Let's play it,' Blake said. 'Come on.'

'How does it work,' she said clapping her hands, watching as Blake placed the record onto the turntable and positioned the needle arm.

In a minute, the room filled with a treasured memory, and they danced together, remembering that special evening in their lives.

'I cannot believe I saw Glenn Miller play live and now he has gone. Life is so unfair,' Alice said once the music had finished.

'Sure is,' Blake said. 'And it can be beautiful, too.'

Alice's mood shifted again at his words. He had this way of lifting her spirits in a second.

'I have another one for you,' Blake said. 'Go sit down and I will put it on.' He pointed to the sofa. Curious, Alice did as he asked.

As she sat waiting, suddenly Glenn Miller's voice rang out loud and clear, offering a message to the Allied forces, hoping they would enjoy the V-Discs made especially for them. Then a piece of music played, and Alice appreciated the poignant moment. After it finished Hardy placed another record on the turntable, and this time it was upbeat. The singer was female by the name of Bea Wain. First she sang, 'Put Your Arms Around Me, Honey' and then 'Comin' In On a Wing and A Prayer'.

'I thought they were appropriate to us,' Blake said shyly, and Alice could see he was unsure of the gifts he had given her.

'They are, they mean something special. I love them all, Blake. How could I not, what wonderful gifts!' she exclaimed.

Dear Diary

Today, Blake brought me a gift so personal to us both, honouring a special time in our lives. I have found myself a truly kind and thoughtful man. However, I am still concerned about after the war. We are winning the battle alongside our allies, and for me, it is bringing about my own internal battle once again. I cannot leave England. Great Britain needs its people to breathe life back into it after the war ends.

I want my breath to reach out and help my country come alive again. To show me where to root myself and feed my energy into her soil. I know, deep down, with or without Blake, I will do this. I will become a librarian, and help those who want to educate themselves, to lose themselves inside the pages of a book, and be the outlet for authors who will write about our battles. I can't do these things in

America. I am a woman of my homeland. My hope is I will enjoy a family to also breathe new life into the heart of a country who stood solid against a tyrant.

In March, a flurry of messages passed through the library and Richard paid her a visit.

'We're winning, Alice. It won't be long before you can dismiss the runners,' he said, touching the side of his nose indicating she kept the news to herself.

By April her excitement grew with each message she sent on its way. Britain and America had Germany trapped between them and the Russians.

Reading between the lines of each secret piece of correspondence, Alice knew her duty to king and country would end in weeks not months, but could not say anything to anyone. Blake and his men were still working tirelessly, and she so wanted to tell him what she knew but she couldn't. In the meantime, whenever he visited he enjoyed her new uplifted mood.

Then the day came.

Churchill announced the end of the war at three o'clock on the eighth of May. After listening to the radio announcement and crying, along with Hilda and Ben, Alice ran to celebrate with Blake.

He picked her up and crushed her lips beneath his.

Alice's joy at being in his arms was dampened when they realised he would return to America once his orders came through. The war was over. They were at the end of their wartime friendship and romance. Their contract of love for the duration was about to expire.

As Alice turned the 'Closed' sign on the door of the library, she felt a mix of emotions – a sense of closure and sadness. The library may have only been closing for the evening, but for Alice part of it was closed for ever – her secret library. Her role as a secret messenger for the SOE had ended, leaving her with a bittersweet feeling of accomplishment and loss.

Her job as librarian would remain and she had taken on the role of a Welfare Support Officer to help people with form filling and official searches for their loved ones – dead or alive.

Richard, Ben, and she affectionately dubbed the shed *The Secret Library*, a name proudly exhibited on a newly created sign by Ben. He hammered it into position above the shed. When Blake next visited he raised an eyebrow in question when he saw the sign.

'The secret library. What is that for, and why is it over the shed? he asked, bemused.

'The sign? A gift from Ben. It is not something I can talk about – even though the war has ended,' she replied with a teasing grin, tapping the side of her nose and laughing, trying to put him off from asking more questions.

'Were you a spy, honey?' Blake asked jokingly, laughing, and Alice stopped for a few seconds to think about her answer.

'Of course I was, darling. Now, shall we listen to music or go for a walk into the village?' she replied.

Chapter Forty-Eight

The evening was one of heartbreak. Blake arrived at the cottage, his face etched with exhaustion. Alice also guessed he had shed a few private tears for his dead colleagues.

From the moment they held one another, Blake also cried for them, their final day together.

'This is it. I have to let you go, Blake. You must return to your mum, let your family nurture you back to health and build a new life—'

Blake kissed her to stop her talking. For Alice the pain behind her ribs was no longer an ache of what was about to happen, it was one of loss. She had last felt it when her grandmother failed to climb out from the rubble.

'I can't bear it, but I also know I cannot change your mind. Alice Carmichael, you have my heart. I cannot imagine a world where you are not ready to chat with me or kiss me. I am no longer a brave man. I will write. You must write back, but when the day comes and you feel you must stop, then stop. I will understand,' Blake said. He pulled her close and they made love for the last time.

It was a gentle, sweet moment with tenderness and a longing for the world to stand still. Alice lay in his arms, exhausted from the emotional upheaval they had brought upon themselves. She tried hard to forgive herself for not giving up her life in England.

'Rest and try to recover from the horrors you have lived with. I know you won't forget me, but please, with my blessing, have a wonderful life,' she whispered.

When Blake finally left, Alice waited until she stared only into a darkness arched by trees. Her legs would not move. Her heart stopped beating. Her world stopped turning.

Dear Diary

He has gone. There is nothing either of us can do but remember.

Remember the warmth of our bodies on a cold night, clinging to hope.

Remember something wonderful that came out of something dark and violent. Proof that life still can be magical, that the world might battle until death to appease the greed and anger of those who seek greatness, but the ordinary man or woman can find love amongst the debris.

Peace.

Will I ever find peace?

Will I ever settle knowing Blake Hardesty has taken my heartbeat, the lifeline to my future, with *him to America. There will never be another man in my life. Never.*

These are not fanciful words of a devastated woman, but those of someone who has enjoyed the love, the romance, let the man go, but is still tied to the memories they made. I will find my path in peacetime.

I am determined to become a guiding light to those who need help. Those who need to find a way into rebuilding their lives as I have to rebuild mine. My day-to-day love will be of a different kind. I will support my fellow man, woman, and the children facing an uncertain future.

But in my heart there is always eternal love for Blake.

From her vantage point, Alice could hear the roar of the engines as the planes took off, leaving behind trails of white smoke. Her legs buckled and she steadied herself against Hilda and Ben.

'Time to go,' said Hilda after they had stared into the empty sky, remembering darker days, and giving thanks to their American allies for their support.

'I can't move,' Alice said, her tears still falling from when Blake had given his last wave and the plane taking him back to America took off into the cloudless sky.

'One step at a time, from now on and through life,' Hilda said, with soft comfort in her voice. In Hettie's absence, Hilda had taken Alice under her wing and proven to be the kind of support she needed. Firm, but with gentle understanding.

'Grieve, and then come 'n find us, girl,' Ben said, tapping her shoulder with affection.

That evening, Alice chose to be alone in her cottage, where she cried for a life altered beyond recognition, and sobbed tears for the loss of Blake.

Gradually, the base turned into a graveyard of machinery that once hummed with activity. For Alice it became a desolate and lifeless place. She never returned to the old hut, nor walked the lanes beside the boundary.

Nothing would ever be the same again.

Slowly she found a way to cope, a reason to get up in the morning. People were desperate for help and guidance, and she threw herself into helping good causes and helpless cases.

People were reunited with loved ones, with their identity, and moved into new homes back in the towns they were evacuated from, thanks to her determination and research.

'You're an angel in disguise,' one woman told her. Alice denied being angelic, but it pleased her she had helped someone find happiness once more.

Dear Diary

Life in the library is busier than ever. Sadly, not everyone comes to select a good read.

Women come to me concerned about their jobs. The men returning home will pick up where they left off, but many of the women will lose their independence and the jobs they value. It is a sad state of affairs. Some women are widowed, and a widow's pension will not be as much as a living wage.

Today, I found a woman's husband for her. He was injured in France. She could not read or write and asked for my help. They are to be reunited. I also found a family searching for a nephew. How it made my heart sing when I learned he had been placed in an orphanage. He is due to live in a home with two cousins around his age group. A family reunited. A child released from the confines of an orphanage, forever wondering what they had done wrong.

Although I sometimes feel miserable about allowing my determination to set down roots in England, I also feel grateful for my courage. It is courage which created my job. I have my certificate. Douglas said I am due a medal, but how am I able to celebrate earning it? Instead, I am grateful to have earned the official title of librarian, and welfare support officer.

Life goes on. As does my love for my beloved Blake. My ground crew hero of Station 139, Thorpe Abbotts.

Dear Gabrielle,

Such wonderful news about the war. Although I am fully aware that some men still battle through the last stages. Horrific stories are emerging, but sometimes I have to stop myself from becoming overwhelmed with the sadness and anger that swells inside of me.

Blake is now back with his family in Ohio, and I am living a life rebuilding those of others in England. All I seem to do nowadays is read official forms from the government, which likes people to jump through hoops just to find out if they have a home to return to – many hundreds do not. I did manage to get through A Hungry Hill by Daphne du Maurier, although I confess it was probably not the right time for me to read a book with such depressing scenes. Nonetheless, I enjoyed it, and it is rare I get to read a book just a year old.

I am delighted to hear you are getting married. How wonderful. Will you visit Scotland? If you do, maybe I can plan a visit to meet you both. I do remain focused on visiting Canada one day, before I am too old to travel.

As we heave a sigh of relief at the prospect of rebuilding our lives. As always I wish you and your family my very best.

Alice.

Four months later, Alice was sitting at her desk when Gladys rushed into the library.

'Alice. Alice. A telegram for you,' she said waving the envelope in the air.

'For me?' Alice tore open the envelope.

She scanned the contents, fully aware of Gladys who stood waiting to hear her news.

'It's from Blake,' she said, unable to stop the wide smile on her face. 'He is flying into Mildenhall airbase tomorrow and wants me to meet him there. Thank goodness I have learned to drive Ben's car; I think it is too far for me to cycle.'

'Oh, I thought it was something important from Hettie,' Gladys said. 'I never realised you still kept in touch with the American.'

'Hettie is fine, I had a letter from her last week. Blake sends me news of his life and family in America. We've remained friends,' Alice replied. 'Thank you for bringing it to me, Gladys.'

She watched as on her way out of the library Gladys stopped to chat with another woman. Alice knew she was the topic of conversation by the way they turned their heads her way now and then.

After work, Alice showed Hilda her telegram.

'I hope he doesn't stir things up and confuse you again, Alice. You are doing so well, my dear. Of course, I'm certain Ben will be more than happy to lend you his car. He filled it with petrol when the airbase offered him a free tankful before they left, but he has hardly driven it since.'

Dear Diary

I will see him again! Blake is flying into Great Britain and wants to see me at a place called Mildenhall. It's not far, and I am no longer nervous on the roads. As Ben said, courage and I go hand in hand through life.

I must be sensible and not let my emotions get the better of me, but it will be wonderful to hear his news. Unless of course he is breaking the news he has met someone, but flying over to tell me is a bit dramatic. There I go again, allowing my imagination to run away with me.

I cannot express the emotions running through me at the moment. Nerves, excitement, and apprehension. But most of all, excitement. Blake is coming back to England and I will see him again!

Standing at the gates of the Mildenhall airbase, Alice felt a mix of excitement and nerves. She was wearing her beloved red polka-dot dress, a favourite of Blake's. Although she hadn't been sure whether to dress up or wear her everyday clothes, she decided that with such an exciting reunion about to take place it was worthy of a pretty-dress moment.

While she was standing and waiting, a large plane flew overhead.

'Your man is on that one,' the guard said with a friendly smile and pointed her in the direction of where she could greet Blake once he had disembarked the plane.

'My friend. Blake Hardesty. We are friends,' Alice emphasised, more to reassure herself of their relationship than the guard on duty.

Time seemed to stretch endlessly as she waited, and just when she thought she couldn't bear it any longer, she glimpsed him confidently striding across the runway and then rushing towards her.

She hesitated. Choosing to wait and see what Blake might be about to tell her, she stood with her heart pounding inside her chest and her skin tingling with excitement.

Alice barely had time to say hello when, in a display of

strength and tenderness, he effortlessly gathered her up in his arms. She blocked out the calls and whistles coming from the spectators nearby.

When Hardy set her down on the ground, it dawned on Alice that he was still in uniform, his military insignia catching her eye as she studied him. He had not received a discharge from the air force. Alice stared at him, taking in what was happening.

She traced her finger over the badges on the lapel of his fresh new uniform.

'What does this mean? Are you back for good?' she asked, unable to keep the hope out of her voice.

'I came back for you, Alice,' he said tenderly.

Alice took a moment before she spoke again. In his arms she suddenly felt whole again. Only Blake could give her the life she wanted, but with him returning to England to stir up her emotions by saying he had come back for her, made her heart ache. Once again she was going to have to turn him away. She could not leave the country she loved, not even for the man she adored. A spark of happiness in seeing him diminished, and she knew she had to approach the subject before getting too caught up in the joy of seeing him.

'Blake, we can't … I cannot come with you. We've been through this before. This is one of the happiest days I have had in a long time, but I must be realistic. I will be miserable company in America. I love you, I do, but this … seeing you here is torture.'

Blake looked at her, then stroked her cheek wiping away the tear which she had failed to hold back, before others pushed their way to the surface. She saw his own eyes moisten, then a soft creasing around them formed and she could not help but smile back at him.

'I am sorry, Blake. Truly I am, but…'

Placing his finger on her lips Blake shook his head.

'No words,' he said and folded his arms around her shoulders drawing her head to him. Alice felt his heart thump inside his chest and listened to the sound, taking it all in. The smell of his uniform, fresh air, and faint aromas of cigarettes and fuel, nothing as strong as she was used to, but it was his smell, her Blake. Enduring another farewell was not easy, but when she drove to the airbase that morning to meet him, she knew there would be one. This was another painful wrench between them, but one she was willing to suffer just to be in his arms once more. She knew other women would have called her foolish and stubborn, and also experienced loss of loved ones, but they probably knew who they were and had other family members. She did not. Her name was all she had. Everything else she was rebuilding.

'You smell beautiful. I've missed you so much, my darling,' he said, as he moved to see her face.

Alice shook her head. 'It's painful. I shouldn't have come. I need to go, Blake. I've made my decision, and you flying in again won't get me on the return flight. I have to be true to myself before I can even think about leaving England. I thought you understood.'

She looked at him, his handsome face smiling back at her. His smile beamed out love and tugged at her heart.

'That smile won't work, Blake Hardesty. Let me go, be kind to yourself.'

Before she could say another word, his lips met hers and she felt their warmth, their tenderness. Gently easing back, she touched her lips and ignored the voice which told her to go to America, to give up her fixation on loving a country over the man who had captured her heart.

'I'm going nowhere, Alice. Not without you. Who would I be without you? The war brought us together and I will not allow peacetime to drive us apart.'

In one swift movement Blake went down on one knee and held out a ring box.

'Blake, no. Please. Get up, don't do this to us. Please.'

Shaking his head, Blake grinned. 'Shhh.'

'Alice Carmichael, will you marry me? Will you become the wife of an American crewman living here, on the Mildenhall base?' he asked, his smile not quite concealing his nerves.

Alice peered into the box and saw it housed a slim gold band, on which nestled a glistening diamond.

'Does the base have a library?' she asked, teasing him.

'It does, but not a secret one. A regular one, with books and shelves … and a position for a cute English librarian,' Blake quipped back.

In that moment, Alice could not have been clearer in her mind. She took hold of his his hands and clasped them to her.

'In that case, the answer is yes,' she said. 'Yes, Blake Hardy Hardesty, I will marry you.'

Chapter Forty-Nine

September 1946

Dear Diary

In five years, I have lost a loved one, a friend, a surrogate sister and many people who gave me the time of day before flying off to defend our shores.

In five years, I have also found my strength and courage, became a postwoman, and a librarian, with a slight twist to her tale.

And in five years I have found the love of a family with no blood ties. People who accepted me as a I am, nurtured and guided me as parents would a child.

Most of all, during those five years I found

my second heartbeat. My Mr Darcy and my latest hero, Ross Poldark, rolled into one.

My Blake Hardesty. My husband.

Today, I am about to share with him my other heartbeat. The one ticking contently inside my womb.

The American line of our family tree is about to expand, and our British one is ready to rise from its roots.

Epilogue

Blake's mother embraced her as they walked through the airport doors.

'Welcome to Ohio,' she said.

Blake's father gave her a bear-like hug.

'Welcome to the family, Alice.'

For a week they enjoyed family life, then spent a week touring various places that Hardy chose to share with Alice. They left with promises to return the following year.

'They are wonderful. I have a large family now. In 1940, I had no one,' Alice said when Hardy loaded the car he had hired.

On the last day of their honeymoon he'd surprised her with tickets to Canada.

'Hilda found Gabrielle's address and she wrote to her. We are expected the day after tomorrow. You will only have two days together before we fly back to England, but I wanted you to have your dream, Alice. You deserved to have your dream,' Blake said, as he took her in his arms. 'I have mine right here.'

'Is there room for one more in your dream?' Alice asked.

Blake's loving kiss answered her question.

Acknowledgments

The moment I heard the stories of the WWII American Eighth Air Force based at Station 139 in 1943, from the knowledgeable volunteers of the 100th Bomb Group Memorial Museum, I knew I had found the place my main character spoke about inside my head.

Set in Thorpe Abbotts, Norfolk, UK, this fictional book takes inspiration from a moment when I stood alone on a deserted runway.

During my research, I explored some emotionally challenging and unsettling areas, where I delved into the lives of heroes and heroines. It is worth mentioning that despite not being mentioned in the story; I hold every one of them in high regard, and offer my utmost respect and gratitude.

Research credits and bibliography

100th Bomb Group Memorial Museum; Common Road, Dickleburgh, Diss IP21 4PH.

Sam and the 100th Bomb Group by Sam Hurry and Malcolm Finnis

McColvin, L. R.: The Public Library System of Great Britain; A Report on Its Present Condition with Proposals for Post-war Reorganization. London, Library Association, 1942.

As always I am grateful to my publisher Charlotte Ledger, the One More Chapter and HarperCollins teams, for their excitement and support whenever I produce another orphan story.

Huge thanks to my fellow author Deborah Carr, for taking the time to cheer me along despite experiencing a devastating personal loss.

To my husband and family for their patience and encouragement. My thanks to my readers for without you I am nothing.

ONE MORE CHAPTER

The author and One More Chapter would like to thank everyone who contributed to the publication of this story...

Analytics
James Brackin
Abigail Fryer
Maria Osa

Audio
Fionnuala Barrett
Ciara Briggs

Contracts
Sasha Duszynska
Lewis

Design
Lucy Bennett
Fiona Greenway
Liane Payne
Dean Russell

Digital Sales
Lydia Grainge
Hannah Lismore
Emily Scorer

Editorial
Janet Marie Adkins
Arsalan Isa
Charlotte Ledger
Jennie Rothwell
Emily Thomas

Harper360
Emily Gerbner
Jean Marie Kelly
emma sullivan
Sophia Wilhelm

International Sales
Peter Borcsok
Ruth Burrow

Marketing & Publicity
Chloe Cummings
Emma Petfield

Operations
Melissa Okusanya
Hannah Stamp

Production
Denis Manson
Simon Moore
Francesca Tuzzeo

Rights
Helena Font Brillas
Ashton Mucha
Aisling Smythe
Zoe Shine

**The HarperCollins
Distribution Team**

**The HarperCollins
Finance & Royalties
Team**

**The HarperCollins
Legal Team**

**The HarperCollins
Technology Team**

Trade Marketing
Ben Hurd

UK Sales
Laura Carpenter
Isabel Coburn
Jay Cochrane
Sabina Lewis
Holly Martin
Harriet Williams
Leah Woods

**And every other
essential link in the
chain from delivery
drivers to booksellers
to librarians and
beyond!**

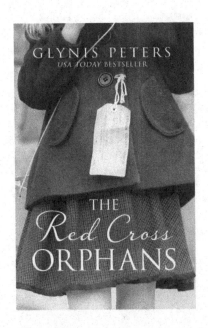

A journey into war, but not one she'll take alone...

Orphan Kitty Pattison is young, naïve and ready to do her bit for the war effort when she volunteers with the Red Cross and pledges to help those most in need. It's one of the most nerve-wracking moments of her life, but then she meets fellow volunteers Joan Norfolk and Trixie Dunn, and a bond of friendship is forged in the fire of life on the wards during the Blitz.

Days are spent nursing injured soldiers back to life and nights are spent anticipating bombs falling from the sky and then trawling through the wreckage to save who she can, but the light and laughter she finds with Jo and Trix see Kitty through the darkest hours.

Available in eBook, audio, and paperback now

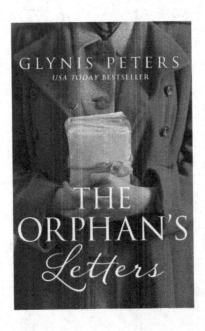

Absence makes the heart grow fonder, but does nothing to heal the pain of spending every minute waiting to hear the worst...

As the Second World War rages on, nurse Kitty Pattison's life takes a nomadic turn as her work with the Red Cross sees her traversing the country, moving from post to post.

With her best friends Jo and Trixie also scattered across the UK, and her soldier sweetheart Michael off on the continent undertaking medical missions he can't discuss, the war takes its toll and long days are followed by sleepless nights interrupted only by nightmares of what she's seen on the wards.

Available in eBook, audio, and paperback now

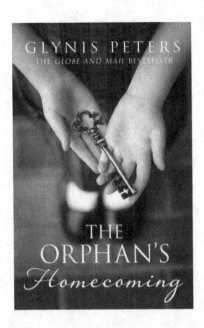

Could the shifting winds of change finally carry Kitty home?

After five long years of endless warfare, Red Cross nurse Kitty Pattison has seen her share of heartbreak and loss. And now, with her beloved fiancé Dr Michael McCarthy recuperating from a head injury across the ocean in Canada, and her dear friends Trixie and Jo scattered to the four corners of the war effort, it's harder than ever to battle through the heavy-hearted moments that mark the passing days.

But as she tends to the lost and wounded, Kitty finds a resilience of spirit within herself she never thought imaginable. Because with everything the war has taken from her, it has also given her a conviction that it can never destroy the things that really matter in life – love, friendship, and hope.

Available in eBook, audio, and paperback now

YOUR NUMBER ONE STOP

ONE MORE CHAPTER

FOR PAGETURNING BOOKS

One More Chapter is an
award-winning global
division of HarperCollins.

Sign up to our newsletter to get our
latest eBook deals and stay up to date
with our weekly Book Club!
<u>Subscribe here.</u>

Meet the team at
<u>www.onemorechapter.com</u>

Follow us!
 <u>@OneMoreChapter_</u>
 <u>@OneMoreChapter</u>
 <u>@onemorechapterhc</u>

Do you write unputdownable fiction?
We love to hear from new voices.
Find out how to submit your novel at
<u>www.onemorechapter.com/submissions</u>